THE MANWAAN SERIES

BOOK - I

RISE OF THE FALLEN

THE MANWAAN SERIES

BOOK - I

RISE OF THE FALLEN

ABHISHEK KRISHNAN

NU VOICE PRESS

First published by NU VOICE PRESS 2023
An imprint of Hubhawks Pvt. Ltd
www.nuvoicepress.com

This is a work of fiction and all characters and incidents described in this book are the product of the author's imagination. Any resemblance to actual persons, living or dead, is entirely coincidental.

ISBN: 978-81-963184-6-8

Typeset by Saanvi Graphics, Noida
Printed at Thomson Press
Published by Nu Voice Press

man.waan

noun

---

1. man-
   MANushya *(human)*
   [only before noun] of or connected with people rather than animals, machines or gods

2. waan-
   bhagWAAN *(god)*
   [singular] (in some religions) the being or spirit that is worshiped and is believed to have created the universe

one

'It is time, Usur,' boomed a voice through the dark and deathly infinite chambers. 'The Council has approved your leadership, and you will be spearheading the first phase of Earth's annexation.'

The king of the Underworld Clan, Usur, smiled as centuries of planning and allegiance finally seemed to be bearing fruit.

'Good to know, Mihaaraji. Will you be joining us? Having you fight shoulder to shoulder with us for the cause would motivate the troops. Nothing would stop us.'

'I'm afraid not. We need to act with great caution lest we alert my siblings. News of the revolution has already reached the celestial abode. If they find out that we have opened the gate, they will fight back. We cannot afford that at this crucial point.'

'We have the numbers, sir.'

'We won't stand a chance.'

'I beg to differ…'

'Usur, you were not appointed to present your opinions.'

'Apologies, Mihaaraji.'

An eerie silence followed which enunciated the constant low-pitched, airy sound that filled the voids of Hell. Almost as if a bed of lava flowed below its surface and a choir of baritones hummed over it. Conversations were crystal clear but silences were deathly. Hell resembled a collection of shiny black stone dungeons engulfed with thick red smoke. Miles below the surface of the Earth, the realm down under boasted multiple levels, almost like floors of a building, hosting various beasts and creatures.

A pungent stench filled the Underworld with intermittent whiffs of rot. The conditions may have been unfavourable, but the inhabitants of this place barely noticed any of its shortcomings.

Having maintained his calm for far too long, Usur was now excited like a kid in a candy store. Conversations with Mihaara got him aroused, but the silence intimidated him. He commanded an enormous army of raging beasts but still did not possess the authority to speak up against the junior Fagir.

Nothing was greater than the cause—the revolution.

'Take me through the plan once again. Step by step.'

'Yes, Mihaaraji. Once the gate is opened at your command, I will authorise the opening of a single portal through which ten to fifteen of us, including me, will enter the human realm. We will first need to find hosts for ourselves. Once we're in their flesh and bones, we will begin carrying out the executions.'

'Remember, Usur. The prophecy states that there will be a hundred and eight of them at any given point. And as soon as Heaven finds out that the number has dropped, it will be restored, which is why you need to be cautious. The executions need to be conducted with great discretion. Many would not have attained their realisation, and those are the ones that must be targeted. You will be no match against those who are even partially realised.'

'Understood, Mihaaraji. Shall I rally up ten Asuras and five Rakshasas?'

'No. The Rakshasas are mindless and cannot be controlled. Make sure all fifteen are Asuras.'

'As you command. The Manwaans won't stand a chance,' Usur sniggered.

'Don't drown yourself in arrogance, Usur. Many have already attained their realisation. And along with my brothers and sisters, they could curb the revolution.'

'Are your siblings expected on Earth?'

'It is possible...'

'We certainly won't be able to face them, Mihaaraji. At least the Manwaans are partially mortal. But your siblings....'

'Which is exactly why you need to be quiet while carrying out the orders. Do not forget that my siblings can also relieve the human hosts of your demonic energy. They could kill you instantly, just by placing a palm on your head and sending a beam of their radiation through you.'

Usur had no response. He began to palpitate and rethink the entire strategy. *What if they encountered an angel from Heaven on Earth? Would the fifteen Asuras be enough? Were they even approaching this the right way?* Doubts began to flood Usur's mind.

'Calm down, Usur. All I need you to do is keep me informed.'

'Yes, Mihaaraji.'

'If there is a sighting of any of our siblings, Saatan needs to be informed.'

Two

'What the hell is the matter with you, Rinad?'

'I'm sorry, sir…' Rinad clenched onto his soiled jeans with one hand while abstaining from making any eye contact.

'What do you mean you are sorry? This is the third time We've found silly grammatical errors. Don't you proofread what you write before sending it in? Thank god I didn't send it to the client. We would've been a laughing stock. Where is your head at?'

It was just another day at work for Rinad.

Being a copywriter at a creative agency only sounded exciting but was as mundane as any other job. Copy That, founded by Mr Mukherjee, the Creative Head and the gentleman currently yelling at Rinad, had recently closed one of their biggest clients. For a small agency, it was a huge deal that eventually manifested itself as pressure on the employees, and Rinad was not the one to handle pressure well.

'I'm really sorry, sir. I haven't been sleeping too well. Of late, my focus has been all over the place…' he brushed his messy hair off his forehead and stroked the large mole on his jawline that was hidden behind his unkempt beard—a sign of the discomfort he was undergoing.

'Stop with the excuses! I want to see the revised copy by 5 p.m.,' he commanded. 'And buy some new shirts, for god's sake! I can see your hairy stomach through those holes.'

Rinad hung his head, gave a slight nod, and walked out of the corner office. Once again, he had been a disappointment.

Contrary to what his boss believed; this wasn't just another excuse. Rinad was in a constant battle with his anxiety, often an outcome of being overwhelmed by any sort of confrontation. Nothing new about it, though. His first tryst with a panic attack was at the age of sixteen—a simple case of not having completed his assignment and being questioned by his teacher in front of his entire class. He was reminded of this suffocating feeling every time he encountered a trigger—a warm sensation against his skin throughout his body, sweat accumulating on his forehead and palms, being short of breath, a rising heartbeat, and feeling like the whole world was weighing down on him.

Ten years later, he had managed to develop his coping mechanisms and dodged himself out of any possible confrontation. Of course, there were times when escaping was not an option. Like in his first year of college, when a gang of college studs cornered and bullied him purely to have a laugh, leading to panic setting in. Or when his girlfriend left him because he wasn't driven enough about his life's goals, as she claimed. He grew up believing that he was just not good enough. While he wasn't a raging extrovert, he was smart enough to hold a conversation until it breached the red zone—the deep-seated philosophical questions which he should have figured out by now. What was he doing with his life? Where was he heading? Such questions were the triggers that he didn't need.

He would toss and turn in his sleep, wake up with cold sweats, and just lie there staring at his ceiling, rubbing his mole with his thumb, waiting for his daily alarm to go off. He seemed to be growing tolerant towards his prescribed medication. Not to mention that his daily weed consumption was at an all-time high. All he needed was a trigger. And just like his teacher from school, the bullies from college, and his ex-girlfriend, Mr. Mukherjee had done just that.

Rinad's forehead started moistening with sweat. He paced towards his desk, opened his bag, grabbed a cigarette box from it, shoved it into his jeans pocket, and darted towards the exit.

'I'm just going to the washroom,' he informed his colleague, who continued working without any sense of acknowledgement.

He ran down the staircase, as he always did since he never had the patience to wait for the lift. The sweat had now covered his face and began to drip from his chin. As he reached the refuge flat of the building, two floors below his office, he shut the door behind him and placed a stone in front of it. The stone was there to warn him of anyone entering while he was there. If someone opened the door, it would hit the stone and make a sound, thus warning him.

The refuge area—an empty, undone flat that was mandatory in high-rise buildings and that was there mainly in case of a fire-related emergency. It doubled up as a part-time smoking lounge for many and acted as a perfect spot for people, mostly men, to relieve themselves. The pipes of the sewage system that ran through the building, normally found behind bathroom walls, remained exposed. The entire flat smelt of urine, so ensuring proper ventilation was imperative unless, of course, one enjoyed the smell.

Rinad walked briskly towards one corner by the window, removed the cigarette box, and pulled out a half-smoked joint and a lighter. The smell of the flat was soon about to change.

He placed the filter end of the joint between his lips and lit it up as he looked out at the towering view.

Just a couple of drags, and life already seemed better.

This was his daily cycle. Half a joint right before work, the second half of the same joint at work right before lunch, one joint right after work, and one before bed. His doctor repeatedly warned him about this addiction and explained how his prescribed medication was pointless if he continued numbing his brain out.

But Rinad was in too deep. Unable to wait for lunchtime due to the trigger activated today, thanks to his boss, a slightly earlier session was necessary.

As he smoked his joint, the sweat faded away, his shoulders relaxed, and deep breaths resumed. His thumb left his mole and his hand lowered. He was aware of the vicious cycle he was trapped in but couldn't help it.

As he stared at the tiny holes on his shirt caused by the burning particles from the joint falling onto it, his phone rang. He hated it when he was disturbed during his "relaxing time." He reached into his pocket and whipped out his phone.

Mom calling...

He swiped the screen to answer it, 'Hi, *ma*. What's up?'

'*Beta*, can you drop by this Saturday?'

'*Arey*...you know I have plans on Saturdays, ma!'

'Just for a bit, Rinu. Please?'

That did it for him. He could never turn down his mother's innocent plea. 'Alright...but I'll leave early. I can't miss my Saturday rager.'

'Yes yes...that's ok, beta. See you then!'

'Bye,' he replied, cut the call, slid his phone back into his pocket, and finished his joint.

Once done, he walked back to his desk, removed his box, and started devouring his meal. It wasn't lunchtime yet, but the munchies had gotten to him. A post-smoking-meal was one of the few joys left in his life, and he wouldn't let anyone or anything interrupt that. It was one of the few remaining joys that helped him get through yet another mundane day in his mundane life.

Three

As the moment arrived, they both stood in front of what was about to be the Gateway of Hell.

Mihaara, standing tall at over seven feet, towered over the five-foot king of the Underworld Clan. While the authority was clearly conveyed right from the beginning, a subtle friendship had brewed between the two over the millennia. Mihaara would communicate the proceedings from the Fagir Council meetings, while Usur shared the happenings from the Underworld. As they exchanged notes over the years, each fuelled the other's ambition. The plan for the revolution kept growing bigger each time.

Usur, a self-appointed ruler, had won the trust of the Council by conveying his belief in the cause. For too long had they been trapped in Hell. For too long had they meandered around the smoky hallways and chambers with no sense of time, place, or purpose. When the seven angels had been cast out from Heaven, Usur understood that this was his only chance. Not only could he strengthen the Underworld's ties with the supernatural powers, but he would also finally have the chance to walk on Earth, much like a free man. Or rather, a being. Asuras and Rakshasas roamed in Hell in a formless manner, almost like levitating shadows. Once unleashed onto Earth, they would be able to possess a host and migrate back and forth at their convenience. But until then, on Earth, they would remain as black and red, thick, glimmering liquid—the only form through which they could cross over and enter the human realm.

Finding flesh and bones was critical.

Mihaara, on the other hand, like all the other angels, remained in full form. Glorious orange wings that spanned nearly five feet on each side; a chiselled, impenetrable body that was, quite literally, a godsend, and powers beyond imagination. It had been over two millennia since the major fallout in Heaven. When the seven angels led by Saatan had been cast out of Heaven, they struck an alliance with the Underworld Clan to stand a fighting chance in their family feud. They fell into Hell and thus, came to be known as the fallen ones or Fagir.

The Gods could not descend upon Earth or Hell, but the remaining seven angels could. They came to be known as Arinch or the worthy ones, denoting that they were still welcome in Heaven.

When the news of this newly formed coalition reached the Gods, they began creating Manwaans—part man, part celestial beings on Earth—as the only solution to help the Arinch battle the enemy, curb the revolution, and prevent the celestial war. On Saatan's orders, Mihaara was bestowed with the responsibility of leading the first wave of this revolution.

They stood there silently. Relishing it. Preparing to embrace the inevitable chaos that was about to follow. Mihaara shut his eyes and began to whisper a *mantra*.

Jagom taram maheeram bhasonayaam
Teem tareem kyoma samo bhasonayaam
Maeka namo jarivyartha sabha kotha bhasonayaam

To Usur, this seemed absurd and ironic.

'Are you praying to the Gods, Mihaaraji?' he hesitantly asked as the Fagir gently opened his eyes. 'I thought the revolution was against them?'

'The mantra that I am reciting invokes other cosmic forces prevalent in this universe, Usur. Forces that are far beyond the Gods.'

Beyond the Gods? Was there even such a thing? Usur thought to himself.

'It is exactly what happens when one bites onto more than one can chew. They create and expect self-sustenance, which can never be the case, and then lose track of it all. They are unaware of many of their own creations. Cosmic forces that they themselves have created and forgotten about. Forces that are lost in the depths of this universe and are now beyond their reach. We Fagir seek refuge in those forces, and will make them pay for this folly of theirs.'

Music to Usur's ears.

Mihaara once again shut his eyes and continued murmuring the mantra. To Usur, it seemed like the same couple of lines were on a loop—the usual nature of a mantra. From the pocket of his angelic cloak, Mihaara pulled out a black and red crystal that was attached to a small golden hilt—almost like a miniature spear.

The Narak Chaab! Usur thought to himself as he stared at it with wonder.

Mihaara held it, like one would hold a flower, and looked towards his commander-in-chief in a meditative state, with eyes half open.

'Are they ready?'

With a smirk, Usur turned his head towards one side and yelled, 'WHAT DO WE SAY?'

'We are ready...'

'Let us out…'

'Let's take them down...'

Voices growled from the shadows with a concoction of laughter and snorts. Fifteen formless Asuras stepped out to take their place by their leader. Even though shapeless, a head, a body, and a pair of eyes could be discerned. All black with hints of red—primarily in the eyes and on the forehead. The pupils were red, and a red line cut through the centre of the forehead area—almost like a red *tika*—a small religious mark.

'Very good,' approved Mihaara as he continued to whisper the next segment of his mantra.

Radho raeka bhasonayaan
Madho raeka bhasonayaan
Jadho raeka bhasonayaan

On completion, the ground began to crack open and a black and red, majestic circular stone structure started to emerge from underneath. The opening got bigger to accommodate the size of the gate, and the parting of the ground filled the air with thunderous sounds. The Asuras were amazed. Only the Fagir had the powers to call upon the Gateway of Hell, and this was the first time it was being done.

Quite literally, a door to their freedom.

They began to jump in excitement as the gate rose and finally, halted. Made of circular patterns and with intricate designs and inscriptions, the only connector between Hell and Earth stood before them. The gate would open to a tunnel—the passageway that connected the gate to the surface of the Earth, and it would then be Usur's turn to create portals that the Asuras could seep through.

'Remember, Usur. Just one portal to begin with. And stealth is the key.'

'Yes, Mihaaraji,' Usur said, and bowed as Mihaara placed his hand on his head. Not once did he imagine receiving blessings from an angel—an ally.

'I'll see you on the other side,' said Mihaara with a contented smile.

At the centre of the structure was an indented spot—a perfect fit for the Narak Chaab. Mihaara held it up, shut his eyes, and proceeded with the last leg of his mantra.

Dhemartha bhasonayaan
Prajaraathy bhasonayaan
Khuladasini bhasonayaan

This time, on completion, the Narak Chaab glowed, and the inscriptions on the gate lit up. Mihaara carefully inserted the key and turned it—three times to the right and once to the left. A pull sucked it in and locked it as the circular architecture of the gate began to unwind one by one. As each piece unwound, a blue light radiated through the cracks. The floors of Hell shook beneath the Asuras' feet, as they laughed with uncontrollable venom and excitement while witnessing the Gateway of Hell being opened for the very first time in all of eternity.

'Good luck out there,' Mihaara said with an almost brotherly smile. Over the years, he had grown to be fond of Usur and his ambitions, like any sibling would be. He looked forward to everything they were going to achieve together.

The prophesied war was about to begin. The end was near, and victory was theirs to take.

'I'll be watching over you. And so will the Council.'

'That is all I ask for, Mihaaraji. *Iaj Raakn Ho!*'

'Iaj Raakn Ho,' replied Mihaara. A war cry created to celebrate the coalition between the Fagir and the

Underworld Clan that loosely translated to 'hail the Underworld.' A phrase conceived to propagate the belief that the ultimate stage of the Dark Ages, or the *Kalyug*, had arrived, and it was time for the Underworld to rule all.

'Iaj Raakn Ho!!! Iaj Raakn Ho!!!' the squadron of fifteen chanted repeatedly.

The gate opened completely, and the Asuras led by their king and commander-in-chief, marched out into the blue light.

Mihaara stood there silently, witnessing the start of the revolution.

One they had been planning for over two millennia.

Four

In one of the narrow alleys of Bandra East, the ground cracked open and shiny black and red liquid seeped through it onto the surface. Usur and Mihaara had finalised this location as the first portal. This particular alley was relatively less crowded, and at the same time, they would gain access to one of the most populated cities in the world—Mumbai.

As the glowing liquid emerged, it began to slither through the bustling streets. The humans of Mumbai had enough going on in their lives—soaring rent rates, traffic, heat when there were no rains, and rains when there was no heat—the list went on. No one had the time to look down and notice the mini streams of thick liquid flowing with lives of their own. And even if someone did, they would easily be convinced that it was nothing but *keechad*—a common sticky dirt sighting during the monsoons.

The liquid Asuras moved at an unimaginable pace—driven by their need to find a host and walk the planet for the first time.

* * *

'How much for half a kilo of potatoes?' an urban woman in her mid-thirties wearing a simple t-shirt and faded jeans yelled through the chaos of the market as she held out her tattered wallet.

'Sixty rupees, madam,' the vendor responded while packing the items for another customer. If you weren't quick, you'd lose the business—the one rule of the fast-paced metropolitan. You answer queries, tally the accounts, and make sure no one robs you, all while tending to three customers.

'It was fifty-five last week!'

'I don't set the rates, madam. But *chalo*, I'll make it fifty-eight for you. Only because you've always been buying from me.'

'Is that all you can do for a loyal customer? Two rup…' she paused midway and began choking as the wallet dropped to the ground from her hands, spilling the coins all over. Her head tilted upwards, and her body vibrated as the veins on her face turned black.

'Are you okay, madam?' yelled the shocked vendor. When he got no response, he burst out frantically, 'Help!! Someone…please…something is wrong with…' he, too, stopped midway and began to choke.

'What are you doing? Will you hurry up?' chided an old, grumpy man who gave in to his impatience and conveniently overlooked what was going on right in front of him.

The vendor and the woman vibrated fervently as screams started surrounding them, breaking through the sound of heavy rainfall. Their eyes turned black, teeth began to elongate into sharp fangs, and pointed black claws emerged from their nails as the black veins spread throughout their brown-skinned bodies. People around them exuded mixed emotions – confused, frightened and worried. The two victims continued to vibrate, went on to assume a crescendo, and climaxed with a final breath, followed by a quick freeze.

A calm suddenly took over them as the teeth and claws retracted, and the veins and the eyes returned to their normal colour. Their heads tilted back down as they stared and scanned each other—top to bottom.

'Nice body,' said the vendor with an abnormally calm and cold smile.

'And you, my king,' replied the woman.

'Let's get down to work,' the vendor commanded, slid across, and exited his small shop.

Both stood there, wriggling their toes and looking at their hands in amusement.

'Amazing!' exclaimed the vendor.

'Right?' retorted the woman as she placed her palm on her cheek and felt skin and flesh for the very first time. People around them, who had been screaming, stood confused but began to calm down on seeing them become normal again.

'Are you two alright? What the hell happened?' the old man shouted.

'Seems like the two of you had a fit. What a coincidence to have it together,' another vendor from the adjacent cart remarked casually as he resumed placing the vegetables on the weighing scale. The bustle of the streets began to pick up and finally reached its normal decibel level. 'You both are okay, *na*?' the vendor continued without lifting his eyes from the scale.

'Never been better,' replied the victim vendor.

Both victims, still in awe of everything around them, began walking away.

'*Oye*...what about your shop? I'm not going to look after it for you.'

No response.

The two humans, now Asuras, marched towards their first target.

Five

Three days later

'Goodnight, *kanna*...'

'*Amma*...it's Friday! Let me watch some more TV, please? It's barely 9.30 p.m.,' said the nocturnal thirteen-year-old to her mother.

'It doesn't matter what day it is. You need to make it a habit to sleep and wake up early. It'll come in handy, especially during exams. Trust me, I've been there.'

With a kiss on the forehead, the mother switched off the main light and shut the door behind her. However, the mischievous teenager immediately reached for her side table, felt around for her phone, turned it on, and started playing on it while hiding under the blanket. The sound was off, but she was deeply engrossed as the light from the phone beamed on her face.

Suddenly, she heard a rustle in her room. Surprised yet curious, she removed the blanket from over her head to look for what she thought might be a rat. As she sat on her bed and scouted the floor, her gaze went to the open window—again, a rare sight. The window was never locked but was never open at night, either. At least it was not a rat, she thought to herself, letting out a sigh of relief as she walked over to shut the window.

'Are you going to lock us in here?'

The teenager turned around in shock, squinting her eyes to look at the dark corner of her room from where she had heard the male voice—one that was not her father's. Two figures emerged from the corner. The speechless girl, now sensing danger, opened her mouth to yell for help. But before she could, a fatal slice from the Asura's black pointed nails landed across her neck.

She collapsed, and a blood pool began to form around her.

'By my count, that's eight. A hundred more to go….'

'Everything is going as we planned.'

'Yes. But let's not get complacent. And there is always scope to do better.'

'Yes, my king,' replied the female figure, as both their nails retracted and eyes turned to normal.

'Let's go. Quickly! Before her parents come in.'

The two of them, a former vegetable vendor and one of his customers, jumped out the window and landed smoothly in the alley adjoining the building, four floors down. A forty-feet jump made with ease.

* * *

Over the next two weeks, similar killings were reported across Mumbai. Right from Borivali to Juhu to Powai to Marine Drive, innocent people were being slaughtered. One case that got reported was even of a six-year-old boy.

Usur's plan was being carried out exceedingly well. The only thing delaying their progress was the Mumbai traffic—a concept that was unheard of in Hell. Adapting to the laws of this new realm wasn't all that hard though. When an Asura leeched onto a host, all its memories would be accessible, making it much easier to blend in with normal, walking, talking humans.

When the Asuras were not busy tracking down an unrealised Manwaan, they would enjoy a ride on the Mumbai Virar local while exchanging body fluids with the hundred others crammed in the train compartment. The smell of sweat from grown men, whom they were smothered against, intrigued them—a sensation they had never experienced before.

Much of their time was spent recreating events that humans would indulge in. They would sit in a *kaali-peeli* taxi and experience the breeze filled with the stench of fish on their faces as they drove by the docks. Some hosts even came with a mobile and a pair of earphones in their pockets, which the members of the Underworld Clan would plug in and shove into their ears to listen to the rhythmic vibrations that were popularly known as "music," while imitating the humans bobbing their heads to it.

They would try to understand the code of conduct followed by their fellow travellers. Like when they crossed the road, they would obediently wait for the colour to change from red to orange to green on the traffic signal before stepping onto the so-called "zebra crossing."

Asuras would even try and put things into their mouths and force them down their throats—a common action practised by humans from time to time, which they gathered from all the memories.

Not like they felt the hunger.

The creatures from Hell didn't feel anything, but pretended like they did anyway.

In one particular skirmish against a young gang of thugs from Dharavi, during another Manwaan chase-down, one Asura even took a bullet to her chest—to no effect. With knives, they would momentarily bleed a black liquid, but that was about it. The immortal members of the Underworld Clan roamed the Earth without a worry, taking down their targets one by one but also taking full advantage of all the materialistic experiences of the human realm.

As the killings increased, cases started piling up at the police stations. Every station began reporting absurd cases of people of all ages being killed. Forensics reported that it seemed like the claws of an animal had done the damage—maybe a new species undiscovered by humankind was on the loose. No one could tell. Relatives of some of the victims cited black eyes, claws, and fangs for teeth.

But, with no evidence to justify themselves. At times, even the forensic experts were convinced that they might have been hallucinating.

* * *

The Asuras gathered around for their weekly midnight meet in a dark alley. They didn't sleep. So, they might as well use the time to serve their mission.

'What's the update?' Usur growled, sporting swanky ripped jeans and a loose Indian cricket team jersey with "Sachin Tendulkar" written on the back. This was his first time on Earth, and he didn't want to be stuck in the dull clothes his host wore. So, he went shopping and, along with all the Asuras, was dressed to kill. Quite literally, though.

'The *vada pav* is certainly a delicious marvel. Especially with the fried chilli,' commented one of them with saliva dripping from his tongue.

'I think we need ice creams in Hell. It does a tingling thing inside my head when I take a large bite. I've never quite eaten anything like it!' said another.

'They'll melt and turn into a milkshake in Hell with all the heat,' jested another, at which all the Asuras burst out laughing. Cracking a joke with human context had become a much-praised talent amongst them.

'About the Manwaans, you fools!' Usur blasted. Even though he enjoyed the occasional human-based joke, he was quick to reorient himself towards the task at hand.

'Ah yes, of course. My king, we've exterminated twenty-one of them. That leaves us with…umm…ninety-one… ninety…eighty-nine…'

'Eighty-seven, you idiot,' boasted another Asura arrogantly.

'Hey! Lay off! My host is not good at this mathematics thing. Test me on any of the capital cities. Or football. I dare you!'

'Silence, you morons!' yelled Usur. 'Have you forgotten the purpose of your visit? Have your fun, but do not lose focus. We've slowed down as it is and are behind schedule. Mihaara will not be pleased.'

'Apologies, my king. We'll do better,' announced an Asura from the back of the herd.

'I hope so. Now…I assume the prospective Manwaan leader has been taken care of?'

Radio silence.

'Please tell me he has been killed by one of you.'

The Asuras looked at each other in confusion. They knew the importance of this target but had overlooked it in all the human-worldly excitement. No one wanted to utter a word, lest they anger their king, who was already on the edge.

Usur slapped his forehead and let out a sigh—a very human way of expressing frustration and disappointment. 'Never mind. You, you, and you,' he pointed out to three of the fifteen. 'Sort this out tonight. And I've changed my mind…don't kill him. I actually prefer him alive. I have questions.

'Yes, my king,' said the three of them in unison.

'You have the coordinates?'

'Yes, sir.'

'Get to it. Now. Iaj Raakn Ho!'

'Iaj Raakn Ho,' the three boomed and scurried away to track down one of their prime targets—the prophesied leader of the Manwaans.

Six

The door opened, and his mom stood there dressed immaculately in a turquoise *salwar kameez* that was embroidered with golden patterns.

'Hi, beta!' she ecstatically leapt in for a hug, making sure her make-up and neatly tied hair bun didn't get spoiled.

While embracing his mother, Rinad had only one thought on his mind. Would she smell the smoke that lingered around him like always? But she was too happy to see him to let any of that bother her.

He noticed her long earrings. 'Why are you so dressy today?' he asked, mildly relieved that his mom didn't immediately pull away because of the smoke smell.

'We've got people over, and we wanted you to meet them,' she replied.

'Arey…why didn't you tell me we had guests? I'm in no mood to meet anyone. And besides, look at me. I look terrible!'

His mom scanned Rinad and nodded in agreement. His clothes were wrinkled with tiny holes, and his face had a general dullness to it—from the pressure in office and the high from weed. He was certain that he could not get through this ambush in a sober state.

'It'll be quick, beta. Come in. Just stay for an hour. You can leave after that,' his mom replied as she pulled him inside the house.

Rinad was greeted with a choir of "Heys" and "Hellos." A bit too much for his stoned mind to process. He sheepishly smiled and waved at everyone sitting in the hall—his dad, an elderly couple, possibly in their late sixties, a younger couple who seemed like they were in their mid-forties, and a young boy and girl, both around ten years old. All dressed perfectly.

The Shahs' house was a massive 4-BHK located in Bandra West. The hall had black leather sofas, beige curtains, and rosewood furniture that complemented it all—a centre table, side tables, and a bar in one corner. A majestic chandelier hung from the ceiling but was currently not switched on as there was enough light radiating from a tall lamp in another corner, setting a "mood" to the room.

'Come!' his dad called out to him and patted an empty spot on the sofa beside him. Rinad went over, placed his laptop bag down, and collapsed on the sofa. On doing so, his dad sniffed and looked at him. A look that said, "I can smell it." Of course, they had company over, and he was in no position to say anything to his smoked-out son.

'This is Ajit and Ramita,' his father said, pointing to the elderly couple. 'That's Karan and Aruna,' he said, pointing to the younger couple, 'and Neena and Amit, Karan and Aruna's children,' he said, pointing to the kids. 'Ajit and Karan are colleagues.'

'Oh...that's nice,' Rinad replied, disinterestedly but with a formal smile.

'So, Rinad...how has work been?' Ajit asked the usual icebreaker in his deep baritone voice.

'Not too bad. The usual.'

'Copywriter in advertising, right?'

'Yup,' Rinad replied. Clearly, a conversation about him had been had before he arrived. And they had been updated with his work profile.

'How long do you plan to stay there?'

'Not sure.'

'You should think about moving to the client side. That's where the money is!'

'I agree,' Karan cut in. 'I made the same jump!'

'Oh...' Rinad replied, again with a disinterested look.

'Do you have any plan in mind?' Karan continued.

And that did it.

The feeling started bubbling up inside of him. He instantly felt like he was being hounded by questions that he had no intention of confronting. His skin started feeling warm, and his breath shortened. As a reaction, his thumb instantly reached for the mole on his jawline and began stroking it.

'Umm...no, not really,' Rinad answered hesitantly.

'Well, you should,' Ajit continued. 'This is the right time to make the jump. Beyond which it may get too late.'

'That's what I told him!' his dad added. 'I even asked him to consider doing an MBA.'

'That's a great idea,' Karan confirmed.

The world began to blur around Rinad as all the voices grew feeble and started getting muffled.

Feeling the sweat beads accumulating on his forehead and his palms moistening, Rinad stood up, mumbling, 'I need to use the washroom,' and walked away from the living room. He darted into the closest toilet, locked himself inside, and stood in the darkness, facing the mirror. He opened the tap and splashed water onto his face. But he got no relief.

The damage was done. He needed a joint.

He wiped his face with a towel and went back into the living room. His mom placed a cup of *chai* and a plate of *pakoras* for him—a delicacy often had during the monsoons, but he couldn't care less. Picking up his bag, he announced, 'Sorry, I got an urgent call from work. I need to run.'

'But Rinad…' his mom pleaded pointlessly.

Before anyone could say anything more, he was gone.

* * *

Just thirty more minutes and I'll have my joint. Rinad thought as he hugged his laptop bag and sat in the bumpy auto rickshaw that took him to his tiny 1 BHK in Andheri East—the only flat he could afford.

As an anxious twenty-six-year-old, escaping from such situations furthered the feeling that he was a nervous wreck. That his life was heading nowhere. Panic attacks at the drop of a hat, barely able to keep up with rent, unhappy with his job, single, but most importantly, purposeless. All this played on his mind as he watched the drenched streets of Mumbai passing by.

The only thing he looked forward to—Saturday nights! His gang of boys met at a local cheap bar and drank till they fell. Not to mention, joints were rolled before drinking, while drinking, and after drinking. It was the only time he felt not-so-bad. And today, being a Saturday, he was slightly jumpier than otherwise.

He got home, rolled his much-delayed post-work-joint with shivering hands, and lit it up. As he smoked it, he slowly began to return to normalcy. Not only had his routine been disrupted, but he had to deal with the arduous task of being answerable to people about his own career graph...

Halfway through the joint, he whipped out his phone, dialled a number, and put it on speaker mode.

'Yo, buddy!' said a voice from the other end.

'Yo, bro! What's the scene? I'm home and ready to rage,' said Rinad with newfound excitement. His friend's voice was the good trigger that he needed at this point.

'Let's meet at yours in an hour-ish? We'll pull one-two and then head to Sagar,' the reply came. Sagar was their go-to drinking spot.

'On scene, bro. *Chal*...I'll see you then,' Rinad replied, cut the call, and went back to his joint.

He smoked, thinking about the roller coaster week that he had had, and awaited the next adrenaline rush for the evening.

Seven

Along with his three friends—Vinay, Jogi, and Param, Rinad followed the Saturday routine to the T. Couple of joints at his flat and then a drive over to Sagar— the budget-friendly restro-bar. For Rinad, hanging out with his school buds meant everything, and looking forward to it made the boring week a tad bit lively. So much so that if the plan ever got cancelled, he sulked in depression and would smoke himself to sleep.

There was a catch, though. The monsoons had set in—a season that Rinad had grown to dislike. The rain did not bother him. It was the erratic lightning. Over the past decade, he had developed an aversion to flashes of lights. Even if someone flickered a torch around him, he would drown in anxiety.

A condition that his doctor called *selaphobia.*

The age of onset of this fear was not clear to him, but it was as real as it got. Any flash of light would act as a trigger. Even the sudden bright lights from the screens in cinema halls would have him feeling uncomfortable. If he had to watch a movie, it would be on his laptop with all his room lights on, just so that any change of lighting in the frame of the film did not feel sudden to his sensitive eyes.

But this would not stop Rinad. On the drive to Sagar during the monsoons, he would simply bury his head into his lap and shut his eyes to avoid any confrontation with lightning. Once he got to Sagar, it was all good. They would sit at a corner table, far away from the window, and all the lights would be on.

'Boss, one *khamba* of Teachers,' Vinay ordered the usual. Khamba being a full bottle, and Teachers being their favourite, affordable whisky.

'And peanuts,' added Jogi.

'And *masala papad*,' added Param.

Each one named his go-to munching item, and Rinad munched on them all. The items arrived, and the drinks were poured.

'Cheers!' said all as they clinked their glasses. And so began the indulgence.

'Guys…I have some news,' said a straight-faced Jogi. When a conversation began with those words, the boys knew something was up. Normally, discussions would be about movies, cricket, school memories, and rants from their work lives. But this seemed like something else. 'I think I'm going to get married,' he confessed.

'Dude, that's amazing!' said an excited Vinay. 'Why do you sound upset?'

'Arey...who wants to do an arranged marriage, man! I was hoping to fall in love...you know...have things happen organically.'

'Bro, that just happens in movies. Nothing wrong with an arranged marriage, man. You can fall in love after marriage too,' a logical response from Param that quickly turned into a jest. 'With your wife, I mean.' As the boys chuckled, Rinad remained relatively silent.

'At least meet the girl first and then take a call?' continued Param.

'I guess so,' replied a half-convinced Jogi. Such a response would normally face a rebuttal from the free-spirited, life-loving Vinay. They all expected him to jump in and say something energy-inducing, but when they looked towards him, they saw him staring at the TV across their table and frowning.

'Dude, what happened?' said Rinad, finally. Vinay gestured towards the TV.

They all looked over. It wasn't just them. The entire bar had its eyes fixed on the TV. One drunk man asked the waiter to turn up the volume.

'...as the number of these mysterious killings increases, the police continue to remain clueless, with the victims' ages ranging from as young as six years to as old as forty-two years. Forensics claim that a certain type of animal was also involved and is one of the common links between all the murders. Marks of claws seem to have been found on the bodies of the deceased. Another link was the fact that all victims were

suffering from an ailment of some sort. Some with diabetes, some with heart conditions, and some dealing with ADHD, anxiety, and depression...but the investigating team has not yet been able to put a finger on the cause or motivation behind these killings. Reporting live from Mulund, Mumbai, with cameraman Ashutosh Patil, this is Ritu Sharma from New India News.'

'What the hell is going on, man!' Vinay cried out.

'This has been going on for over a week,' commented Param. 'Sounds like some psychotic killer with a well-trained dog or something.'

Rinad felt a sinking feeling in the pit of his stomach as he quietly sipped his drink.

Humans have a special gift of listening to their gut—one of the features that set them apart from animals. Possibly where the saying "listen to your heart" came from. When something felt right—it could be felt in the gut, in the skin, in the flesh, and in the bones. And the same goes for when something felt wrong. And Rinad was feeling the latter.

His nights normally were troubled due to nightmares—arbitrary visions of killings, bloodshed, and destruction. Of course, nothing was discernible—owing to him being stoned out of his mind every night. Weed was known to be a dream blocker, and without it, he would toss, turn, sweat profusely, and have horrifyingly lucid nightmares. Sleeping sober was never an option.

'Dude, are you okay?' Jogi interjected. 'Why are you holding the glass to your mouth like that?'

Rinad shook himself out of it and realised the rim of the glass barely touched his lips, and he was frozen in that position. 'Oh shit, sorry…didn't realise I was doing that. Just got a weird feeling about the news.' His friends were taken aback by this comment of his as he barely followed the news, let alone be affected by it.

'Have you been following this story?' asked a surprised Vinay.

'Not really…but…umm…it just seems awful,' replied Rinad unsurely, merely covering up his surprised reaction. 'Forget it, na…so what's the girl's name?' he shifted the focus of the conversation as their indulgence continued.

The session continued till roughly 1 a.m., which was when the lads were drunk out of their minds. They could sit there till dawn, but the bar had to close, so the boys had no choice but to head back to their mundane lives. As Jogi drove around a small section of Andheri East—making sure to avoid any interception with the cops, they rolled and smoked their last joint for the night before each one got dropped off—Rinad being the last one.

'See you, brother. Next Saturday?' slurred Jogi.

'For sure, man! Let me know how it goes with the girl. And get home safe,' replied a high-out-of-his-mind Rinad.

'Done, bro!!' Jogi sped away after Rinad got off on the other side of the road opposite his building's gate. With great struggle, he began to cross the road, barely able to maintain his balance.

Just then, he noticed a pair of headlights speeding towards him from one end of the road. He had barely gotten halfway across, so it felt like a wise decision to go back and wait for the vehicle to pass. He stumbled back just in time, but strangely, a huge white van—almost like one of those delivery or courier vehicles, pulled over right in front of him.

The door slid open, and two figures got out and darted towards him. His vision was blurred, his mind went hazy, and he could barely make sense of what was happening. Before he knew it, one of the figures pulled out a wooden stick-like object, raised his arm, and forcefully landed it across Rinad's head.

He was out cold.

Eight

HOLY SHIT!!! Have I been abducted? Rinad thought to himself. As he slowly regained consciousness, he gathered that his hands and legs were tied, and his mouth was wrapped tightly.

He lay there for a while, trying to observe the surroundings as the feeling sank in. Rinad began to rethink his entire life and the role that karma played in it. He didn't owe anyone any money, nor had he caused anyone any harm. Maybe his ignorance of the real world and desire to always escape from it had gotten him into this predicament. Basically, karma came back and bit him like a serpent.

As he gained some energy, he began wriggling around in an attempt to free himself. The parched throat due to the alcohol made him cough fervently, and he began to regret the overindulgence. He noticed the two figures sitting right beside him and exchanging glances between him and the road ahead but was still unable to discern what their faces looked like. If he made it through this alive, he would need to remember the faces so that the cops could track them down. He thought calculatingly as the intensity of his wriggling steadily increased, which eventually caught the attention of the two figures.

'Stop it!' yelled one, in what sounded like a feminine voice. Rinad paid no attention to the instructions and continued squirming. He even attempted to scream through his gag.

'I won't say it again!' continued the voice. To no effect. This cued the other figure to reach under his seat, remove the same stick-like object, and whack Rinad, whose yelling now crossfaded into painful moans along with tears that began to roll down his cheeks.

The figure didn't stop at this.

As the beating continued, Rinad managed to sneak a glance. Now that the figure was closer to him. He didn't seem to be wearing suspicious clothing of any sort. In fact, for a captor who was in the middle of an abduction, it was quite absurd that he didn't even wear a mask to cover his face. From the little that he could gather, the face looked like that of an innocent, middle-aged man. As he continued getting beaten, Rinad thought that these were possibly newly inducted goons on a first-time abduction who were just looking to make a quick buck.

'*I don ave ay muny, lease le me go…aargh*!' Rinad cried out loud in a muffled manner through the gag as blows landed on him. The male figure showed no mercy and continued beating him up.

'That's enough!' interjected the female voice. 'Usur asked us to bring him in alive.'

'Then ask him to shut the hell up!' the car hit a speed breaker, and everyone banged their heads on the top.

'Oops...sorry guys,' said another male voice casually from the driver's seat.

'Does your host even know how to operate one of these things?' asked the female voice as she rubbed the top of her head.

'I checked his wallet, and he has this thing called a driver's licence. He seems to know his way around the wheel.'

'Keep your eyes on the road. Let's not draw any unwanted attention to ourselves,' commanded the female voice.

'Got it!'

'And step on it, will you?'

'I'm trying! But if I go too fast, I'll miss out on these bumpy things...umm...' the driver paused midway as he searched for the word in his host's memories, 'speed breakers!! That's the one.'

None of this made any sense to Rinad, who continued to lie there in pain. To begin with, they were having pretty nonchalant conversations for abductors. They didn't really sound like your quintessential thugs.

Who were these people referring to when they said hosts? And what in god's name did they want from him? he thought.

He had no answers.

Thankfully, the beating had stopped, and Rinad knew better than to continue wriggling. Someone called Usur wanted him alive, but in what state was not clear from the conversation that he overheard. In any case, he was outnumbered. Saying or doing something unrequired could trigger these people to leave him in a worse state.

He thought it best to stay silent and leave his life in the hands of fate.

Nine

As Rinad continued to wait in pain, he felt the van slow down.

This is it. I'm now going to be presented to this Usur fellow, who'll probably extract the little money I have left. What if they ask me to call my parents and make them send in lakhs or crores of rupees? And what if they just kill me after getting the money? There is no way this is going to end well!

The anxiety began to kick in, and beads of sweat began rolling down from his temples. This was the last thing he needed. A panic attack.

Not now, not now, not now!!! He yelled in his mind as the bubbling started rising within him along with the tingling warm sensation against his skin.

Normally, a joint would have done the trick. Or his SOS medication, which he barely used, as he preferred a high to calm him down. But at this point, anything would've been better than nothing. And he really couldn't expect any sympathy from his abductors—*oh, our poor little abductee is having a panic attack…let's release him, or maybe give him a joint or stop by a medical store to get him his medication so he could be more accommodating.* That was definitely not going to happen.

All he could do was breathe, like his therapist constantly asked him to do. Of course, she would ask him to stay away from medication and weed as much as possible and try and overcome an attack by purely breathing. But Rinad always chose the easier way. As he lay there like a vegetable, he thought this could be a good time to try the highly recommended breathing technique. And so, he began. Slow and deep breaths.

In, 2, 3, 4…hold, 2, 3, 4…out, 2, 3, 4…hold, 2, 3, 4…

A futile effort, however. Rinad discontinued the attempt and went back to awaiting what fate had in store for him.

'That was quick,' said the female figure doubtfully. The van had slowed down, but the journey was shorter than what they had planned for.

'Umm, not quite,' responded the driver.

'What do you mean?'

'We haven't reached yet. There's a random vehicle that's blocking the road.' Rinad was induced with a ray of hope at what he had just heard. If there was one last chance to escape, this was it, he thought to himself. He summoned all the remaining energy that he had and began yelling through his gag and shaking as hard as possible. He figured that maybe the person blocking the route would notice the entire van moving, and if they heard a bit of his screams, they would definitely suspect something.

'Stop that,' yelled the figure who was holding the stick. When Rinad did not follow the instructions, hard blows landed on him yet again. The little remaining energy that Rinad had also faded away, and he began to quieten down.

'Just go around it...quickly!' commanded the female voice. Just as the van began to move towards one side in an attempt to dodge the car blocking them, two men dressed in black robes with vague black markings on their hands and faces got out of the vehicle. They reached into their baggy coats, pulled out a gun each, and pointed them towards the white van. It looked like a clear challenge. They were not going to let them pass.

'Okay, something is not right,' claimed the driver. 'We better go check this out.'

'Stay in the car and make sure he remains quiet,' sneered the woman to the man keeping charge of Rinad. The driver and the woman proceeded to get out of the van and walk towards the armed men. As the man watching over Rinad peeked outside to stay up-to-date with the happenings, Rinad also managed to sneak a glance—still hoping he would get saved. He saw his two abductors marching towards the armed men.

Bang!!!

The triggers were pulled, and his abductors were hit. But they just stood there. Both looked down at the bullet holes engraved on them and looked back up at the black-robed men. Enraged, Rinad's prospective saviours looked at each other in fear. They had hit the target but to no effect. Rinad couldn't believe his eyes. These were not humans. He had gathered that they were not wearing any armour of sorts. They were literally in casual attire—t-shirts, shirts, jeans, and so on.

The armed men, now perplexed, continued firing more bullets towards their targets—who were now marching towards them with great angst. Their guns emptied, and before they could pull out another weapon, the abductors extended their claws and, with just three blows, managed to exterminate their opponents. The two men dropped dead, and Rinad, who had just witnessed this mini-skirmish, lost the little ray of hope that he had.

'There's one more on the driver's seat,' said the abductor driver.

As the two abductors walked towards it, the door opened, and another long-haired, black-robed man got out, this time with a sword. He began taking blows at the two of them. He seemed more skilled than the recently killed ones and, after much effort, managed to pass the sword through the woman right above her navel.

She looked at the wound and then back at him. Unaffected.

'Is that all you've got?' she sniffed arrogantly and proceeded to whack him across the face with her claws. He was sent, almost flying, to the ground. As he lay there with scratches on his face trying to muster up his strength to fight back, the woman pulled the sword out of her stomach and raised it to finish the fight. Just as she was about to, they sensed a pair of headlights coming from a distance.

'Leave him...let's get out of here. We're risking the mission!' said the driver. The woman paused for a second and threw the sword down—realising that he was right. They could not afford to get caught. The two of them jogged back into the van and sped away after the random car passed them.

Thankful that his life was spared, Jaffer collected himself and managed to sit up against the wheel of the car. As he continued to bleed profusely, he reached into his trouser pocket and removed what looked like a dilapidated cell phone, and proceeded to dial a number.

'Sorry, Guruji...I...I wasn't able to save him,' Jaffer said in a hushed tone as he held onto his ribs. 'But they're heading towards the Sassoon Docks. You should ask your students to get there quickly—these Asuras are extremely powerful and won't keep him alive for long.' As a reply came from the other end of the call, he continued, 'I'll survive. Make sure Rinad does too.'

He cut the call, held onto his stomach, and drove away.

Surreptitiously, from behind the wall of a nearby building, a police officer had witnessed everything that had just taken place.

Ten

Rinad opened his eyes slowly. He had lost track of the number of times he fell unconscious and was quite surprised that he was still alive. He looked around and found himself in an old, empty warehouse.

'Where is Usur?' said the Asura holding the stick.

'He will be here. Have some patience and stop asking me again and again!' the female Asura yelled. 'Oh…good morning! Someone seems to have woken up from his nap,' she continued and noticed that Rinad had regained consciousness. She walked up to him and lifted his face with one hand. The female Asura extended her black claws on the other hand and placed it by his jaw as her eyes turned to a haunting shade of black. Rinad, now fully aware of his surroundings, was breathing heavily and shaking with fear. Unable to believe what he saw, he tried crying out for help, which cued the woman to press her claw hard onto his cheek.

'Enough! Don't make me do Usur's job. He wanted to kill you himself. It's such a shame that a pretty face will cease to exist,' she grinned as she ran the claw from her index finger down his left cheek—resulting in a long scar that began to bleed.

It did look like she was tempted to rip his flesh apart.

'Maybe just one nice blow,' she said, raising her hand to deliver it across Rinad's face.

Bam!!!

The ceiling blasted open, and the quiet room was flooded with commotion. It was too much for Rinad to handle, considering the state that he was in. As he watched with disbelief, two masked figures—a towering, gigantic male with wings and a slick female with a bob cut perched on the former's back—landed smoothly and confidently, implying that they had clearly done this before and were prepared for what was about to follow.

The male spread his brown wings and started battling two of the three abductors. He, too, seemed to have claws.

Why the hell does everyone have claws? Rinad thought to himself.

He wasn't too surprised, considering how the entire night had unfolded up to this point. From their movements, it seemed like the two figures had come to his rescue.

The woman drew out a small silver stick with two black dots on either end from her back and held it in her left hand. To the layman, it looked like nothing more than a tiny steel rod. She raised her right hand with her five fingertips stretched and pointed towards the female

Asura, who suddenly stopped midway through her charge and held onto her stomach. Her face began to convey a feeling of discomfort rising within her, and in seconds, she fell to her knees and began throwing up. With the Asura handicapped, the bob cut woman charged towards her and jumped in the air. She transferred the silver stick to her right hand, pushed on the black mark with her thumb, ejecting a long, sharp blade, and landed a fatal blow across Asura's neck, severing her head.

Meanwhile, the towering, winged man was a fair match for the two male Asuras. He was big and didn't move as fast as the woman, but his blows seemed lethal. He landed a side kick on the abdomen of one of his opponents, who flew to one corner of the room, and now had all his attention focused on the other. As the Asura raised his hand to attack, the winged giant caught hold of it, twisted it down, and severed his head from the body with the claws of his other hand.

Just as he finished the second Asura, the third male came running back from the corner. As he charged, he suddenly stopped midway as a feeling of discomfort surged within him. Eventually, he too started throwing up—the woman had orchestrated her trick. Consequently, the male figure flew in the air and, once again, sliced the head off from the body.

As Rinad sat there tied to the chair with a gag in his mouth, he looked at the three heads that had been separated from the bodies. What freaked him out was that the bodies were still in motion. They flapped around like fish out of water.

'I had him, you know,' said the male figure.

'I know. I just saved us some time,' replied the woman.

'So, I'm counting that as my kill. Two for me and one for you...'

'Ugh...whatever,' the woman rolled her eyes, least bothered.

The two of them turned towards Rinad and walked up to him. The woman was roughly five feet tall. She had to hunch a bit to get a closer look at his face while the giant had to stoop down a considerable distance.

'Are you okay?' the woman asked in a warm yet matter-of-fact tone.

Rinad, who was shitting bricks, had absolutely no response. He passed out yet again.

'I think you scared him,' sniggered the male.

Eleven

At the Bandra police station, Sub-Inspector Virat Pawar huffed his way in. His mind was still whizzing from all that he had witnessed the previous night—not to mention he was also slightly hungover. He refused to believe that it was the alcohol that had him in a daze. Drenched in sweat and with barely any sleep, he walked into a corner office that had the nameplate "Inspector Manohar Deshpande" on it.

'Sir…may I come in?' he panted, intimidated by his big, short-tempered boss.

'You're already in, Pawar. And how many times do I have to tell you to knock?' Deshpande responded, twirling his thick moustache without breaking his attention from the paperwork that he was deeply engrossed in.

'Sorry, sir, but this is urgent.'

The number of killings was on a steady rise. The cases kept piling up. The police department had no leads and was absolutely clueless, leading to all the officers being overworked and infuriated. When a case remained unresolved, Deshpande's anger only built up like a pressure cooker, ready to explode at a moment's notice. No one wanted to be at the receiving end of his fury—resulting in everyone steering clear of him during times of crisis.

Virat Pawar was Deshpande's right-hand man. Shorter in height, he too donned a thick moustache, inspired by his senior Inspector, whom he idolised above any other. Pawar was a law-abiding citizen and refused to report to officers who took bribes—one of the reasons why he kept shifting branches. He was in no position to complain about his seniors, so the least he could do was find one who had similar ideologies and whom he could look up to.

Enter Deshpande—the most honest cop in all of Mumbai, as some would argue. He was known to have refused a ten-lakh bribe as an offer from one of the local notorious goons in exchange for allowing the distribution of hashish in certain pockets of the city. Not just that, he had even arrested them. When this story reached Pawar, he realised that he had found his mentor and, since then, had been Deshpande's loyal associate. After winning his trust, Pawar was ready to face all of Deshpande's wrath but knew that deep down, his boss had a gentle side to him.

'*Kay aahe*, Pawar? Can't you see I'm busy…' Deshpande boomed.

'Sir…this is important. I saw something strange last night,' Pawar replied hesitantly.

'Were you drinking?'

'Umm…'

'Pawar…how many times have I asked you to stop drinking?' said the teetotaller Deshpande as he sighed and rubbed his temples to relieve himself of a throbbing headache. 'How do you expect me to believe anything you say? However strange it may be, you were drunk. And this is really going to hamper your performance in the long run. Mark my words!'

'Sir…I didn't drink too much. Just…slightly…'

'Ugh…tell me.'

'Sir…I was in town with my friends and, after we finished, I was walking back to take a cab. Just then, I saw a white van being stopped by another car in the middle of the road. Three people from the car, who were dressed in black, had a fight with two people from the van…'

'So? Just file an FIR. What's the big deal?'

Pawar just stood there, unable to say anything. He knew he risked being called mad by his supervising officer but, he also knew what he had seen.

'Pawar…kay aahe?

'Sir…th…the people from the van had black claws, fangs, and even black eyes.'

Deshpande froze.

These descriptions had been heard a couple of times before but had always been outrightly dismissed. Now that it was coming from his trusted associate, he had reasons to believe it.

'Did you smoke something, Pawar?' said Deshpande, wanting to be absolutely sure.

'I wish I had, sir. And please trust me...I was not even that high,' Pawar defended himself and proceeded to whip out his phone. He went over to Deshpande's side of the table and continued as he showed the video to his boss, 'See, sir. It's a little blurry, but I tried to zoom. If you look carefully, you can see the claws.'

'Who are these guys in black robes? Why do they have these tattoos on their faces?' Deshpande asked as he squinted his eyes to grab all the details of the recording.

'No idea, sir. I think someone was in that van. It was shaking a bit. Maybe they were kidnapping someone or something?'

Deshpande sat there and rubbed his moustache a couple of times without batting an eyelid. 'Hand me those files in the first drawer,' he pointed to an old steel drawer rack that had all the ongoing, unresolved cases. Pawar opened the rusted, squeaky drawer, grabbed a bunch of files, and handed it over to Deshpande, who then began reading some of the pages meticulously while Pawar stared at his face to study his reaction.

Deshpande glanced swiftly over the pages, then stopped, and his brows furrowed.

Pawar could discern that his boss had had a major realisation.

Maybe all those people who reported the black eyes, black nails, and teeth-like fangs were not hallucinating. No one took those people seriously. It was time for this to change. But if this was true, what were these things with black eyes and nails? And about fangs? Was this some random hybrid between man and animal? Deshpande's head was whizzing with unanswered questions.

'What is it, sir?'

'Pawar…we have shit loads of work to do.'

Twelve

Rinad opened his eyes and found himself in a small, dullish room with grey, textured walls and a relatively low ceiling. It seemed barren—except for an empty study table in one corner with a mirror on top of it and a small cupboard beside it. He laid on a comfortable bed with white bed sheets, and on a small glass shelf at the top right corner, adjacent to the entrance, were three small portraits. From where he was, he couldn't see the portraits clearly.

As he rubbed the mole on his jawline while scrutinizing this unfamiliar place, flashes from the previous night were whizzing through his mind. Everything had happened too quickly for him to fathom it all properly. However, he finally felt well-rested. No body ache, no headache, nothing. He felt normal.

He sat up on his bed and noticed his reflection in the mirror by the wall across. His face was perfectly intact. He recalled receiving blows all over his body and expected scars and bruises. Surprisingly, there was nothing. He quickly scanned his entire body to check for the same, but not a single wound.

Instead, he looked and felt fresh as ever.

He stood up slowly and stretched himself out to properly awaken from his much-needed sleep. As he heard the creaks and cracks from his body, he turned to the tiny portraits on the glass shelf. Portraits of the holy triumvirate—Brahma, Vishnu, and Shiva—the three main Gods, about whom he and many others like him had been taught while growing up. Each of the portraits had a tiny red, finger-imprinted mark. It seemed like the red powder that people normally applied on their foreheads in temples—the *kumkum*.

This put Rinad in a pickle. The people who supposedly rescued him were skilled warriors, and here, this simplistic room with pictures of the three Gods—the creator, the preserver, and the destroyer—gave off more of a saintly vibe. It didn't seem to add up. Rinad didn't know what to make of it.

He proceeded towards the door and slowly opened it, revealing a huge room with a large dining table in the centre. From a distance, he heard a couple of voices. He couldn't see anything, so he strained his ears to try and pick up as much of the conversation as he could.

'You were not supposed to kill them. We're not here to do that,' said an old, raspy voice.

'What else were we supposed to do, Guruji? They would've not hesitated to kill us. Why should we go easy on them?' replied a familiar male voice, aggressively.

'Your job was to injure them at the most and rescue Rinad. If not, what differentiates you from the Asuras?'

Rinad froze for two reasons. Who were these people, and how did they know his name? And Asuras? These were terms he had heard as a part of his bedtime stories. When he was a kid, his grandmother had told him stories in which Asuras would normally be the antagonists of the narrative. The evil guys.

Of course, it was all a myth. Or was it?

'Guruji…technically, we didn't kill them,' said a mildly familiar female voice.

'What do you mean?'

'We severed the heads, but the bodies continued to move after we did. It's almost as if life still coursed through their veins. I don't think these Asuras can be killed.'

'Hmm…but still, the heads can never be stitched back. Remember, they're still humans, and if there is the slightest chance of keeping them ali—' the old man stopped mid-sentence, and a deathly silence took over. 'It's okay, Rinad. You can come out. We know you can hear us.'

Rinad gasped. It was pointless trying to escape the obvious fact. He had been caught eavesdropping.

'Don't be scared. Come out,' continued the old voice. A slightly reassured Rinad started walking towards the direction where the voices came from. He crossed the huge dining area, and as he approached the wall that separated it from the adjacent section of the house, he felt the space open up. He entered the living room to find five expectant faces looking straight at him. He started palpitating, and the anxiety started taking over. He wasn't used to having so many eyes on him.

Of all the faces present, only two were familiar, the man and woman who had saved him from those vicious creatures. Asuras, as they apparently were. Just as he saw their faces, it started coming back to him. The man had wings and claws, and the woman made the Asuras throw up just by pointing her hands at them, he recollected, and as he caught a closer glimpse of them, he realised that besides that, they looked pretty normal.

The man was ginormous and wore a multi-coloured tank top and black harem-type trousers. He had short, spiked hair, and his face was rugged with a thick but well-kempt beard below his long-pointed nose.

The woman was sleek and quite a stunner with flawless skin, light brown eyes, and an enunciated jawline—features that Rinad had not noticed the night before. She sported body-hugging black track pants with a grey zipped-up jumper which complemented her bob cut. Of course, this was not like the last time he saw them when they were dressed in costumes and masks.

Sitting on the sofa across them were two oddly similar-looking individuals—a man and a woman, visibly younger than the others in the room. They both had curly hair and tinier body frames than everyone else. Their noses and ears were uncannily similar—one could have swapped them, and no one would have been able to tell the difference.

Besides that, they didn't have any other noteworthy features and wore a simple T-shirt and shorts each.

The living room had black leather sofas around a tiny centre table, where the four sat comfortably. At the head of the centre table was a short, old man, possibly the one who had spoken to Rinad and the one who was being referred to as "Guruji." He had white hair all over, a long, well-kempt beard, and wore a yellow baggy robe with stripes of orange on it—almost like a saint. He stood there with a warm and gentle smile on his face. All eyes were on Rinad, but he was the only one smiling.

'Please…take a seat. We have much to discuss,' the old man said calmly.

Rinad's eyes darted across the room, searching for an empty spot. On one side, there was a long couch with the two look-alikes on it, with room for one more. On the opposite side were two single couches with the winged man and the bob cut woman on each. There was a single couch behind where the old man stood, but it felt like he was in the middle of an important discussion and couldn't be seated for it.

Feeling everyone's eyes on him, Rinad slowly walked over to the long couch and sat on the end that was closer to him.

Noticing the sweat on Rinad's forehead, Guruji broke the uncomfortable silence, 'Would you like something to eat?'

Thirteen

Lunch was served, and Rinad ate his heart out. Salad, soup, chicken, *paneer kebabs*, *dal*, mixed vegetable *subzi*, *dahi*, *roti*, and rice—a meal containing all the required macronutrients that skilled warriors would need to consume as well as a lavish variety fit for a king.

Rinad ate like he hadn't eaten in days. The others slowly put morsels of food into their mouths as they stared at Rinad, who was relentless. As one morsel entered his mouth, the next one was being prepared on his almost overflowing steel plate. Guruji slowly ate small portions of rice, dal, and dahi, but was still the first one to finish.

Eventually, when the sound of cutlery and chewing faded out, Rinad realised that he was the only one left.

'Sorry…I'm really hungry,' Rinad said with his mouth full.

'Please take your time. We have nothing better to do,' said the winged man with a straight face and a sarcastic tone as he kept popping the paneer kebabs from the serving dish into his mouth, even though he had finished his meal.

'Yuva…' chided Guruji.

'Sorry, Guruji,' he said, licked his fingers and sat still.

'Please don't mind him. You haven't eaten since last night, so eat till your heart and stomach are full,' Guruji said with a mild chuckle.

Rinad smiled while nodding and picked up his pace of chewing. After a few minutes, he swallowed his last morsel, had a glassful of water, and let out a deep, satisfied sigh followed by a closed-mouth burp.

'You know…you shouldn't have so much water after a meal,' Guruji said without wiping the smile from his face.

'Sorry…ji…G-Guruji,' Rinad said hesitantly.

'You don't have to call me that yet. Someday, if you feel like it, you may.'

Rinad nodded sheepishly.

'Would you like some more?'

Rinad shook his head vigorously, indicating how full he was.

'Good. So, first of all, welcome to Manbhoomi. This is where we live, train, eat, and sleep. Basically, this is our home. And now, you too are a part of it. The room you were sleeping in will be yours from now on.'

'Why am I a part of it? I have a home...'

'We'll get to that. You won't be able to go back to your home anymore. Lest you face another encounter with the Asuras, who you've been warmly introduced to, I believe. Of course, we can bring all your things here.'

Rinad started worrying. It seemed like his relatively settled life was about to be disrupted, and that was not something he was prepared for.

'This is Nivedita or Nivi, and that is Ashwin or Ash. They're twins.'

That explains why they look so similar! Rinad thought to himself.

'I believe you've already met Yuva and Maya.'

Rinad looked around and gave a formal smile to all of them. Nivi and Ash beamed warmly and excitedly. Maya responded with a slightly formal smile, while Yuva couldn't care less and continued to stare coldly. Although this intimidated Rinad a bit, he quickly realised that Guruji was the one in charge here, so he didn't let it bother him too much.

'Rinad, there's something very important that you need to know. Now, I want you to take your time in processing what I'm about to say.'

Rinad's curiosity peaked. *What Guruji was about to say would be the answer to all his questions—who these people were, who the Asuras were, and why, in god's name, was everybody after him?*

He leaned in as the tension built with Guruji's unrequired and elaborate pause.

'Like the four of them and many others, you have been chosen to be a Manwaan.'

Rinad did not react. This was the first time he had heard that word, and had no clue what it meant.

'What's a Manwaan?' replied a confused Rinad.

Guruji chuckled, 'Let's take a walk, shall we?'

Fourteen

'How about we start with a tour of the house?' Guruji asked as he picked up his walking stick and exited the dining area.

'Okay…' said Rinad, shrugging his shoulders. Each piece of information was blowing his mind, so the order of events didn't matter anymore.

'You've seen the dining area, the living room, and, of course, your room,' Guruji continued as Rinad followed.

From the dining area, they crossed a foyer at the entrance of the house and walked through a doorway that led to a large area that looked like a classroom. Many plastic chairs were spread all over in a disorganised manner, much like they would be once a class was dismissed and students ran out immediately, with some chairs stacked on the side and a big whiteboard with a duster and different coloured markers.

'This is where we have our discussions.'

Rinad looked at Guruji curiously.

'Discussions on strategies,' continued Guruji.

Rinad remained confused.

'Battle strategies.'

Rinad's eyebrows raised, 'What exactly are Manwaans? And what do they do?'

Guruji smiled yet again and started walking towards the back of the classroom. His warm and innocent reaction began to annoy Rinad. He wasn't getting the answers he wanted, and a smile was not sufficing. As Guruji reached the back wall, which was textured and orange, he looked down and shoved aside a piece of the carpet covering the entire classroom floor—to reveal a square translucent glass. As he carefully stepped both feet on it, light beams began to scan it—horizontally and vertically.

This was a first, thought Rinad. He had heard of face and retina scans but never soles-of-the-feet scans. Additionally, the so-called "Manbhoomi" had a very simplistic aura to it. One would not expect high-end tech gadgets after having been in one of the under-whelming bedrooms, making it feel slightly out of place.

On completion, the walls parted open to reveal a dark void. Rinad gasped at the spectacle. Secret doorways suggested that there was something much bigger at play here.

'Watch your step,' Guruji cautioned as he disappeared down into the darkness. Rinad inched towards the doorway and found a flight of steps leading downstairs, with each step illuminated at the edge.

'What are you waiting for?' yelled Guruji as his cracked voice echoed through the chamber downstairs—it sounded like there was a huge room there.

'Coming!' Rinad yelled back, unsurely. He held the railing and walked down, step by step, making sure not to trip and fall. When he reached the bottom, all the lights went on, and Rinad stood there facing what seemed like a large training area. Almost the size of three football fields, the entire area was divided into grass, concrete, and rocky sections.

'I definitely did not expect this,' exclaimed Rinad.

'I am sure!' chuckled Guruji. 'This is where we train. Of course, on Sundays, the grass section doubles up as a football ground. So far, the teams have not been even, considering there were five of us. Now that you're here, we could have a fair match with three on each team!'

Rinad wasn't sure what to be more shocked about—the fact that this old man with hunched shoulders, carrying a walking stick, played football or that he assumed that Rinad would be around on all the forthcoming Sundays to join them.

'You play football?' asked a wide-eyed Rinad.

'Oh…you'd be surprised to see how good I am!' grinned Guruji.

The house seemed rather small compared to this humongous area. On one end of the field was a line of scarecrow-type figures with red circles on them.

Must be for target practice, thought Rinad.

Right next to it was a make-shift gym—a few dumbbells, a barbell with a couple of weight plates, a pull-up bar, and a bench. Adjacent to that were a bunch of weapons—bows and arrows, swords, knives, nunchucks, and whatnot—all neatly organised.

'No guns?' smirked Rinad.

'No need for them. Only humans use guns.'

Rinad froze.

A statement like that implied that there was something inhuman about all of this. Flashes of the night of his abduction started coming back to him. Things were starting to make sense, but at the same time, they were getting more nonsensical as the events progressed.

The feeling started bubbling. Panic started taking over.

'Calm down, Rinad. We're getting to it. I have a lot to tell you. I am just warming you up for it. And a word of advice…don't try and fight whatever you see or hear. Accept it. Believe in it. That'll be the first step in the right direction for you.'

Guruji's words were soothing. In an attempt to calm down, Rinad began to consciously take in a couple of long, deep breaths.

In, 2, 3, 4…hold, 2, 3, 4…out, 2, 3, 4…hold, 2, 3, 4…

As he repeated this a couple of times, he felt his chest getting lighter and the tension in his muscles slowly fading away. He surprised himself with the fact that his therapist's breathing technique worked, as he had barely used it in the past. The few times he had tried it, he would give up before it could even have its effect. Of course, he still missed his weed. And it helped that Guruji's words felt therapeutic too.

'We've got two more rooms to see. Let's go. Quickly!'

Two doorways adjacent to the flight of stairs led them down here. Guruji proceeded towards the doorway that was closest to it, opened the door, and walked in. When Rinad entered, he witnessed, yet again, another large room.

'How many large rooms do you have in here?'

'We tried to be modest with the house, you see. Don't want to be drawing too much attention to ourselves.'

Makes sense, thought Rinad.

This room, however, was more of a laboratory. Rinad was never into science but could tell that experiments were conducted here. Test tubes and beakers all over the place, an operation section, and multiple glass jars with different coloured chemicals. A haven for scientists.

'I know you're not big into science, but this is where some of the most important work is done.'

How does he know that I'm not into science? Rinad's thoughts were clearly expressed on his face.

'You think we don't know about your likes and dislikes, Rinad? I don't mean to come off as intrusive, but we know almost everything about you, you see. How you hate science, your job at Copy That, how many joints you smoke in a day…'

Rinad was speechless and slightly embarrassed. He didn't like people knowing about his addiction.

'Don't worry. You won't have to develop an interest towards science. In fact, besides Ash and Nivi, none of us are good with it. They are the smart ones. Each of us has a role to play, but it is important to have a basic understanding of the roles that your comrades play…in case you need to step in someday.'

'If I ever have to step in and mess around with these chemicals, that'll be the end of this place,' smirked Rinad.

Guruji chuckled, 'Let's hope we never reach that stage.'

'But what kind of stuff do you do here exactly?'

'Right from experimenting with explosives, creating weapons, and treating injuries…this room takes care of it all.'

'Building explosives?'

Guruji smiled. 'Don't worry, Rinad. We're not the bad guys. We are just preparing ourselves to face them.'

Rinad looked unconvinced.

'Let's go to the last room. Hopefully, things will seem more justified then.'

'If you say so,' Rinad replied with a lack of faith. He wasn't sure if anything could ever justify the building of explosives and weapons, but it didn't look like he had much of a choice. He hesitantly followed Guruji into the last room.

As Guruji opened the door, a passageway lit up that led to another opening. On crossing it, Rinad stood in front of a huge circular area.

His jaw dropped.

Along the periphery of the room were five tall glass boxes with spotlights above them. In each was a different coloured body suit, a face mask, and a bunch of accessories placed neatly on the bottom shelf.

'Costumes?' asked Rinad.

Guruji smiled and nodded his head, 'Costumes!'

Fifteen

'Sir…he's here!' yelled Pawar after banging open Deshpande's door.

'How many times have I told you to knock, Pawar!'

'Sorry, sir…but he's here!'

'Yes, you already said that,' Deshpande was on edge about a last-minute meeting with ACP Kamat. The fact that his superior had decided to drop by the Bandra police station was a rarity in itself. Further, it being without prior notice, made Deshpande tense. He knew that the entire police force was on high alert because of the steady increase in the arbitrary killings, and considering Bandra was witnessing the highest numbers, he knew what was coming. Deshpande took in a deep breath to clear his mind, prepared himself for the storm, and stepped out to welcome ACP Kamat.

'Stay right outside my door and make sure the CCTV footage on your laptop is on standby. Let's keep this smooth,' he whispered to Pawar, who bobbed his head and jogged away to prepare. Just as he sat down at his desk, he stood up again, along with all the other officers present at the station. Overlapping voices of "Good afternoon, sir" echoed as everyone synchronously saluted.

ACP Kamat had entered the station.

A tall, lean gentleman with well-kept salt and pepper hair, a moustache and a perfectly fitted uniform, ACP Kamat had a rather calm demeanour—something that everyone was well aware of and respected him for. He was followed by two junior IPS officers who carried files with them and seemed to have an air of arrogance, unlike their superior.

Calmness and humility came with experience and maturity, and one could tell that ACP Kamat embodied the same. He responded to all the police officers with a smile and asked them to be seated while his juniors barely acknowledged anyone.

'Good afternoon, sir!' Deshpande banged his feet in attention as he stood outside his office and saluted his senior, who he deeply revered.

'*Aur* Deshpande...how are you?' Kamat responded with a smile. Deshpande almost melted with the warmth that Kamat exuded.

'Not too bad, sir. Please come in,' Deshpande smiled respectfully and showed the three of them the way in. Kamat took a seat while the two junior officers stood behind him on either side.

'How have you been, sir?' Deshpande continued. 'We started to miss your presence at our station.'

Kamat chuckled, 'I miss being here too, Deshpande. But it's been a bit crazy of late.'

'I can imagine, sir. Shall I get you something? *Chai*, coffee, water?'

'I'm good. We need to check on Juhu, so let's get to it,' Kamat said, immediately stiffening up. 'What in god's name is going on, Deshpande?'

'I'm lost myself, sir. We've never seen anything like this. The number of reports have been increasing drastically…'

'Especially in Bandra,' Kamat cut in. Deshpande pulled on his collar to escape from the warmth that crept in. A cloud of embarrassment and failure was being cast over him. He was at a loss for words.

'I'm sorry, Deshpande. I did not mean to put you in a spot. But this is the first time we have been concerned about Bandra. We've been so proud of all the work you have done up till now. But now that these killings are getting out of hand, my superiors are beginning to wonder if your plate is overflowing.'

'It's not that, sir. We've been looking out for clues that may lead us to possible answers, but things don't seem to be adding up. Let me show you, sir,' Deshpande said as he stood up and walked over to his steel drawer stand. He opened the middle drawer, took out a bunch of files, and placed them on his desk. While this was just to show the number of reports, he simply gave the topmost file to his commanding officer. As Kamat focused and went through the contents of the report meticulously, his face crossfaded to one of disgust and hopelessness.

This was Deshpande's cue.

'And that's just one case, sir.'

'*Hey bhagwaan!*'

'There's more, sir…if you will allow me.'

'Please.'

Deshpande walked over to his door and gestured Pawar to come in. He pointed towards his table, signalling Pawar to keep the laptop before Kamat.

'This is Sub-Inspector Pawar, sir.'

'Good morning, sir. I mean…afternoon, sir,' said an intimidated Pawar. But Kamat's smile eased him out instantly. He placed the laptop on the desk and looked towards Deshpande for approval. Pawar hit play after Deshpande nodded.

Kamat shifted to the edge of his seat. The two junior officers' cold expressions transformed into worried looks.

A mother and her ten-year-old son were crossing an alley when they were intercepted by two figures. One was dressed casually in jeans and a T-shirt, and the other in shorts and a shirt. There was a brief exchange of words, after which the mother dropped her shopping bags and began to step back in what seemed like fear. She stood in front of her son in an attempt to protect him, but what followed indicated that she was the one who needed the protection. While the images seemed blurry, it was discernible that the nails of the two figures began to extend. One of the figures landed a deathly blow across the mother's neck, and she fell against the side of the wall, leaving the child to fend for himself. Both the figures stared at the boy for barely a minute. They looked at each other, shook their heads, and fled away.

'This was from an alley in Bandra East, sir. We were lucky to have one of the shop vendors share the CCTV footage with us.'

'But why did they spare the child?' Kamat said in an almost-choked voice.

'That's what I'm confused about, sir. We even did a background check on the woman in case she had any criminal records or owed money to someone. Nothing. She's absolutely clean. We also tried looking for the culprits but could not trace them,' Deshpande replied.

'And what the hell were those claws!' Kamat didn't seem to acknowledge what Deshpande had to say. He was overwhelmed with questions but got no response from anyone.

'Sir, Pawar even witnessed this first-hand.'

'What do you mean?'

'Pawar!' Deshpande gestured him to recount his experience. Of course, Deshpande had instructed him to leave out the drinking bit as such reports were frowned upon.

'Sir, I saw exactly what you saw just now. Some of these people were in a white van. I think they were kidnapping someone. They were intercepted by another bunch of skilled warriors.'

'Skilled warriors?' questioned Kamat suspiciously.

'Yes, sir. I could not tell who they were. But they were dressed in black robes and had black marks on their faces.'

'Hmm…strange. Carry on.'

'They tried to battle these people but were no match. The people from the white van had long black claws, black eyes, and even black veins that began to appear on their necks as they started fighting. That's all I could make out, sir.'

Just then, the door banged open, and a constable barged in. He looked scared at first and got even more intimidated by the tense atmosphere in the room.

'Sorry to intrude on your meeting, sir,' the constable said hesitantly and looked towards Deshpande, aware of his hatred towards officers who did not knock.

'It's okay, go on,' Deshpande replied, trying to maintain a calm composure in front of his supervising officer.

'Sir…we've received one more report. The location is just around ten minutes from here.'

Deshpande darted a look towards Kamat, expecting an order.

'Let's go,' commanded Kamat.

Sixteen

Three police jeeps rushed to the location that was sent to them. The people of Mumbai were slowly becoming more aware of these killings, and word of any new incidents travelled fast—something that worked in the police's favour.

As they arrived at the location, they parked the vehicles outside an alley and the officers marched in with Kamat and Deshpande leading the way towards a crowd.

'Move please!' boomed Deshpande.

As the swarm of people parted, two officers stood there, towering over a body lying in a pool of blood. They saw the senior officers walking in and, on sneaking a glance at their insignias, slammed to attention with a salute. With a gesture, Kamat signalled them to be at ease. He and Deshpande glared at the horrendous spectacle in front of them.

'He was seventy-three, sir,' said one of the officers who had been at the site from before.

Kamat nodded slowly.

His city was falling apart, and neither he nor his superiors could do anything about it.

'Did anyone witness this?' asked Deshpande.

'That gentleman says he was here,' replied the officer, pointing towards a man standing in front of the crowd. The man was in tears as he stared at the body.

Pawar walked up to the man and slowly began the standard investigation process, 'Sir, I'm Sub-Inspector Virat Pawar, this is Inspector Deshpande, and this is ACP Kamat. Could you please narrate to us whatever you saw?'

The man looked up with a forlorn gaze and fumbled for words.

'It's okay, take your time,' said Deshpande.

The man, roughly in his early forties, took in a deep breath, exhaled, and closed his eyes. After seeming slightly calmer, he began, 'My father and I were taking a stroll. We decided to cross this alley to get to the other side when these three strangers confronted us. I knew something was wrong because of the way they looked at us. I offered them money, but they weren't interested. When I tried to have a conversation to understand what they actually wanted, they simply pushed me aside and went for my father. And then…' the man choked as his eyes flooded before he could finish what he wanted to say and broke down.

'I'm sorry for your loss,' Deshpande responded awkwardly. He was not used to comforting victims during such situations. 'By any chance, did you notice anything strange about the perpetrators?'

The man sniffed his nose and wiped his tears. 'They wore normal clothes, which seemed odd considering they were murderers. And they even had long black nails. They didn't use any weapon, just their hands.'

'Did you see their eyes changing colour?' asked Pawar.

'I didn't notice. My attention was on my father....'

'What about their teeth? Or neck?'

The man shook his head. 'Their backs were facing me, so I could not tell.'

A silence followed.

'Are these the same people who have been all over the news?' the man asked bitterly. Pawar and Deshpande darted a look towards each other. A look that seemed to have answered the man's question. 'Well, you can tell everyone that they're no animals. They're mere human beings, maybe part of some terrorist group who like to grow their nails and kill innocent people so that it seems like an animal has done it.' The rage in his voice steadily increased, and soon, he was yelling with fury, 'Don't let them get away with such heinous crimes!'

'Sir...please calm down,' Pawar tried to console him. None of the cases were being resolved, and it seemed like the capabilities of the police forces were being doubted. To top it all, an angry victim yelling at a crime scene would only worsen the situation.

'No! I will not calm down!! Don't try and bury this by saying an animal did it!! Do your goddamn job. If you had done it well so far, my father might have still been alive!'

The two officers who were overlooking the body came over and started consoling the man as he continued screaming. Pawar was at a loss for words. He looked over to his Inspector for a command, only to find him teary-eyed and dumbfounded.

As a dejected Deshpande walked back to his jeep with revenge on his mind, a loud scream was heard from nearby. Everyone who was gathered around the body popped their heads towards the direction of the sound.

'Help! Help!!'

The screams continued.

'It seems to be coming from there, sir,' Pawar said, pointing to an adjacent alley.

'You two, stay here,' Deshpande told the officers who were there at the crime scene. 'Rest…follow me. *Chal*, Pawar!'

Deshpande and Pawar sprinted towards the direction of the sound, followed by six armed officers, joined by ACP Kamat at the back. As they entered the lane, they found two bodies on the floor, with a woman frantically crying for help. Pawar looked around and saw three figures exiting the alley from the other side.

'There, sir!' he yelled and began running towards them before even completing his sentence. Nine officers, including Kamat, Deshpande, and Pawar, chased the figures. As they came onto the main road, Pawar saw them running into the crowd and continued to lead the way.

All the officers had their guns on standby.

'Move!' shouted Pawar.

They weren't going to let the culprits escape this time.

The three figures sped into another alley, hoping to escape. As the chase continued, the three finally met with a dead end. The guns clicked into standby, and the officers took their positions, finally cornering their targets. An iota of the sensation of victory came over Deshpande. The criminals who were trying to escape were cornered. The six officers stood in front and inched towards the criminals with loaded weapons as their three superior officers gave the orders from behind.

'*Thaamba!*' commanded Deshpande, asking his comrades to stop and hold their positions. 'Drop your weapons, if you have any, and turn around slowly. Nothing hasty. We will not hesitate to fire!'

Silence.

No response.

The figures stood still, facing the brick wall.

Deshpande gestured to one of the officers to fire a warning shot. The officer aimed towards the corner of the wall, making sure not to hit the killers, and fired.

The figures did not flinch.

'Leave us…or else we will have no choice but to kill you,' growled one of the Asuras.

'I'm afraid that's not possible. In case you haven't noticed, we're the ones holding the guns. Surrender yourselves…there's no way out,' commanded Deshpande.

They turned around in the most composed manner. As they began to assume their complete demonic potential, their nails elongated, and their eyes turned dark as black veins emerged on their necks.

The officers briefly lowered their weapons in shock, unable to believe the spectacle.

The figures roared, and Deshpande yelled, 'FIRE!'

A round of bullets were unleashed on the Asuras. The officers recovered from the recoil of their guns immediately and awaited their next orders. They were stunned to see that, even though all the bullets had hit the targets accurately, the figures seemed unaffected.

There were tiny black patches at the spots where the bullets had hit. But there was no blood dripping, not even a scar.

'Our turn,' grinned one of them. The perpetrators marched up to the six officers and decimated them in two effective blows from each.

Six able-bodied, armed officers dead. In under five seconds.

Realising that no hope was left, Pawar got behind an enormous green trash collector while Kamat and Deshpande stuck themselves to the walls.

One Asura began to march towards Kamat, but the other one stopped him and shook his head. He gave in, and the three creatures, now with a clear path to escape ahead of them, morphed back into their human forms and sprinted towards the exit of the alley, leaving the three senior officers unharmed.

Deshpande and Kamat were shattered.

They had lost some of their most capable men, and the guilt of not being able to do anything about it crept in. Their eyes flooded as they stood there dumbfounded by the proceedings that had unravelled in front of them. Deshpande dropped his head and bent over with his arms on his waist, feeling sick and disgusted from all the bloodshed. His breaths shortened, feeling choked at the hopelessness of the situation.

They had witnessed a bloodbath. What was worse, they finally knew what they were up against. To which they were no match.

Pawar crawled out from behind the trash bin and walked over to Deshpande, trembling and awaiting an order.

Taking the cue from Pawar, Deshpande mustered up the courage and stood up straight. He followed this with a few conscious and forceful breaths to restore his energy and walked up to his commanding officer.

'Kamat sir…give me two weeks. I'll get to the bottom of this,' he said in a choked voice. He could barely get words out of his mouth. The need to avenge his late officers seemed to be the only thing motivating him and giving him the strength to speak up.

'Don't act in haste, Deshpande,' replied his commanding officer hopelessly as his eyes flooded. 'Did you see what those things did?'

Deshpande did not respond. He realised that he might have spoken too soon. Barely two minutes ago, the bloodbath had occurred, and there he was talking about the next step in the plan.

However, this was no time to mourn.

Each minute they wasted meant putting many more lives at risk. Kamat might have been more sensitive towards the situation, but Deshpande had to be more pragmatic about it. In a soft tone, he spoke up, 'It's not in a haste, sir. I assure you. I do need your approval on something, though.'

Deshpande's rational approach slowly rubbed off on Kamat. Even though lives were lost, they had to get to the bottom of this.

'Anything that will help you resolve this,' Kamat said with forced optimism.

'I'd like to hand pick and put together a special force… with your permission.'

'Sure. How many officers do you need?'

'Thirty, to begin with, sir.'

'You have my permission.'

Seventeen

'That's Yuva's...and that's Maya's, right?' Rinad said, pointing out to two of the five costumes.

'Correct. I am guessing you remember them from last night?' Guruji responded with a smirk on his face.

'Kind of. Why do we...I mean...you...need costumes?'

Guruji stood there with a gentle smile on his face.

The time had come.

'Rinad, what I am about to tell you might be a bit unsettling and hard to believe, but it is as real as it gets. Let me start with this...do you believe in God?'

Rinad shook his head, 'Not really. I guess I'm more agnostic about it. I question God's existence, but I do believe that there is some kind of a greater power that's beyond our understanding.'

'I am glad! We can work with that. You see, Rinad...the title that is given to it could differ from person to person, but at the end of the day, each individual is surrounded by a single force...belief!'

Rinad frowned. He was expecting a deeper and more philosophical answer. Certainly, there was more, he thought.

'Belief?'

'Belief. It is what drives people; it is what comforts them. Some people focus the energy of belief towards the idea of a God. Some, like yourself, towards an intangible greater power. Some, towards love…but everyone gets on with their lives with the idea of belief. Some people thank God when they're happy, as they believe God is responsible for their happiness. Some pray to God when they are low, as they believe God will uplift them from that state. Everything is centred around the idea of belief.'

'Okay…' Rinad said, confused.

'So, Rinad, I want you to believe. Believe in yourself, in everything that's happening around us and, most importantly, in what I am about to tell you,' Guruji concluded.

'Sure.'

'To believe is to be close to God.'

Guruji paused as he knew Rinad would need a minute to let that sink in.

Rinad's eyes darted from one side to the other, trying to solve this conundrum.

Guruji continued, 'When one believes, one feels empowered. One experiences a strong force running through their veins…maybe even feeling enlightened… euphoric…satisfied! These are the sensations that take one closer to God. So, to believe is to be close to God. Are you with me till here?'

'I think so,'

'Questions?' said Guruji, giving Rinad an opportunity to clear his mind.

'So according to what you're saying, as long as you believe, you'll be close to God?'

'Precisely,' Guruji said with a content smile. He was glad that his pupil seemed to be imbibing what he meant to convey.

'So, you don't need to believe in God, per se. You just need to believe in…well, something…anything…' Rinad reconfirmed with increased enthusiasm.

'Sure.'

'Hmm…'

'But the idea of belief is inevitable. And that's God's doing.'

'Okay…now you've lost me.'

'I am glad. But I need you to believe,' Guruji chuckled.

Rinad frowned.

Guruji had this annoying habit of trying extremely hard to be funny at the worst moments.

'I apologise, but I was only partially joking,' continued Guruji as he tried to contain his chuckling. 'The fact that we feel…that we have emotions aligns with the notion that there is, in fact, a God.'

'So…we feel because there is a God?'

'Why else? Or rather, who else would enable us to feel? We could have just been rocks or leaves or some other substance incapable of feeling. Why were we blessed with this ability to feel? Because someone wanted it to happen. Someone made a choice. And who is that someone?' Guruji paused expectantly, hoping for an answer from his newfound disciple.

'God?'

'Precisely. God. And, thus, what might the conclusion be?'

Another expectant pause.

'That…there is a God?'

'Correct. I need you to believe more, but we can work with this.'

Rinad released a deep breath, almost like he had run a marathon.

Guruji smiled, 'Would you like some chai?'

Eighteen

The sun began its day's descent as Guruji and Rinad strolled across the lawns of Manbhoomi. Surrounding the house was a row of thick bushes with a jogging track that ran along the border of the premises. The entire area must have been the size of three football fields, with the house occupying only around one-tenth of it at its centre.

The huge lawns must be to cover up for the massive underground training arena, thought Rinad.

At the edge of the lawn was another thick row of bushes. Flowers bloomed everywhere, mostly marigolds, jasmines, and indigos, and in one corner of the lawn was a large Banyan tree with dense roots hanging from it.

'I'm guessing that's where you attain Nirvana?' jested Rinad.

'Something like that,' Guruji replied with unusual seriousness.

'Also, where exactly are we?'

'Dahisar. At the far end of it.'

'Wow. I think it's my first time coming to this side of Mumbai.'

'I am not surprised. Did not expect much else from a Bandra boy.'

Rinad frowned.

Being called a "Bandra boy" was akin to being called "from a privileged background" in many ways. Most people from Bandra, especially Bandra West, were well-to-doers, and even though Rinad didn't identify himself with that anymore, as he lived in Andheri East, it didn't change the fact that that's where he grew up. Such a comment still pinched him.

They both walked around slowly and sipped on their hot tea. Rinad was still processing all the information that he had just received. As they strolled, they saw Yuva, Maya, Ash, and Nivi jogging on the tracks that ran through the middle of the huge lawn. All of them wore track pants and hoodies. As the four of them were jogging, Yuva darted a poker face towards Rinad, who quickly looked away.

'Doesn't he have wings?'

Guruji chuckled. 'He sure does. But that does not mean he should forget how to run!'

'Good point.'

'How are you feeling?' Guruji asked, hoping he could continue his teachings.

'The chai is helping for sure.'

'Good. Can we continue?'

'I guess…'

'Wonderful. Now, what are your thoughts on angels?'

Rinad stared at Guruji. 'I mean, you've convinced me that there is a God. I'm assuming there are angels as well?' he said with a shrug.

'Well assumed!' chuckled Guruji. 'You see, Rinad… after the Gods made everything—this planet, this universe, us humans—they needed someone to look after it, quite simply put. The Gods' celestial radiation is too powerful for them to be able to step onto this realm. Earth would implode if they did so….'

'Hold on…you keep saying *them*, and *they*. You mean there are multiple Gods?'

'There are multiple perceptions of God. Think of it as energy. It cannot be singular. It is a collective force. One source, many forms.'

'Hmm…and male or female?'

'There is no way to tell. But the way each person sees God is the way God is for you. Did you notice anything different about the three portraits kept on the glass shelf in your room?'

'Not really…'

'Well, have a look the next time. We call them Brahma, Vishnu, and Shiva for convenience, but if you look closely, you will notice that each one is an *ardhanarishwar* form.'

'What's that?'

'Half man, half woman. Each individual gives the form of God, but the source is one. And it has no gender attached to it. It is a combination of all genders as well as none. Each person views God in their own way—Hanuman, Lakshmi, Ganesha, Saraswati—whichever resonates with you becomes your God.'

'Hmm…interesting.'

'You'll understand this better in just a minute. Coming back to angels….'

'Right.'

'Angels form the bridge between the Gods and humanity. Whether it's carrying out celestial proceedings or communicating God's messages to humans, angels are the only ones who can do it. Are you with me?'

'Yes…so far, so good.'

'Good. Now, Heaven used to have fourteen angels. You were always fascinated by history, right?'

'How did you kno…never mind,' Rinad rolled his eyes. He knew the answer to that question.

Guruji chuckled. 'We're going to dive into a bit of history now, and I need your full attention.'

By this time, they had completed a lap around the house and had arrived at the Banyan tree.

'Have a seat,' Guruji pointed to a section of the stony structure that surrounded the tree.

'My first step towards enlightenment!' jested Rinad.

'We'll see,' Guruji said with a mild squint in his eyes. It was almost as if he was hoping for Rinad to attain the said enlightenment.

'Over two millennia ago, a war broke out in Heaven, and seven of the fourteen angels were cast out. The seven

Fagir, as they came to be known, were sent to Hell—the home of the Underworld Clan comprising of Asuras, Rakshasas, and many more creatures. While the Fagir were in their eternal exile, they formed a coalition with the Underworld Clan and, under the leadership of Saatan, the first of the Fagir, began to plan a revolution against the Gods and the remaining seven Arinch, the worthy ones, to claim back what they felt was rightfully theirs. Vengeance consumed them, and the alliance strengthened them. With time, the revolution against Heaven magnified into the annexation of Earth and Heaven. The Fagir, along with the Underworld Clan, planned to take over the two realms that were out of their reach, and, well, we fear that day has come. It looks like the Asuras have entered our realm. Rinad, we believe we have entered the dark ages, or the *Kalyug*—popularly known to be the last cycle of the universe's existence. But more appropriately, it is the era of the Underworld. Where the Underworld rules all.'

Rinad sat there with his jaw dropped.

'Too much?' Guruji said with a soft smile.

'No…I mean, kind of…I mean…so the killings, the people who abducted me last night, they were…' Rinad gulped.

'I am afraid so,' Guruji replied with sadness in his eyes as silence brewed between the two of them.

He then mustered up a soft smile.

'Let's get some dinner, shall we?'

Nineteen

As the two of them walked back in, they were welcomed by the four Manwaans who were already seated at the dining table. It seemed like they had been waiting for a while.

'Finally!' exclaimed Yuva. 'That took longer than expected.'

'We barely got halfway through,' remarked Guruji.

'Well, we're all starving. Can we eat, please?' Maya said as her tummy rumbled.

'You could've started off, and we would've joined you,' Rinad said relatively more confidently than before. Right after uttering those words, he realised that this was the first time he had directly spoken to the four of them.

'We always eat together,' Nivi said with a pleasant smile.

It also seemed like each person had a designated place at the table. Yuva and Maya would sit on one side, Ash and Nivi on the other side—Ash opposite Maya and Nivi opposite Yuva and, of course, Guruji would sit at the head of the table—leaving one spot for Rinad, across him—the same seat he had sat at for lunch at the six-seater table. As he started peeking into all the dishes laid out in front of him, his expression turned into disappointment, especially after the lavish lunch he had been presented with. There were three large bowls—one with plain *dal-khichdi*, another with mildly spiced curd rice, and the third with a subzi—primarily comprising of cauliflower, peas, potato, and carrots.

It had been nearly twenty-four hours since Rinad had last smoked a joint and dinner without a smoking session before it was not part of his daily routine. Even though he was hungry, the desire to eat was not at its fullest. And to add to this, even the food did not seem all that appetising.

Of course, he was new here, and it would have been rude for him to comment on any of this.

He stared at it as the others started serving themselves.

'We usually have a light dinner, you see,' Guruji said with a smile after observing Rinad's reaction. 'It is not good to eat food that is rich or spicy at night. It must be kept simple so that your body can digest it easily. You better start getting used to this.'

Rinad nodded and began to serve himself.

Each one had just a plate to themselves, except for Yuva, who had an extra bowl by his plate.

Maybe he needs some extra protein, considering his size, thought Rinad, trying to amuse himself.

'So where did you reach in today's discourse?' Ash chuckled and asked Rinad in a pseudo-dramatic manner.

'Well...umm...we spoke about the coalition between the angels and the Underworld Clan,' Rinad looked towards Guruji for approval. With the overload of information, he feared that minute yet important details might be missed. Given the situation, that could not be afforded. Guruji smiled and nodded, gesturing him to carry on.

'...and the Asuras have started attacking people on Earth. I think that's about it,' once again, he looked at Guruji for approval. Guruji nodded and smiled.

'That's it?' said a surprised Ash. 'You really do have a lot left.'

'They haven't reached the *masala* yet,' Yuva said with a tiny grin on his face.

'The masala?' asked Rinad.

'The masala!' said an excited Nivi. 'It's the most exciting part of anything—a dish or a story.'

'Oh...' Rinad semi-chuckled.

'Without which you don't really get the true flavour of the dish,' Yuva said with his mouth stuffed.

'And...umm...what is the masala? Because everything up till now already seemed...masaledaar.'

Everyone at the table chuckled as Rinad tried to speak their lingo, wanting to convey that he had received a strong enough dose of the "masala" from what Guruji had told him thus far. Anymore, and he would have to deal with heartburn. Metaphorically speaking.

'Guruji will reveal all of it to you,' Yuva continued as he reached into the bowl that was kept by his plate, picked up what looked like a tiny piece of meat, and held it close to his ear. 'Govi! Govinda!!' he yelled.

'Don't shout, Yuva!' said an annoyed Maya.

Who is Govinda? Rinad thought to himself as he waited for someone to show up.

Just then a sound echoed through the house.

'Kaww…Kaww…'

A crow flew in from one corner of the ceiling and perched itself on Yuva's shoulder. It picked on the piece of meat offered by its master and devoured it.

'*Shabaash*!' exclaimed Yuva as he patted the crow on its head.

'Kaww…Kaww…'

'This is our new friend. His name is Rinad. Rinad, say hi to Govinda.'

Rinad was slightly confused.

Yuva had just asked him to greet a crow.

'Umm…hi…Govinda…'

'You can call him Govi if you like.'

'Okay…hi…Govi…I didn't see him during lunch.'

'He likes to travel around during the day.'

'Oh…how nice…' Rinad said awkwardly.

'Kaww…Kaww…'

'It's his first day. Obviously, he'll be scared,' Yuva continued his conversation with his buddy.

'You can communicate with him?' asked a wide-eyed Rinad.

'Yup.'

'Is it with all birds?'

'Nope. Just him. I can understand what other birds say, though.'

'That is so bizarre…but pretty awesome too.'

'Kaww…Kaww…'

'Shh!! Don't be mean, Govinda!'

'What did he say?' Rinad cut in.

'He said that…you won't hang around. You don't have what it takes, and that you're going to run away.'

Silence took over the dining table as an awkward subject was broached.

'Why would he say that? I made it this far, didn't I? If I had to run away, you really think I would have stayed for dinner?'

'It's barely been twenty-four hours, Rinad. And you haven't heard all of it yet. Besides, don't take Govi too seriously…he tends to make quick judgements.'

'He's a bloody bird…who is he to…'

'Don't you dare talk to him like that!'

'That's enough!' commanded Guruji. 'Focus on your food. Nothing else.'

'Sorry, Guruji,' said Yuva and continued to alternate between feeding Govi and eating his food.

'Sorry, Guruji,' whispered Rinad and went back to his food.

The silence that followed stretched into an uncomfortable one. Rinad soon realised that he had over spoken. He was new here and had to be more courteous. If he planned to stick around, he needed to ensure he didn't arouse any ill feelings from anyone at Manbhoomi.

With great difficulty, he managed to break the silence.

'Why the name Govinda?'

'Was that an apology?' Yuva grunted.

'Was that not clear?' Rinad rolled his eyes and shook his head.

Yuva smiled and continued, 'It's because I love Govinda,' a sign of acceptance of the apology.

'Who?'

'The actor,' Maya said with a poker face.

'He's his favourite. You should see him working out to "*Main toh raste se jaa raha tha.*" It's quite an annoying spectacle,' added Nivi, as she quoted one of the actor's most popular songs from a movie titled "Coolie No. 1".

'Kaww…Kaww…'

'He says he likes the name. It suits him,' translated Yuva.

'Kaww…Kaww...'

'And that he can be *Kauva* No. 1.'

Everyone laughed and carried on eating. Eventually, they all called it a night and retired to their rooms. Rinad prepared for his second night, feeling slightly more warmed up to the new place and the people that he was about to go on a journey with.

Twenty

As the lights went out, Rinad tossed and turned in his bed while rubbing on his mole. The cold sweats took over, and before he realised it, his pillow was drenched. He needed his regular dose of weed to sleep well. He hadn't slept sober in years and did not intend on starting now.

Not to mention that the amount of information he had been bombarded with earlier was too much to process.

Was he really a Manwaan? How was this going to affect his life? Would he ever be able to live the life he used to? And were the Asuras going to come after him again?

Questions kept whizzing through his mind, and slumber seemed far from possible.

He stood up, switched on the light, grabbed a water bottle from the study table, and walked to the glass corner shelf with the three portraits. As he pulled up the bottom of his t-shirt and used it to wipe the sweat off his forehead, he sipped on the water and had a closer look at the three

Gods, as Guruji had asked him to—Brahma, the creator, Vishnu, the preserver, and Shiva, the destroyer. Only this time, he noticed the ardhanarishwar form that Guruji had spoken about.

Each God was made up of equal halves of a man and a woman. He wasn't quite sure who the women were. Possibly their better halves—Brahma's wife, Saraswati, Vishnu's wife, Lakshmi, and Shiva's wife, Parvati.

He had never really been interested in the idea of God, but his conversation with Guruji had got him intrigued. As he stood and stared at the portraits, he took a couple of deep breaths.

In, 2, 3, 4...hold, 2, 3, 4...out, 2, 3, 4...hold, 2, 3, 4...

Eventually, a calmness began to take over. The sweat receded, his muscles relaxed, and he soon felt much better. And possibly ready to sleep.

As Guruji said, maybe all Rinad needed was belief.

To believe.

He needed to believe in the existence of God, his purpose and destiny in this world, and that there was a reason he was chosen to be a Manwaan—whatever that was. He still had no answer as to what that was.

All he knew was that he was one.

And that his life might not be the same anymore.

With these thoughts, he switched off his light and tucked himself inside his blanket to finally get some much-deserved shut-eye. He had a big day ahead, with a lot more information to process and, hopefully, many more answers that would lead to some clarity.

He had to prepare himself for it.

Within minutes, he was fast asleep.

The first sober sleep he had had in years.

Twenty-one

'Those imbeciles!' growled Usur as his voice echoed through the alley. The Asuras had gathered for their weekly midnight meeting, where each shared their reports from the past seven days.

'They had one job to do!' continued Usur. As he puffed, an eerie silence followed. 'None of them made it?'

'No, my king,' a voice spoke from amidst the platoon of twelve Asuras. 'Their hosts' heads were severed from their bodies. They were no match for whatever they were up against.'

'Could the humans have done this?'

'I highly doubt that, Usurji,' continued another. 'We were up against a bunch of cops the other day...the humans are weaklings. No way they could have done this.'

'Then it must be *them.* They know that we're here,' Usur continued in a contemplative state.

'Who, my king?'

'The Manwaans.'

Silence brewed.

The Asuras began to have a faint understanding of what they were up against. Even though they had done their due diligence on the Manwaans, they never knew what to expect from those who were realised. Arrogance had led members of the Underworld Clan to believe that nothing or no one could be as powerful as them.

'Give us one more chance, Usurji,' boasted another.

'That's all we have. We've already lost three of our comrades. Anymore, and that'll be it for us. And Mihaara will not be pleased.'

No one responded. All were in agreement.

'You...and you...' he pointed to two of the remaining twelve, 'I want you to go and inspect his house, gather as much information as possible about this prophesied leader of the Manwaans, and stay ready. Do not assume your demonic forms in front of anyone else...we can't afford to blow our cover. Speak to his neighbours, do whatever you must. And this time, when you see him, kill him immediately. No need to bring him in alive. No delaying!' commanded Usur.

'Yes, Usurji,' said the two in unison.

'And tread carefully. These Manwaans seem to be realised. You will be no match for them.'

'We promise to be careful.'

'Good. Iaj Raakn Ho!'

'Iaj Raakn Ho!' they responded and ran off to take care of what their comrades could not.

'What about us, Usurji? What should we do?' continued another excited fellow Asura.

'Wait,' said Usur with a hint of fear in his voice.

'We may need reinforcements.'

Twenty-two

The ground cracked open, and fire began consuming all areas of the land. Blood-soaked, lifeless bodies lay all over the place as the city was being torn down. While the Asuras slaughtered anyone who came in their way, giant, translucent creatures nearly 300 feet tall, with wings and horns, emerged from the cracks of the ground and unleashed themselves on Earth.

Rinad saw this and fled in the opposite direction. There was no escaping this time. The biggest creature, which seemed to be the leader, leaped towards him and pinned him down. The creature, red with curled horns and a long, pointed tail, pressed its foot on Rinad's chest, carefully avoiding his face.

'I've waited for this day for a long time…' the creature growled.

'Rinad! Rinad!!' a voice shouted, calling out to him.

Rinad tried to escape, but the creature had him locked down.

'Rinad! Rinad!!' the voice continued, but this seemed like the end.

The creature drew its blazing sword, lifted it in the air, and brought it crashing down, severing Rinad's head.

Rinad jolted up on his bed, covered in sweat.

'Nightmare?' a smiling Guruji asked as he stood at the doorway of Rinad's room.

'Umm…I…I…d-don't know…I guess so…' said Rinad, recovering from the experience.

'Hmm…when was the last time you slept without smoking?'

Rinad stared at Guruji sheepishly.

'Ah! So that could be the problem. I am sure it will get better with time.'

'But why such terrible nightmares? I saw the Asuras tearing down our homes. And I even saw these massive creatures with wings and horns walking around. There was fire all over…the ground had cracked open.'

'Wings and horns?' Guruji asked suspiciously.

'Yes. One of them even had a tail. That one chased me down and killed me. I mean, in my dream.'

'Hmm…' Guruji's eyebrows tightened.

'What?'

'Nothing,' dismissed Guruji. 'Do not read too much into it. But please stop smoking. If you want to achieve your full potential, you must refrain from intoxicating yourself.'

'Sure,' Rinad said in an unconvinced tone. A part of him did not want to deal with this conversation. He simply said what his listener wanted to hear.

'Now, let us go? We have much to talk about!' Guruji pressed on.

'Sure. Breakfast?' Rinad asked.

'As a Manwaan, you should no longer be eating breakfast.'

'What? Really?'

Guruji chuckled, 'I am just kidding. Life is not going to be all that terrible, you see.'

Rinad frowned.

'Apologies. You seemed like you could have used a good laugh. It is set up on the table. Get ready, have your stomach's fill, and meet me under the tree. I'll be there.'

'Okay.'

As Guruji left, Rinad wiped his sweat again. His body still felt a bit tired due to the lack of sleep. He mustered up some strength, showered, and got ready.

He went to the dining area, sat down for breakfast, and observed the spread in front of him.

Not too bad! Rinad thought to himself, admiring an assortment of fruits, bread with jam and butter, boiled eggs, *idli*, and coconut *chutney* to go with it.

Without further ado, he began indulging.

While doing so, he noticed Govi perched on top of a tall light in the corner of the room.

'Kaww…Kaww…'

'I hope you're not saying something bad.'

'Kaww…Kaww….'

'I wouldn't know if you were…' Rinad tore a tiny piece of the idli and held it up, hoping to make peace with the bird. Govi flew in and landed on the table next to Rinad's plate. He grabbed the piece of idli with his beak, dipped it in the chutney on Rinad's plate, and gobbled it up.

'Smart bird!'

'Kaww…Kaww….' Govi responded and flew off.

'You're welcome, I guess!'

Twenty-three

'How was breakfast?' Guruji asked as Rinad approached the tree.

'Wholesome and tasty,' said Rinad with a satisfied smile.

'As it should be! Now, are you ready for the masala?' Guruji chuckled.

'Bring on the masala!' said Rinad with a smirk. Guruji's sense of humour had started to grow on him.

'What was the last thing we spoke about?'

'You told me about the history of the angels, their coalition with the Underworld Clan, and how the Asuras have entered our realm....'

'Right. Moving along. Even though the coalition was meant to be a secret, news reached the heavenly abode. The Gods feared that they might be outnumbered. They could not step on Earth and fight against the revolution whenever it would happen, and the Arinch would be no match against the coalition. This would mean the end of everything that had been created. So, they began building their army on Earth.'

'Army on Earth?' said a confused Rinad.

'Manwaans.'

'Oh!'

'Half man, half celestial.'

'Like…half God?'

'You could say that. Over the years, the Gods kept creating Manwaans on Earth. They were never sure when the uprising would start, but they had to be prepared and would send the *Svargeeya Amrit* with the angels.'

'Svargeeya Amrit?' interjected Rinad.

'Celestial nectar.'

'Oh…'

'This was poured down the throats of humans, making Manwaans out of them...'

'Hold on…so someone poured this Svargeeya Amrit down my throat, and I didn't know about it?'

'An angel did. And there's no way you could have found out.'

'And on what basis are these humans chosen?'

'That is something we're not entirely sure of.'

'Hmm…okay.'

'The prophecy states that at any given point, there must be a hundred and eight Manwaans. Not more, not less. So even if any Manwaan passes on, another Manwaan is created immediately as a replacement.'

'But why a hundred and eight?'

'Multiple reasons. Hundred and eight is known to be a number that governs many forces of the universe. For instance, we have a hundred and eight vital points of life forces in our bodies. It is the basis of all creation."One" represents divine consciousness, "zero" represents null, indicating that everything is temporary, and "eight" represents the infinity of creation. The distance between the moon and the Earth and the sun and the Earth is a hundred and eight times the diameter of the moon and the sun, respectively. It is even said that a hundred and eight nerve channels converge in our body to form the heart chakra. These are only a few reasons why this number holds great significance and is followed by many cultures. There are a hundred and eight Upanishads, stars in Chinese astrology, beads on a *mala*, images of Lord Buddha, repetitions of a mantra, sun salutations in yoga, and the list goes on.'

'Whoa!' Rinad gasped.

'There are also a hundred and eight stitches on a baseball!'

'What does that have to do with this?'

'Nothing…it is just a random interesting fact. Thought I could lighten the mood with it, you see,' Guruji chuckled.

Rinad frowned at first but followed it up with a smile, acknowledging the fact that Guruji consciously attempted to keep it light.

'Over the centuries, many Manwaans were created, some reached their realisation, but none had a chance to serve the great revolution,' Guruji continued, 'until now. You see, Rinad, it is possibly the first time that the gates of

Hell have been opened wide enough to let the Underworld Clan out.'

'Possibly?' Rinad butted in.

'There have been unsuccessful attempts with their own sets of unexpected consequences…but let us not get into that right now. We need to focus on the matter at hand.'

Rinad shook his head vigorously, implying that he was trying to absorb everything like a sponge.

'Now, when a human consumes the Svargeeya Amrit, they undergo many changes. Obviously, it is quite an unnatural experience for the mind, body, and soul. The human form was not built to accommodate celestial energy in any capacity, so the trauma is inevitable.'

'What sort of trauma?'

'It could be anything—anxiety, depression, ADHD, stomach issues, body parts giving way—absolutely anything.'

Rinad grew quiet. Finally, he had an answer to his recurring anxiety and panic attacks. He had never experienced anything as a child, but as the years passed, the anxiety increased and got the best of him.

Maybe it was because of this? Maybe the Svargeeya Amrit was poured down my throat when I was around ten years old? He thought to himself.

'Many Manwaans do not make it, you see,' Guruji pressed on. 'The ailment or side effect becomes too much for them to handle. Many of those who survive do not have their realisations and continue to battle their ailments or suppress them with drugs or intoxicants—weed, alcohol, medicines—or anything external that relieves you of the pain or provides an escape.'

This is making so much sense! Rinad thought to himself.

He finally understood the need for the relief that weed, or his medication, provided.

'I know what you're thinking…' Guruji smirked.

Rinad smiled sheepishly.

'You see, Rinad, if you continue to consume substances to relieve yourself, your tolerance towards them will increase over time. You will eventually numb yourself out and never attain the totality of the potential you were destined for. Escaping is never a solution. You need to face the light and, most importantly, you need to…?' Guruji stopped midway, hoping Rinad would complete the sentence.

'Umm…quit smoking?'

'Yes, that. But the word I was looking for is "believe"!'

'Ah, yes…of course.'

'When people do not believe in themselves and the true depths of their potential, they resort to all forms of escapism in an attempt to pursue pleasure. Nothing could be further from the truth. If anything, this leads them away from the idea of pleasure, you see.'

Rinad's eyebrows tightened as he processed all that Guruji had to say.

'You know, there is this common notion that people die when they stop breathing. Sure, they cease to exist at that point, but they truly stop living when they stop believing. And that is why I started with the idea of belief. Does it seem to add up now?'

'I...guess so. But you're saying that some Manwaans don't survive because of the intensity of the side effects of the Svargeeya Amrit. If any form of drug or intoxicant offers them the possibility of an extended life, shouldn't they take it?'

'At what cost? Living a meaningless life, constantly complaining, being a burden to everyone around you? Is that not extremely selfish?'

'Maybe...but it wasn't their choice to become Manwaans. It was almost forced upon them. Isn't that unfair? Shouldn't they be the ones in control of their lives?'

'Rinad, the biggest fallacy surrounding us is that we have any sense of control. Our destiny is written out for us. Before we are even born, everything that happens is pre-ordained.'

'That's bullshit!' Rinad quickly covered his mouth realising the language he had used.

Guruji chuckled.

'I'm sorry. I meant that can't be possible. That would mean we have no free will.'

'You are right. We do not have any free will. Think of your life as a book. All you do is turn the pages. Day by day. That is all that you are doing. Do you think the choices you make, good, bad, or ugly, are made as a result of your own free will? If yes, I am afraid you are gravely mistaken, Rinad. Every choice you make has already been made for you. You are simply acting it out, as it has been written out.'

Rinad's jaw dropped. 'But that's ridiculous. What's the point of even living then?'

'To let go of the idea of control and simply live each moment. Not thinking about the past or the future, and playing your part in the present. The sooner you come to terms with this, or the sooner you believe, life will open itself up to you. Stop worrying about the outcome because it is not in your control anyway. Just do. Keep doing. Only this way can you fulfil what you were destined for.'

A silence followed as Rinad got lost in his thoughts. Guruji did not interrupt. Indeed, this was a lot to process, and he felt Rinad should be given the required time to do so.

They both sat there quietly for several minutes.

Rinad then let out a deep sigh. 'So, now what?'

Guruji smiled. 'Now, I've told you about the creation of Manwaans. Do you not want to know what happens after they attain their realisation?'

Just then, it all came back to him. The night from the warehouse, Yuva and Maya's tricks. All of it.

'Special powers?'

Guruji's smile widened. 'More like heightened capabilities.'

'That sounds like a fancy word for the same thing.'

Guruji chuckled. 'Let's take a walk.'

Twenty-four

Rinad followed as Guruji led the way back into the house and further into the study room.

'Are we going down?' said Rinad excitedly. The training arena had fascinated him, and he wanted to have a second look.

'Yes. I'd like you to see something.'

Guruji stood on the feet scanner, and after a couple of beeps, the door slid open. As they walked down, sounds of battle were heard—clinks from the contact of weapons, grunts heard from the participants, and much more.

'What the hell is going on here?' exclaimed Rinad as he walked down, and the sounds grew louder.

'Training. You'll be starting soon.'

As they reached down, Rinad noticed the four Manwaans training fiercely in combat. Yuva was mid-air, and his wings were flapping mildly to maintain his position. He was on one end of the rocky section, while Nivi was at the other, launching wooden arrows at him using a bow. With each arrow launched, Yuva would flap his wings into a summersault and catch the arrow with the claws of his feet.

'At least give me a challenge, yaar!' he boasted and hurled the arrow back at Nivi, who calmly took a step aside and caught it at the side of her abdomen.

'You don't need to do summersaults to dodge an arrow, show off!' yelled Nivi.

'Kaww…Kaww…' a familiar voice came from the corner.

'Exactly! See…even Govi feels you're going too easy on me,' replied Yuva.

'How about I shoot some metal arrows? Don't blame me if it pierces your arrogant heart.'

'Charming, aren't they?' Guruji jested.

'Very,' said Rinad. He then noticed the other two engaged in an intense combat further down on the grass section. Maya and Ash didn't bat an eyelid as their gazes were locked onto each other. Maya held a spear with a blade on one end. The same spear she had used the night Rinad was rescued. Ash held a pair of nun chucks—one in each hand. Like a martial arts master, he spun them around his torso.

Maya stepped in and wielded her weapon. Ash countered it with a flick from the nun chucks. As Maya took a slightly offensive stance, her spear moved so rapidly that it was almost invisible to the human eye. Any other person would have fallen in just the first or second swing—but not Ash. The quicker the action of the spear, the quicker the nun chucks flicked them away. Maya swished it across his legs, and Ash hopped over it. She went for the neck; the spear got entangled in the nun chuck, and she swiftly retreated for a microsecond and jumped back in.

It was a dance. Almost meditative. For several minutes, the frequency of the clinks of the weapons steadily increased and echoed through the training arena.

Finally, Maya stepped back and smirked.

Ash smirked back.

She held the silver hilt of the spear in front of her and pushed the black button on the other side. Another blade emerged. She now stood holding a double-bladed spear.

Ash held the nun chucks in front of him and pressed the buttons on them. A pointed edge emerged from each nun chuck on the attacking end.

It was on.

The room grew quiet.

Yuva descended while Govi perched himself on his shoulder. Along with Nivi, they, too, brought their attention to the fight.

This time Ash stepped in.

It was his time to play the offence.

He wielded the nun chucks, and Maya used her weapon to defend herself. The nun chucks came flying towards her head, and she ducked down. She returned it with a stab at the shoulder, but the nun chucks flicked it away and came for her chest. She backed away.

The fight continued.

Once again, they danced together.

However, something different seemed to unravel. Maya's moves started getting more aggressive. Her gaze got more agitated, and she began to lose patience. The battle did not end, and she started panting while Ash remained meditative. When she went in for the stomach, Ash stepped to the side and, once again, entangled it in his nun chucks. This time she was unable to retract it. Left with no other option, she released her right hand from the spear and pointed it at Ash. Ash dropped one nun chuck and grabbed his stomach in pain. With no time to waste, Maya landed a roundhouse kick on the other nun chuck, and it went flying out of his hand. She released her hand, and just as Ash recovered, he opened his eyes to find himself facing the tip of Maya's spear. Pointed right in the middle of his forehead.

He stood there. Holding his stomach. Enraged.

'We're not supposed to use our capabilities,' he grunted.

'All's fair in love and war, Ashoo,' Maya responded with an evil sweetness.

'Maya!!' Guruji's cracked voice boomed through the arena. She immediately released her weapon and stood straight with her hands behind her back.

'Sorry, Guruji,' she said softly.

'Anger will drown you. Do not let it get the best of you.'

'Yes, Guruji,' she said apologetically, then turned towards Ash. 'Sorry.'

'It's chill,' Ash responded coldly and looked away. Maya noticed this and forced herself to hug him. Something she didn't indulge in too often.

Ash chuckled and hugged her back. 'Wow…you really must be sorry.'

'I am. I don't know what happens to me sometimes…'

'It's fine. Chal…let's go wash up and lay the table for lunch.'

'Phew! That got intense,' Yuva whispered aside to Govi.

'Kaww…Kaww…'

'Govi says you've gotten better at your combat,' he shouted out to Ash.

'Why, thank you, Govi!' Ash bowed his head in jest.

'It's true…you had me today,' Maya confessed. Ash blushed, put his arm around Maya, and all four Manwaans, along with Govi, walked towards the stairs.

'Are you coming for lunch, Guruji?' Nivi asked.

'We'll be there in a bit,' Guruji responded.

'See you, man!' Ash held up a closed fist towards Rinad.

Rinad responded with a fist bump. 'See you! Good stuff!'

Ash winked, and the five left Rinad and Guruji to continue their conversation.

Rinad traced them and waited for them to leave the arena. 'What happens when she points her hands the way she just did? I saw her do something to the Asuras in the warehouse as well….'

Guruji smiled. 'Maya has a very unique ability, you see. She has the power to influence the internal organs of living things.'

'Whoa!'

'Yes. It's quite something.'

'Like…any internal organ?'

'Soon enough. She's only partially realised.'

'Realised?' Rinad interrupted.

'Realisation is the process through which Manwaans attain their true and total capabilities.'

'Oh…'

'As of now, Maya can control only the liver and the large intestine to a great extent since they are the bigger organs. But once fully realised, there would be no limit to what she could do. Even as a child, she unknowingly gave headaches to the kids with whom she got into a scuffle. Right now, she's able to strongly influence only the digestive system. Any idea who her celestial parent is?'

'What do you mean?'

'Well, when the Svargeeya Amrit is sent down, it normally carries the traits of a particular God, who ends up becoming the celestial parent of that particular Manwaan.'

'I thought you said there is only one God?'

'One source. Many forms.'

'Oh…who?'

'Yama.'

'The God of death?'

'Correct.'

Rinad grew quiet for a couple of minutes, and Guruji did not interrupt him. After having processed this, he continued, 'How does a Manwaan know who his or her celestial parent is?'

'You will know it only when you have attained a certain degree of your realisation.'

'Hmm...' Rinad pondered. 'Do you know who's mine?'

'We tried making an educated guess but cannot say for sure.'

'Who did you guess?'

'We are not supposed to tell you that. It is your responsibility to figure it out for yourself.'

Rinad frowned.

'What about Yuva? Was he born with those wings?'

'No. He developed his wings when he was around ten or eleven. Yuva is blessed with extraordinary strength as well, you see. Not just that, but he can also understand what birds say to each other. And, as you have noticed, he can speak with Govi. Honestly, I am quite excited to see how his abilities develop.'

'Who's his celestial parent?'

'Would you like to guess? Strength and flight. Who do you think it could be?'

Rinad shrugged his shoulders. 'I'm sorry...I'm not very good with this.'

'Not to worry. Vayu!'

'The God of wind?'

'Correct.'

'Hmm…makes sense. What about Ash and Nivi?'

'Interestingly, they have the same abilities. Their celestial parents are the Ashwini Twins. Not only do they have the ability to heal, but their blood has healing capabilities too!'

'So, they can never die?'

'Not to my knowledge.'

'Hmm…'

'Also, they are extremely smart. A gift that not many people have,' Guruji chuckled. 'As I mentioned earlier, they are the ones who set up the laboratory and the ones who build the weapons that we use.'

'I was going to ask about that. I've never seen weapons like those…like Maya's spear or the bladed nun chucks Ash was using.'

'All credit goes to Ash and Nivi!'

'Cool!'

'They also run a small homoeopathy clinic and try to help out people as much as possible. In fact, they both are even professional doctors!'

'Whoa! Doctors by day and weapons manufacturers by night. That's amazing!'

Guruji chuckled. 'Yes, they are quite extraordinary. They are the most realised of the lot. Even though they are the youngest. No one here is fully realised yet.'

'And how does one achieve this realisation?'

'Through extensive meditation and training. Although, none of the Manwaans till date have reached their full potential. Although, none of the Manwaans till date have reached their full potential.'

'There are seven levels of realisation?' Rinad asked, dumbfounded.

'Correct.'

'And I'm assuming you start from one and keep climbing the ladder from there?'

'Not necessarily. You could skip levels.'

'Hmm…what levels are Yuva, Maya, Ash, and Nivi at?'

'Yuva and Maya are at level three, and Ash and Nivi are at level four.'

'Interesting.'

'Now, Rinad…I want you to take the whole of today and soak in everything I have said. We shall begin your training tomorrow, and I will need your full focus. We do not have much time on our hands. I need us to be prepared for when the Asuras make their next move.'

'What if I don't want to be a Manwaan? I'm not sure I'm quite cut out for this lifestyle.'

'It is your destiny, Rinad. And it is inevitable. I would also like to bring to your attention that there is something unique about you. You are the only unrealised Manwaan that the Asuras did not kill. They took you in alive. And I need your cooperation to help me find out what they want from you. They could have killed you instantly. But they chose not to. And I need to know why.'

'Okay.'

'And they will not leave you alone, Rinad. They will keep coming after you. If nothing, I need you to attain a certain level of your abilities so that you may protect yourself.'

'Sure,' said Rinad semi-enthusiastically.

'But to begin with, I need you to…'

'Believe?' Rinad smiled.

'There you go. Now, go get some rest,' Guruji concluded and walked back into the house.

Twenty-five

Once again, Rinad tossed and turned as the sweat accumulated on his forehead. He wasn't ready to put in the efforts required to become a so-called "realised Manwaan". He was content with his job at Copy That, with his boss being displeased with him every now and then. It seemed like an ordinary life back then. This seemed like too much of a commitment. Too much of a responsibility.

As the pillow got drenched, Rinad sat up with an intense contortion to his face. He wiped the sweat with the palm of his hand and looked at his phone.

2:00 a.m.

He had a tiny little duffle bag that Yuva and Maya had brought from his home. He pulled it out from under his bed, removed the few clothes from the cupboard, dumped them in it, and zipped it up.

He once again picked up his phone and made a call.

'Yo!' said Jogi from the receiving end.

'Yo, bro! Are you sleeping?'

'I was just about to, man. What's up?'

'Bro…I really need a favour. Can you please pick me up? It's really urgent.'

'Sure, bro. Where are you?'

'Somewhere outside Dahisar. I'll send the location pin.'

'Dahisar?'

'Yeah, man. Long story…come quick, na?'

'Haan…I'll be there in around an hour.'

'Cool! See you, bro.'

Roughly forty minutes later, Jogi called Rinad, telling him that he had arrived at the location. Rinad opened his room door and checked to see if anyone was awake. He didn't want to be intercepted by anyone. Especially Govi—who would then caw and wake up the whole damn house.

Silence.

Everyone was asleep.

He crept outside, opened the main door, and closed it quietly behind him. Outside the huge lawn, he saw the familiar car waiting, giving him an instant sense of relief.

Jogi's car! He thought, ran towards it, and opened the door to find Jogi sitting in the driver's seat.

'Bro…what place is this?' said Jogi as he looked around in amusement.

'I'll tell you. Just start driving.'

'Sure. Do you want to spark?'

Rinad looked over and saw a neatly rolled joint held up in front of him.

'Umm…' Rinad stared at it uncertainly. A bit of a shocking reaction to Jogi.

'What happened, man?'

'Nothing…I'm not sure if I should.'

'What? Why? All okay?' Jogi shrieked. This was the first time he had seen Rinad having second thoughts about smoking a joint. And it felt unsettling.

Rinad didn't bat an eyelid. Guruji's words were on his mind, and he was torn between relieving himself with the high and the pure guilt that would follow if he did. He was escaping confrontation, yet again—by leaving Manbhoomi, fleeing from the universe's plan for him, and considering numbing his brains out with the weed. All of this came screaming at him, and the feeling started bubbling within him due to the conflict. Warmth against his skin and rising palpitations. He stared at his weakness as his breathing got shallow and his palms moistened. The world started weighing down on him as he felt the pressure of the responsibility of making the right choice.

Should I do it? Run away from my so-called "pre-ordained destiny"? What if it's all just a hoax? But the Asuras are not a hoax…I've seen them with my own eyes. So, everything Guruji said must be true. But why can't I live a normal life and do whatever I want to? Who are they to decide my fate? Multiple questions overlapped in Rinad's mind. All he did was stare at the joint, but these existential questions were whizzing by. And his response to the joint would be symbolic of being an answer to all of them.

Screw it!

Rinad took the joint, and Jogi lit it up for him. As he took the first drag, his shoulders relaxed, and the sweat from his forehead receded.

But something was different.

Even though the obvious sensations of his anxiety faded away, the heaviness on his mind did not lighten. A lump formed in his throat as he welled up from the guilt. He was far away from being relaxed, and it felt unusual.

He had failed yet again.

This was possibly the first time Rinad didn't feel "good" after getting high. Of course, he wasn't one to communicate any of this. Rinad simply sat there silently as a gamut of sensations coursed through his being.

As he went through this, he suddenly snapped out of it and realised that he wasn't being his usual self, and finally gestured for Jogi to start driving. Jogi hit the pedal, and they took off.

'What's going on, man?' asked a confused Jogi.

'Where do I start from, bro…' said Rinad hesitantly, trying to force the words out. He was in no mood to talk. Besides, he did not want to give away much. Not like Jogi would have believed him. Irrespective, the discretion of the "celestial plans" seemed important, and Rinad did not want to be the one to break that.

'It's a rehab centre of some sort,' Rinad lied. 'I thought I could go there and quit pot, but it just didn't feel right.'

'Oh!! That's why you hesitated to smoke!' Jogi thought out loud.

'Umm... yeh,' Rinad was pleasantly content with how Jogi justified Rinad's response for himself.

'Why do you want to quit pot, bro?' asked Jogi, surprised.

'Just…' Rinad fell short of answers. He tried hard to change the topic. 'So, did you meet the girl you were talking about?'

Twenty-six

Once he was dropped off, Rinad ran up to his house. He entered, reached for his stash, and fervently rolled himself yet another joint. The damage was already done. There was no point holding back now. As he lit it up and puffed on it, he began putting more things into the duffle bag that he carried with him from Manbhoomi—a knife from the kitchen, all his stash, and the required paraphernalia, a couple of change of clothes and his laptop. He had decided to go to his parents' place and stay there for a few days. No one would be able to find him there, he assumed. He also had to reconnect with his boss to ensure he didn't lose his job. He figured he'd have some peace of mind there and could handle all these things.

'We've been waiting for you…' a voice growled from his bedroom.

In an instant, Rinad knew who it was.

Asuras.

His breathing got heavier, and sweat began to emerge. Seeing it as the only chance for survival, he darted for the front door. Only to find another female Asura awaiting him. He turned around and saw the other male Asura inching towards him from his bedroom. Jumping out the window was not an option. He would die instantly.

Rinad was trapped.

He had no choice but to fight.

This might be a good time for me to have my so-called realisation, he thought to himself.

Else, he would be no match for the two Asuras.

As they cornered him, their eyes turned black, black veins emerged on their necks, and nails elongated into black claws.

The knife! he realised.

He swiftly reached into his bag, took it out, and pointed it at the Asuras. Alternating between each one with his trembling hands.

'That's cute,' the woman hissed. 'Well? Are you going to use it or just keep pointing it at us?'

Rinad gathered the iota of courage he had and went in for a stab. The knife pierced the woman's left shoulder, and Rinad retracted it immediately. His eyes started welling up. He had barely hit anyone, let alone stabbed.

However, to no effect.

She didn't flinch. A couple of droplets of black liquid, but that was about it. The woman just stared at the knife and then looked back at him.

'Now that's just rude. Didn't your mother ever teach you not to hit a woman? Oh well…my turn!'

She removed the knife from her shoulder, only to reveal a black mark that the stab had left behind. She raised her hand and landed it on his right shoulder.

'*Aargh!!!*' he yelled and fell against the wall behind him.

'This time, we don't have to bring you in alive. But we're going to take our time and enjoy every second of this, oh leader of the Manwaans!' she snarled.

The male Asura raised his hand and landed a slash across Rinad's face. His elongated claws ripped into his cheeks, and blood dripped from his face and shoulders. He began to howl in pain.

'Help!! Help!!!' he shouted.

'Stop it!' the male rumbled.

When Rinad kept screaming, the woman Asura held him by the jaw with her right hand and pierced his gut with her left hand.

This was it. Possibly the penultimate blow.

She twisted her hand as the elongated claws ripped through his flesh, causing a pool of blood around him as it dripped from his abdomen. Finally, she retracted her hand, and Rinad collapsed to the ground. Smothered in blood and almost unconscious.

'You know, I wish he was at least slightly realised,' said the male casually. 'At least we would have had more of a challenge. This was way too easy!'

'That it was,' the woman smirked. 'Would you like to do the honours?'

'It would be my pleasure!' The male Asura raised his

hand to finish the task that Usur had ordered them to carry out.

Just as he was about to land the fatal blow, a golden-white light filled the room. Too bright for anyone to adjust to quickly.

The half-conscious Rinad and the two Asuras squinted their eyes while trying to understand where the bright light was coming from and adjusting to it simultaneously.

No one could make out a thing.

Just as soon as they started getting accustomed, the light faded away. A hard blow landed on the woman's stomach, making her collapse while the man's head was rammed against the floor.

In seconds, both the Asuras were pinned down to the ground with a palm on each of their heads.

The darkness of the room emerged again. Rinad was able to catch a blurry glimpse of what was happening. A somewhat middle-aged man in golden-white attire, radiating and well-sculpted, had forcefully held the Asuras down. Rinad could not discern much more, but it seemed like someone had come to his rescue.

The Asuras growled and grunted. They shook vigorously and tried hard to break out of the grip, but they were no match for the man, who easily held them down.

The man proceeded to close his eyes. As he did, the palms of his hands, which had the Asuras pressed down, began to glow. Once again, golden-white radiation emerged from it. The intensity of the beam strengthened and reached the peak of its crescendo.

Zap!!!

Black and red shiny, thick liquid splattered against the walls of the house and began to drip towards the floor.

The bodies of the Asuras, flapping fervently until now, suddenly reached a calm state. The man removed his hands from their faces, and the two perpetrators rose and stood on their feet.

'What happened?' cried the woman.

'Where am I?' the man choked. 'Who are you?' he asked the woman. 'And you?' he asked the man. 'And you…oh my god! You're b-bleeding. So much blood…what the hell happened here?' he cried.

They both were in tears and unable to fathom what was going on around them.

'You both were victims of a terrible kidnapping,' Rinad's rescuer said in an extremely calm and soothing baritone. 'Please…go back to your homes and get some rest. Everything is fine now.'

The two former Asuras, now humans, scurried out of the flat.

Unable to make sense of any of it and with no energy left in him, Rinad's eyes began to shut.

'You're going to be fine, Rinad,' the man's voice echoed but grew faint as Rinad lost more and more of his consciousness.

'You're going to be fine.'

He could barely hear the voice anymore and finally collapsed.

Twenty-seven

'Gentlemen, I'm sure you all know why you are here. You have been handpicked to solve one of the most devastating cases that Mumbai has ever seen. Our city is burning, and I will not let that happen!' Deshpande banged his table as he addressed his team of thirty, who were tightly crammed into his office. The rate of killings had moderately reduced, but the total number of victims until now was enough to incite the men in uniform.

Pawar stood by his side with rock-solid attention. Having experienced these inhuman creatures in person, he and Deshpande were dumbfounded. Even though they had to save their city, the priority was to identify what these things were and how they could be stopped. Or, at least, weakened.

'Pawar and I have encountered these things first-hand, and I assure you all, it is unlike anything we have ever witnessed. Have a look,' Deshpande said, turning the laptop screen towards the group and hitting play. The same videos that he had played for ACP Kamat.

Their faces morphed as the videos played on.

'As you can see, gentlemen, these…creatures…are not human. Black eyes, long claws; I've never seen anything like it. We don't know what they are, and it's our job to find out. Bullets have been ineffective on them. Do we face them hand-to-hand? Do we use grenades? I have no clue. We have noticed one thing, though. They are on a mission and do not intend to harm anyone who is not an active target. Now, here's what I want you to do. I want you to look at all the records and track each and every case in detail. Pawar will assign the cases to each of you. Speak to the relatives or friends of the victims and find out their past—where they went, who they met, and why they were targeted. While some of you will focus on that, a few of you will need to direct your energy towards discovering who or what these creatures are. For that, I need you to do an in-depth investigation on all the people who have gone missing in the past few weeks. Once you have done that, get the details of all those people, and let's see if there is any connection between them and these creatures.'

'Sir, why do you think there will be a connection between missing people and these creatures? You said they are inhuman,' one of the officers interrupted Deshpande, who rolled his eyes and looked at Pawar.

'Well, Pawar here believes that maybe these humans are possessed. Honestly, I would have thought him mad, but after seeing these things, I feel anything could be possible and would like to be extra sure. Maybe we need to work with *pundits* and exorcise these possessed people…who knows?' Deshpande responded as he rubbed his forehead. A part of him couldn't believe that he was even uttering these words. He had always been extremely practical, and ghosts and spirits were beyond his scope of belief.

Pawar, on the other hand, had the tendencies of a dreamer. Being a member of the police force urged him to stay practical, but this seemed like a situation that required an out-of-the-box approach. Thus, he put forward his theory regarding ghosts and possession. Deshpande had no clarity or answers whatsoever and had no choice but to consider Pawar's suggestion.

'Any more questions?' grunted Deshpande.

Silence filled the room.

'Fantastic. I would also like to add that we need to be absolutely discrete about this. Remember, the people look up to us, gentlemen. If they find out that we are helpless or that we're dealing with…ghosts…or whatever, they will lose faith, and the city will plunge into chaos. Do not engage with any of these creatures if you come across them. No firing. All we need now is information. Is that clear?'

Silence.

'Is that clear?' Deshpande boomed.

'Yes, sir!' the resounding response came in unison and filled up the room.

'Good. Pawar…I'll leave them with you. Good luck out there, gentlemen. You are dismissed.'

The troop of thirty slammed into attention and was led out by Pawar for further briefing.

Deshpande sat there in stillness.

Ironically, praying for some answers.

Twenty-eight

'Rinad!'

Guruji woke up with a start. He had sensed that something was wrong and ran over to Rinad's room, only to find it empty.

A worried Guruji paced with his stick and gathered his four students in the living room. Govi was also perched on the sofa's handrest and tried to make sense of the situation.

'Yuva, Maya...you need to find him.'

'Why should we, Guruji?' yelled Yuva as he stomped around the room. 'He's a bloody coward. He's no Manwaan. Let alone the prophesied leader. With all due respect, I think you've got this one wrong, Guruji.'

'Why would the Asuras chase him then?' Nivi butted in calmly.

'I don't know. They're brainless creatures...maybe that's why?' yelled an enraged Yuva.

'Why should we help him if he doesn't believe it himself, Guruji?' Maya said in an irritated tone. She was, however, more composed than Yuva, who was seething with rage.

'We rescued him once, and he has absolutely no gratitude. Maybe he wants to get himself killed…'

'Yuva!' Guruji rumbled. 'You need to calm down! Put yourself in his shoes to try and understand what he must be going through. You all had issues accepting it at first, did you not? Be patient with him.'

Yuva bowed his head, surrendering his argument, and went and collapsed on the sofa. Govi took off from the handrest, perched himself on Yuva's shoulder, and rubbed his jawline with his beak. His own way of consoling his master. Yuva took in a couple of breaths and patted his trusted sidekick, calming down steadily.

'We need to believe in him if we need him to believe in himself. Now, Yuva, Maya…will you go get him please?' said Guruji in his therapeutic tone.

There was silence in the room.

Maya finally spoke up, 'Yes, Guruji.'

Whoosh!!!

Just then, she was interrupted by the sound of a flapping of wings from outside the house. Considering the sound was heard in the living room, everyone assumed that it was a large set of wings. As they all walked towards the front of the house, they noticed golden-white light seeping in through the gaps of the main door. The glow receded, and the knob of the door was turned from the other side. As the door was pushed open, a mid-sized, slightly muscular man with curly hair stood at the doorstep.

In his arms—an unconscious, blood-soaked Rinad.

A sense of worry took over the room. Everyone wondered if Rinad was alive or not. But as the man walked in, they noticed Rinad's belly moving up and down.

Breathing. He was still alive.

The man gracefully walked all the way in and placed Rinad on the couch. He didn't seem to be bothered by the state he was in. Almost as if he knew that he could be cured here, which was, in fact, true. He wore white clothes made of what seemed like silk with streaks of gold. The clothes fit well in the torso area and at the top and bottom of his limbs but were slightly baggy in between, almost like harem garments.

He turned back and scanned everyone in the room, including Govi.

All eyes were on him.

No blinks.

The Manwaans were mentally prepared for some form of an attack from the stranger and remained on the edges of their toes. The man then began to inch his way towards Guruji. The room got tense. They had been taught to expect the unexpected and always be prepared. And that's what they did as they watched the stranger walk towards the man who had taught them this. The man came close and towered over Guruji, who remained unintimidated and did not flinch.

Finally, in a deep baritone, the man spoke up, 'You run a tight ship around here, old friend.'

Guruji smiled, 'My house, my rules.'

They both chuckled and embraced each other.

The four Manwaans and Govi looked at the two, shell-shocked.

'Kaww…Kaww…'

'I have no idea!' Yuva whispered to his sidekick.

'How have you been, brother?' the man continued. The word "brother" being said in the way a friend would say it to another, rather than actual brothers.

'Did he just call Guruji brother?' Ash whispered aside to Maya. Maya shrugged without batting an eyelid. No one was used to their teacher being referred to as anything but Guruji.

'I have been good, Milaayak. How have you been?' replied Guruji.

There was a sudden gasp in the room.

All five pairs of eyes, including Govi's, popped from their sockets as they were made aware of who stood in front of them.

Milaayak.

One of the seven Arinch. In their living room.

Everyone's posture immediately changed into one which paid respect to the celestial being that was having a tête-à-tête with their Guruji. Their chests and shoulders were relaxed, arms behind their backs and heads slightly bowed. They had only heard stories of this benevolent being. And now, they were in his presence.

'Not too bad. He's on the couch,' Milaayak continued.

'I can see that,' Guruji chuckled. 'I am sorry about that. He needs some more time. Nivi...can you please attend to him?'

'Yes, Guruji,' said Nivi, pacing into the living room where Rinad lay unconscious.

'It's not his fault. It's nearly impossible for unrealised beings to believe in all of this,' Milaayak continued while deviating his vision from Guruji and addressing everyone else in the room. It was almost as if he had heard the heated conversation that had consumed the place just a minute ago, sensing the Manwaans' lack of faith in Rinad. 'But you need to get him ready soon,' he continued, 'we're running out of time.'

'Is it Mihaara?' Guruji asked in a hushed tone. However, it was enough to send a chill down everyone's spine.

Mihaara was a name that the Manwaans had studied in their sessions with Guruji. The theory lessons had taught them all there was to know about the great celestial revolution and all its major participants, or rather, the protagonists and antagonists of the bigger plot. Of course, they never had any visual cues and didn't really know what anyone looked like. All their learning was purely through text. They did not know much, but they knew enough.

Mihaara.

One of the seven Fagir who was in charge of leading the revolution against Earth and Heaven.

'I'm not sure,' replied Milaayak in a dejected manner. 'He's not on Earth; that I can certainly say. And the Fagir

Council has built a protective shield to prevent any more information from slipping out. I'm not able to make it through that force field. All I know is that he's sent a squadron of Asuras to Earth.'

'Yes, we're aware of that,' replied Guruji as he grew pensive, realising that whatever plans he had, had to be expedited.

Meanwhile, Nivi was healing Rinad's wounds, as Guruji had asked her to. He was doused in blood and had deep cuts on his left shoulder and stomach and scratches on his face. The one on the stomach looked the deepest, so Nivi attended to it first. She sat on the edge of the couch and placed both her hands, face down, an inch above the wounded area, and closed her eyes. As she did so, a fluorescent yellow-green light began to radiate from her palms. She consciously deepened her breathing. The glow brightened, and the torn skin and flesh began to inch back to seal themselves together. By the time the glow subsumed, the wound was no more there. The skin seemed as good as new. Nivi's breathing had turned into a slight panting. She had a couple more to go. She gathered her breath and moved her palms to his shoulder. The glow radiated, and the skin and flesh sealed themselves up.

Sweat began to accumulate on Nivi's forehead, and she was depleted. The deeper the wound, the more it would demand of her. Only the scratches on the face were left. She moved her palms to his face, and the glow radiated yet again.

From the dark, Rinad felt a warm sensation on his face and began to regain consciousness. When his eyes opened slightly, he gasped for air and turned his head to one side, away from the light he saw.

'What's that?' he cried.

Nivi gently opened her eyes and let out a deep breath, 'You're not done yet. The scratches on your face still need to be healed.'

Rinad began to make sense of what was happening. He calmed down and turned his head back to the centre without saying anything. As Nivi placed her palms on the scratches, he noticed the sweat accumulated on her forehead. The glow radiated; this time, Rinad could hear the skin and flesh on his face joining together. The glow subsided, and Nivi opened her eyes and removed her hands.

'Done!' she said in a breathy voice and a partial smile.

'Thanks. Is it tiring?'

'Your stomach and shoulder took some work. If you hadn't gotten here in time, you probably would've died.'

'Oh…who brought me here?'

Nivi gestured towards the other room, where voices were spilling over from. Rinad leaned forward and strained his ears to pick up as much of the conversation as he could.

'How long do you think he'll take to attain a level of realisation?' the baritone voice came from the other room.

'I can't say,' Guruji's voice replied.

'Well, my cover is blown. They are going to know I'm here. They will send reinforcements.'

'Did you have to compromise your discretion?'

'He would've died.'

Rinad sat up feeling mildly rejuvenated but hung his head in dismay. He was being blamed, and it was all because he attempted to escape. He stood up and began to walk slowly towards the voices. Nivi followed behind in case he fell because of his weakness. As he got closer, he noticed everyone standing in a position that conveyed respect to the new guest, who was facing away from Rinad while chatting with Guruji.

'All better?' Guruji tilted his head to one side and smiled.

Guruji's smile made Rinad feel even more terrible. Not only had he compromised the angel's stealth, but also proved his lack of faith in Guruji. But there stood his teacher. Welcoming him back with a smile when he deserved to be reprimanded.

Rinad gave a partial, guilt-filled smile and nodded back.

All eyes shifted focus and were now on Rinad. The Manwaans were not pleased. The moderately muscular, seven-foot man turned around, and it all came screaming back to Rinad. This man had saved him from the Asuras. And from what he had just heard, he was meant to be in hiding and had blown his cover while doing so.

'Thank you…and sorry,' Rinad said sheepishly.

A soft smile dawned upon the man's face. He didn't say a word but nodded, gesturing it was alright.

'I'm Rinad.'

'I know,' the man replied, continuing to smile.

'Of course.'

'Do you plan to escape again?'

Rinad shook his head fervently.

'Great. In that case, I better head back. I need to keep my siblings posted. I'll pop back in soon. See you, brother.'

'See you soon, old friend. Please look over us,' Guruji replied to him.

'I always do! Oh, and Rinad, we all hope you find the strength to believe. We're kind of depending on it.'

With that, he looked up and jolted his shoulders.

Whoosh!!!

Glorious golden-white feathered wings flung out, each wing roughly five feet long. As he slowly flapped them, the room began to glow with a golden-white light that was being emitted from Milaayak. His feet gradually lifted off the floor, and he levitated for a few seconds.

Zap!!!

He was gone. And the light went with him. Almost as if vanishing into a tiny golden dot on the ceiling. Gradually, the room returned to normalcy.

Rinad stood there, confused.

'Okay! Who the hell was that?'

It still hadn't struck him.

Twenty-nine

'An Arinch?!'

Guruji nodded.

'You mean…one of the seven Arinch?'

Guruji continued nodding.

'So, when he said that he had to keep his siblings informed, he meant more angels?'

Guruji nodded still.

'And when he flew up, he went to the Heaven?'

Rinad was overbrimming with questions.

'Why do you sound so surprised? After everything that Guruji has told you?' Ash asked in a mildly displeased manner.

'It's just a bit surprising that an angel was in this house. That's all,' Rinad replied in a slightly hushed tone. He still felt guilty about what he had put everyone through and could not speak up.

After Milaayak's departure, everyone gathered in the living room to discuss what must be done next. Rinad had yet to begin training, and the other Manwaans had to keep practising. Even though they were partially realised, Guruji was unsure if they were ready for the battle. Their best bet was to keep getting better till the fateful day arrived.

'Kaww…Kaww….'

'Govi is asking if we'll need to face Mihaara,' Yuva translated what his sidekick had to say.

'Who's Mihaara?' Rinad whispered aside to Nivi. She seemed like the only one he could speak to at this point, considering she never got angry and always spoke in a composed way.

'The Fagir who's leading the revolution,' she replied.

'Oh…I see….'

'Are you kidding? Do you think we're in any state to face Mihaara? I mean…this guy couldn't even face two Asuras,' Maya exclaimed.

'Can you stop saying it like it's my fault?' Rinad replied with increasing anger.

'I'm not blaming you. I'm just stating the facts. You are not ready! Neither are we!'

'But I'm sure Milaayak will be there to help us in case Mihaara shows up, right?' Ash spoke up unsurely.

'Let's hope so,' Maya said while rolling her eyes.

Just then, everyone noticed that Guruji hadn't said a word.

He sat there in silence. Looking at one point on the centre table, lost in deep thought.

'Guruji, you haven't said anything,' Yuva said softly.

No response.

'Guruji?'

'Hmm?' he finally responded.

'What do we do?'

Guruji took in a deep breath and let it out, almost as if he was clearing his mind, and finally spoke up pensively. 'If Mihaara is made aware of Milaayak's whereabouts, which I am sure he will be, he will expedite his plan.'

The Manwaans stared at Guruji expectantly.

'There is only one thing we can do,' Guruji continued, 'train and be as prepared as we can.'

There was a slow and silent collective nod in the room. Their options were limited, and all they could do was do their best.

And so, it began.

Thirty

Over the next few days, the Manwaans trained intensely. Four to five times a day. Guruji worked extensively with Rinad, hoping he would attain a certain level of realisation; even though a few days were not enough, however powerful or prepared a Manwaan was. Guruji knew that Rinad's chances of being prepared were slim, and chances of him realising his powers were slimmer, but he would not give up hope.

He would not give up on his students.

With the other Manwaans, he wasn't too worried. With a couple of days of focused, rigorous training, they could polish themselves up, and he was sure of that. But Rinad would need a lot more than that.

'Focus on your breathing, Rinad. Bring all your attention to the surface of your nostrils and feel the cool air going in and the warm air coming out,' Guruji said in his soothing voice during Rinad's session on meditation.

Rinad itched his left arm.

Back to stillness.

Rinad shifted his weight to adjust his position.

Back to stillness.

Rinad sniffed and wriggled his forehead.

Back to stillness.

'You are not letting go, Rinad!' Guruji said firmly.

'But I'm not holding onto anything!'

'Yes, you are. You are focusing on everything but your breath. If you truly had all your attention on your breathing, you would not be itching and shifting your weight,' Guruji said strictly.

'Sorry,' Rinad said while he kept his eyes shut.

'Relax your forehead.'

'It's relaxed.'

'No, it's not. I can see tension between your eyebrows. Relax them.'

Rinad raised his eyebrows, almost like stretching a muscle, and relaxed them back down.

'Whatever thought comes to your mind, just let it pass by. You are not here to be affected by it. Simply observe it,' Guruji continued on seeing that Rinad had achieved some level of stillness.

'But I feel itchy…'

Guruji frowned.

'If an itching sensation arises, observe it. If you stay on the outside, you will not be affected by it. Relax your jaw.'

Rinad's mouth opened by a quarter of an inch.

'Make sure the breathing is absolutely smooth. Right from when you begin the inhalation, reaching the peak, the transition to the exhalation, and all the way to the end of it. Let there be a flow, and let it flow smoothly.'

Rinad continued breathing, trying to smoothen it out as much as possible. On reaching one of the peaks of his inhalation, he let out a forceful exhale, collapsed his head as a sign of surrender, and opened his eyes. As Guruji looked at him sternly, Rinad shook his head and looked back in a way that gestured his giving up.

'I can't do this. I've never meditated in my life!'

'There is a first time for everything,' Guruji interrupted.

'How is this going to help me fight the Asuras anyway?'

'Meditation is the path to your realisation which will help you identify and understand your celestial parent and your capabilities.'

'Is there no other way?'

'There is.'

Rinad looked at Guruji expectantly.

'If you are pushed to any extremity…emotionally…you could attain a certain level of realisation. But that is not healthy and is certainly not sustainable. You cannot resort to it every time you need to reach the next level.'

'Why not?'

'Imagine what you will need to do to reach your highest potential! Where you will need to go! It will not be safe or healthy to go there. You may break.'

Rinad sat there silently under the tree. Obviously, he did not want to break.

'What do you want me to do?'

'Try,' replied Guruji, 'and believe!'

'Of course.'

'For the rest of the day, I want you to focus just on this. I am confident your combat skills will improve, but I need you to connect with yourself. If you are not able to do that, everything else will be irrelevant,' concluded Guruji and stood up to leave.

'Wait…where are you going?'

'I have other students to attend to, you see.'

'You want me to continue by myself?'

'You want me to spoon-feed you throughout?'

Rinad frowned.

'I have told you what needs to be done. Now work on it by yourself.'

Rinad stared speechlessly as Guruji began to walk away. Just then, he remembered something he had heard during his last attempt to escape.

'Guruji!'

'Yes?'

'The other night, when the Asuras were trying to kill me, they called me the leader of the Manwaans. What's that supposed to mean?'

Guruji smiled.

'I think it's pretty self-explanatory,' he said and returned to the house, leaving Rinad scratching his head.

Thirty-one

'Guruji...how do you expect me to attain the true potential of my capabilities without actually practising the extent to which they can be used?'

'True power comes from awareness, Maya. You need to be in control. If you are not in control, you will never reach the level you were meant to.'

Maya stared at Guruji, unconvinced.

The four Manwaans and Govi were in the training arena two days after Milaayak's visit. Each session consisted of an hour of meditation, an hour of warm-up with conditioning, and an hour of intense combat training. Guruji would mostly be present for the last segment.

Rinad, however, was still focusing on his meditation and preliminary training that included running around the house and short, intense body-weight workouts that Yuva had written down for him, primarily comprising of burpees, squats, push-ups, pull-ups, sit-ups, and leg raises.

Guruji looked over to the other side of the room and yelled, 'Are you ready, Yuva?'

'Why must I be the guinea pig?' he mumbled.

'Kaww...Kaww....'

'Stop flattering me...I'm not the strongest. Okay, maybe I am.'

'Kaww...Kaww....'

'This is going to be so much fun!' Ash said as he bounced in excitement.

'Do you have to be so sadistic?' Nivi asked, unable to bear the excitement Ash was exuding.

'*Yen yepodhum ennoda excitementa kollarae?*' Ash rambled.

'*Yenna nee kozhanda madhiri nadandhikarae!*' Nivi rambled back.

'*Onakkum yennoda vayasu dhaan,*' Ash snapped.

'Hello...*onna vidae yenakku moolae rombave jaasti,*' Nivi snapped back.

'*Vaaya moodu di!*'

'*Nee vaaya moodu da!*'

'Ugh! I hate it when they do that. Can't understand a thing!' Yuva shook his head and whispered to Govi, who was perched on his shoulder as the siblings squabbled. The Iyer twins had a tendency to transition their conversation to Tamil. Especially when they fought. Apparently, negative emotions such as anger and frustration were best expressed in one's mother tongue.

'Would you cut that out and let me focus!' Maya growled from the other end. 'I still can't believe those two are more realised than me,' she whispered aside to Guruji, who chuckled.

'Now, Maya…I do not want you to inflict any pain. All I want you to do is feel Yuva's large intestine. Feel it like you are in it. Feel the movement of the food through it, the blood that surrounds it, and the vibrations that it experiences from the pumping of the heart. Be one with it. If you are able to do that, nothing can stop you,' Guruji whispered.

Maya looked at Yuva with laser-sharp focus.

'Okay, buddy. This is it. She's going to squish my intestine. It was nice knowing you,' Yuva whispered to Govi.

'Kaww…Kaww….'

'I am not being melodramatic. How dare you?'

The twins stood on the side and watched carefully.

The tension in the room could be cut with a knife.

Once Maya seized her focus, she raised both her hands. Slowly, sweat began to accumulate on her forehead, and her breathing transitioned into panting. Her hands began to tense up, and her entire body started to tremble.

'Breathe into it, Maya,' Guruji's muffled voice echoed.

Maya consciously performed a couple of deep breaths, following which the trembling reduced, and the tension faded away. Her eyes slowly began to close, and her jaw dropped slightly as she relaxed further into it.

'Good. Now, with every time you inhale, feel yourself going deeper and deeper,' Guruji's voice continued as it got more muffled and indistinct.

Rightly so, with each breath, Maya felt the burden lifting off, and she began to go deeper into it as everything around her started to blur, as if being sucked into what she was focusing on. Before she knew it, she was transported to a dark void.

There was absolutely nothing there except for her and Yuva's large intestine.

She scanned the organ from top to bottom and smiled to herself. Never had she been able to do this before.

To everyone else in the room, Maya's body had suddenly relaxed and was scanning thin air. At least, that's what it looked like from the outside. Of course, in her mind, she was looking at the intestine. The mild smile was not just in her head but was visible on her face too. Everyone could tell that she was in.

'Very good, Maya,' Guruji's voice echoed all around her. 'Now all I want you to do is stroke the organ. Remember, you don't actually need to touch it, but you do need to feel the contact on the palm of your hands.'

Maya raised her hands and swiftly placed them in position. To everyone else in the room, it seemed as though the weight of her palms had increased exponentially.

'Ouch!!' Yuva yelled, holding onto his stomach.

Maya retracted her hand.

'Easy, Maya. Gently. The more softly you touch it, the stronger you will be able to impact it. Try it again,' Guruji's voice echoed.

This time, Maya slowly raised her hands, with her palms relaxed, and gently placed them in position. After staying there for a few seconds, she wriggled her fingers.

'Ooo…that tickles…' Yuva said as he chuckled.

Maya increased the pace of the wriggling.

Yuva's chuckles crossfaded into laughter, 'Oh, stop it… hahaha…it's tickling…stop it!!'

This time, Maya began to shake her fingers at a quick pace but still in a gentle manner.

Yuva's laughter assumed a crescendo and began to echo throughout the arena. It was almost uncontrollable, 'Stop it. I can't take it anymore…hahaha…ha…ha…' The intensity of the laughter began to peak and finally culminated with a mini explosion.

Maya snapped out of it and was back in the room, frightened. She was worried she had hurt her fellow Manwaan. She looked at Yuva, who was bent over, holding his stomach with his head almost touching his knees. Guruji and Maya, on the other end, were too far away to discern what had happened.

Ash figured it out, 'Did you just shit your pants, bro?'

Yuva raised his head and was red like a tomato.

The room burst out into laughter. Ash and Nivi were rolling on the floor, Maya clenched her stomach, and Guruji tried to maintain a decent composure while laughing, even though he was failing miserably. Even Govi flew around hysterically—his way of conveying that he, too, could not control his laughter.

'That's not funny,' an embarrassed Yuva yelled in a half-choked voice. 'Guruji!!'

Guruji tried to gather himself, 'I am sorry, Yuva. But it is a little funny. Come on, have a laugh.'

'This is not done, Guruji,' Yuva yelled and awkwardly ran out while holding onto the back of his pants, trying to ensure nothing dripped from anywhere. Govi flew after to look after his mighty master, who had just gone loose in his pants.

As the laughter subsided, Maya smiled to herself with pride. She had effectively attained a new level of realisation, at least with her capabilities.

'Do you understand now?' Guruji asked in a hushed tone as he looked at his student with pride.

Maya didn't say a word. She nodded with contentment while continuing to smile.

'Only when you are in control can you do the unthinkable, Maya. If you act from a place of irrationality, you will only cause pain to others and to yourself. Now that you have a glimpse of how to control your abilities, you will be able to give it the direction and the impact that you desire. Keep working on this, yes?'

Maya nodded.

'Good. Now go help your friend clean up. I am sure he is very upset with you.'

'Yes, Guruji,' Maya giggled and ran upstairs.

Thirty-two

The next day, Ash and Nivi dragged Guruji downstairs to their laboratory.

'What is it now?' Guruji asked.

'We've been working on something, and we'd like you to have a look, Guruji,' Ash said excitedly.

'Is it another weapon?'

The Iyer twins looked at him sheepishly.

Over the past few years, Nivedita and Ashwin had juggled between being at Manbhoomi and running their boutique homeopathy clinic, Ashnivi Homeopathic Centre. They attained the first level as kids back home in Chennai when Ash met with a terrible accident while riding his bike, and Nivi accidentally cured him by placing her palm on his wound. What they took time with, was comprehending that they were born with a layer of a special tissue that ran throughout their bodies and was nestled between the dermis and the subcutaneous layer of their skin. Guruji had jokingly named it the Iyer tissue and the Iyer blood, which was more like a yellow-green serum.

Their self-healing abilities also got stronger as they achieved higher levels. At their current stage, small scars and bruises would heal instantly, but bigger ones took time.

Both studied to be doctors. Not like they needed to. The serum that flowed through them had the ability to treat anything, possibly even cancer. But to ensure that they didn't draw any unwarranted attention to their inhuman abilities, they obtained their degrees before practising. All they had to do was procure the plain homoeopathy white pills. While the other doctors would meticulously make a mixture of chemicals and pour droplets into it, the Iyer twins simply had to use the serum that ran through them instead, and it would cure any disease.

An unfair advantage but quite a marvel.

However, despite this unique gift, the twins always felt inadequate. Especially when they were in the presence of powerful Manwaans like Yuva and Maya. They felt their capabilities could do a lot of good but fell short when it came to effectiveness during battle. And to overcompensate, the abnormally smart twins would create unique weapons that would not have been imagined otherwise. They created Maya's unique double-bladed spear, Ash's bladed nun chucks, and Nivi's boomerang blades—a pair of circular blades that were designed in an aerodynamically efficient manner, which only the two of them knew how to use. When practising, they would keep switching between the nun chucks and the boomerang blades, sometimes training with one of each.

But this was not enough.

They would keep experimenting and would come up with deadlier unique weapons each time.

'What's wrong with creating weapons, Guruji?' Nivi asked softly. She could never assume a harsh tone but spoke up when she needed to.

'I fear you might get too dependent on them,' Guruji replied calmly.

'But then, how else are we supposed to fight in a battle?' Ash butted in.

'I am not asking you not to use them. Just don't obsess over them. Anyway...what have you two Einsteins conjured up this time?'

The twins chuckled as they entered the lab and walked over to one of the penultimate counters in the room. Ash bent down, opened the cupboard that was at the bottom, and placed a palm-sized triangular instrument on the table along with a square-shaped, yellow-tinted monocle that was attached to a white body and a piece that went around the ear, like the curved end of a spectacle. The triangular piece had a handle attached to it, where the palm could be inserted, and on the handle, right next to the thumb, was a button.

Guruji stared at it with a poker face.

'Guruji...presenting the audio destroyer!' Ash announced in a dramatic manner.

Guruji continued to stare unflinchingly.

'Tch Tch Tch...I told you, *da*...that name sounds terrible,' Nivi commented while shaking her head in disapproval.

'*Aye...idhu romba nalla paeru dhaan*,' Ash rambled.

'*Nee yedheyo kolla pandra maadhiri irukku*,' Nivi rambled back.

Guruji stared with a poker face, allowing the twins to transition back to English for his benefit.

'*Podi!* Why don't you come up with a better name?'

'Trust me, I will. Carry on for now.'

'Guruji, we thought that if we were to battle hundreds of Asuras, we need to be better prepared,' Ash continued. 'With the nunchucks and boomerang blades, we won't really be able to cover much ground, so we came up with this beauty.'

'We devised a way in which we can send targeted ultrasound frequencies at decibels that would be harmful to a human body,' Nivi took over. She picked up the triangular device and held it closer to Guruji. 'Through this tiny hole, the ultrasound waves get emitted when we push this button,' she said, showing the handle, 'and with that glass piece, we can control the decibel level, ranging from 120 to 180, and the frequency, ranging from 20 kilohertz to 50 kilohertz. Not only that, but we can lock in multiple targets and send rays of ultrasound waves directly at them, so it doesn't spill over and harm anyone else.'

Ash took over. 'Of course, we can also target a wider range rather than individual candidates in the case of multiple Asuras or something. So, what we plan to do is, Nivi and I will hold onto one nun chuck and one boomerang blade each, and we'll have this on as well. We could shoot the ultrasound rays at the Asuras, handicap them, and before they can regain their senses, we could finish them off with our weapons.'

They both paused to hear from Guruji.

Guruji took a deep breath in.

'Interesting.'

Ash and Nivi looked at each other with soft smiles on their faces.

'So, this will not actually kill them, but impair their hearing and distract them from their surroundings?' Guruji asked.

'Exactly!' Nivi's enthusiasm grew on receiving a certain sense of approval from her teacher. 'We might even be able to kill them with it if we toggle the decibel level to 180. But we haven't been able to test that. Not really sure how we could test its effects either.'

'Guruji, we also want to integrate some form of a gun into this piece. We would be able to handicap and kill them instantly while targeting them accurately. But we didn't have the time to work on that. We would need a few more weeks,' Ash concluded.

'We do not have that kind of time. But this is good. Keep the decibel level low. Do not work with levels that you have not been able to test. The last thing you need on a battlefield is to encounter side effects that you may not have accounted for,' Guruji said as he picked up the piece and started observing it closely.

'Yes, Guruji,' the twins replied in unison.

'Can I ask you both something?' Guruji asked thoughtfully as he squinted his eyes and continued observing the newly invented weapon. The twins nodded and leaned in.

'You both are possibly two of the sweetest youngsters I have met. But you build these weapons that cause so much pain. And you have been doing this repeatedly. It says a lot. Why so much rage?'

The twins fell short of words. Ash was not very good when it came to justifications, so he looked over to Nivi, who he depended on during such situations. Nivi, taking the cue from her twin brother, spoke up to explain. 'Guruji, we're extremely proud of our capabilities, we don't want to let you or the others down, and we want to be useful when it comes to fighting the Asuras. How can we be of service if we depend purely on our healing abilities? At least with these weapons, we feel slightly more empowered, and we won't need to depend on others when it comes to facing the Asuras.'

'Hmm...do you really believe that?'

This time, Ash nodded in a subtle manner.

'Very well. Whatever keeps you happy. But I never want you to forget how special you are and the role that you play,' Guruji continued. 'When life needs to be saved, no one can be more useful than the two of you. Please keep that in mind.'

The twins smiled and nodded as Guruji turned and began to walk away.

'Oh…and one more thing,' he said as he stopped at the doorstep, 'you have one more ability that you never give yourselves credit for…'

The twins listened on, intrigued.

'You both are abnormally smart. And there are more ways than one in which that could be useful,' Guruji concluded and left.

The twins smiled, let out a contented sigh, and got back to putting this heightened capability of theirs to use.

As they continued working, Ash slowly raised his head and said, 'How about an *Audicapitator*?'

Nivi looked at him with pursed lips.

'It's almost like audio plus decapitator,' Ash continued.

'Not bad,' Nivi bobbed her head in agreement.

'Works for now. Audicapitator it is!'

Thirty-three

'I think we should place a round of bets,' Ash whispered excitedly.

'*Dai*...don't be mean!' Nivi chided him.

'I'm in!' Maya said with a grin.

'That's the spirit! So, what should we bet on? I say we bet on the number of places he bleeds from,' Ash continued.

'Ugh! That's gross! Something less grotesque, please?' Maya responded with a shudder down her spine.

'Okay. How about the number of times he gets back up?'

'Ooo...that's interesting.'

'I say he won't get up more than two times.'

'Hmm...alright, I'll bet against that.'

'Perfect. So, if he gets up the third time, you win. If not, I win,' Ash concluded.

'You guys are sick!' Nivi interjected.

'What are we betting on, though?' Maya said with rousing amusement.

'I call shotgun on Yuva's back whenever we fly out with him. You take the leg.'

Maya grew pensive. She knew this was a tough decision to make. Yuva, being the biggest, tallest, broadest, and the only one who could fly, would carry the other three on his back whenever they flew out. Now that there were four of them, two would need to hold on to his legs, who would be dangling mid-air, and two onto his shoulders, who would have his back to rest part of their bodies on. Up till now, the ladies would get one shoulder each out of courtesy, and Ash would hang from one leg. It was a tough choice to make.

'Fine. But if I win, you will permanently be on the leg and can never use that in a bet again,' Maya said with a grin.

This meant dangling from Yuva's leg for the rest of his life in case he lost this bet. Ash thought to himself and after much contemplation, he accepted, 'Deal!'

They both shook on it and shifted their views towards the arena where Yuva and Rinad stood facing each other.

Yuva, towering at almost eight feet, and Rinad standing at roughly five feet eight inches. Guruji stood on Yuva's side, near the staircase, with his hands behind his back and chin lifted, almost in an observing stance.

'Are you ready, Rinad?' Guruji yelled from across the room.

'No!' Rinad responded as his voice shook. He looked up and saw Yuva grinning at him.

'Well, time is running out. It's time you take a few blows.'

'What?' Rinad shrieked. This was possibly the most violent statement that he had heard from Guruji.

Bam!!!

A blow landed on his face, and he went flying down.

'Yuva! I did not ask you to begin!'

'Oops...sorry, Guruji. I thought that was my cue,' Yuva grinned unapologetically.

'That's one down,' Ash whispered to Maya.

'I can count,' Maya hissed.

'Ouch!' Rinad groaned. 'At least let me get ready, man!'

'No one is going to wait for you to get ready, Rinad,' Guruji said nonchalantly. 'So, here's what we're going to do. To begin with, all I want you to do is deliver one punch on Yuva. One punch...absolutely anywhere.'

A near-impossible task.

Yuva folded his arms and smirked arrogantly as Rinad mustered up his strength to stand up.

'You've got blood dripping from your nose,' Yuva sniffed.

Rinad wiped the blood, clenched his fists, and started inching towards the winged giant.

'Only defend, Yuva,' Guruji commanded.

'Not to worry, Guruji,' Yuva yelled back.

Rinad stood close enough to have to tilt his head up to look Yuva directly in the eyes. He could feel the warm breath blowing down from his opponent's large nostrils. He proceeded to raise his clenched fists and assumed an offensive stance.

'Go for it,' Yuva whispered arrogantly.

Rinad shot his right hand towards Yuva's abdomen, who simply stepped aside to dodge it. He tried shooting the left hand. Same thing. This time Rinad took a second to choreograph a triple punch.

I'll give one with the right hand, which he might dodge... one with the left hand, which he might also dodge...but then I'll follow it up with an uppercut on his giant jaw. He'll never see that coming! Rinad thought to himself.

And then he went for it.

First punch—dodged successfully. Second punch—dodged successfully. Finally, a hopeful Rinad went for the final uppercut. Yuva simply smacked it aside with his left wing with just enough force to send Rinad to the floor.

Bloody hell! So, this guy can use his wings as arms? So that means it's almost like he has four arms!

'That's two,' Ash whispered excitedly.

Maya didn't respond.

The frustration was getting to Rinad. He was easily outmatched. He thought maybe he should just go for a burst of punches. The chances of at least one of them hitting Yuva were minutely higher. So, he went for it.

A quick succession of roughly thirty punches. All dodged with ease, but Rinad didn't stop. Yuva would step away and dodge the punch, using his hands and wings to flick them off, all with a strange calmness. He defended like a ninja. Finally, he flew a few inches off the ground and caught Rinad's approaching right hand with his left foot, making sure the claws didn't pierce into his skin.

Rinad stared at his legs. *So, he can also use his legs to catch. Great!* he thought.

'Is that all you've got?' Yuva sniggered and let go with a jolt.

Rinad took a second, caught his breath, and resumed his punches. They were weaker than before, considering he must have tried nearly fifty punches up till now. Yuva stayed levitated, folded his hands, and used only his legs to flick the punches away this time, as his wings flapped slightly to hold him in position.

Rinad finally gave up.

On seeing this, Yuva landed and stood waiting for his opponent's next unsuccessful move.

Rinad, drenched in sweat, went for one last blow, and Yuva caught his right arm with his left hand an inch away from his chest. He then brought in his right wing and used the feathers at its tip to wipe Rinad's sweat off.

'You seem to be getting tired. Shall we call it a day?' Yuva chuckled.

Just then, a thought came into Rinad's mind. He observed the wing with his peripheral vision, casually lifted his left hand and plucked one of the feathers out.

'Ouch!' Yuva yelled and pushed Rinad away.

Rinad went flying to the floor, but he, along with the rest of the room, burst out laughing. Maya, Ash, and Nivi slowly clapped as Yuva turned red with embarrassment.

Guruji also quivered with laughter while trying to hold it back. Yuva looked around, unsure how to react, but finally came to terms with it. He walked over to Rinad, who was holding his stomach from uncontrollable laughter. He finally calmed down and noticed a grumpy Yuva standing tall and looking down at him.

The entire room got quiet.

Everyone wondered how Yuva would respond. Rinad stopped his laughter and prepared himself for a punch from the giant.

Guruji leaned in as well.

'You cheated,' Yuva sniffed. 'But…all is fair in love and war. So, well done,' he extended his hand out to Rinad, who smiled, caught hold of it, and stood up.

'I win!' Maya cheered.

'Sure, but it wasn't really a fight,' Ash rolled his eyes.

'Still!'

Nivi smiled with a glimmer of pride, 'But that was a smart move. I wonder how none of us ever thought of it.'

Thirty-four

Rinad laid down after another tiring day of training. The meditation, or the inability to do so, was taking a toll on his mind and the combat training on his body. It had barely been a week, and he already felt like he needed a break. The thought of doing this for the rest of his life seemed to be a difficult one to digest.

The only upside was that his lifestyle had improved significantly.

Guruji had strictly asked him to stop his weed consumption and medication as it would interfere with his ability to reach his realisation. While the first few days seemed impossible, his mind slowly began clearing out. He was sleeping well and felt much better.

But tonight, he couldn't sleep.

A certain sense of joy ran through him. Even though he was nowhere close to having his realisation, he was making slow progress, and more importantly, for the first time in many years, he felt a certain sense of being. A certain sense of purpose. He felt like he was responsible and part of something much bigger. His identity was being defined, something he had yearned for a long time. He decided to celebrate this euphoria with a meditative midnight walk.

Rinad opened the door and walked towards the balcony of the living room. He noticed a broad structure that had wings on its back sitting there. He couldn't make out much in the darkness but figured it was Yuva. He was wearing a tank top like he mostly did, just so it didn't get in the way of his wings. Yuva was sitting with his chin resting on his interlocked fists, with an elbow resting on each thigh. He seemed to be lost in thought but looked peaceful.

'May I join you?' Rinad whispered, trying not to break the calmness of the environment.

Yuva simply shrugged his shoulders.

Rinad sat on one side of the ledge, slightly squeezed. Yuva noticed this and gently moved to the other side, making room for Rinad.

'Thanks!'

Yuva nodded. He clearly wanted to be with himself and his thoughts.

Nearly ten minutes passed without either saying a word. Both were lost in their own worlds. But strangely, there was no awkwardness in the silence.

'How are you doing?' Yuva finally spoke up.

Now, this came as a shock to Rinad for two reasons. One, Yuva never started conversations, especially with Rinad, and two, he had asked about his wellbeing, which he never seemed to care about. Until now!

'Umm…what?' asked a surprised Rinad.

'How are you doing?' Yuva repeated.

'Not too bad. Getting there, I guess…'

'Good.'

'It does get overwhelming at times, but it's better than before.'

'Good.'

Silence.

'Did you also have to deal with any sort of side effects?' Rinad softly broke the silence.

'Every Manwaan does,' Yuva replied with a poker face.

Rinad continued to look at him expectantly, hoping for a more in-depth answer to that question.

'I used to overeat,' Yuva continued.

'That's barely a side effect. I overeat all the time after getting high. I mean…when I used to get high,' Rinad said sheepishly.

'I'm sure it wasn't like how I used to. No amount of food was ever enough. There have been times when I've eaten so much that I threw it all up.'

'Well, you're in great shape.'

'Now. I used to be an obese child. Food was my best friend,' Yuva said sombrely.

'Oh! What made you stop?

'It was Guruji who pointed out that I was only trying to fill a void. Since then, I never overate.'

Rinad smiled on hearing that this giant creature sitting next to him had dealt with his share of struggles. Everyone faced issues, and it felt comforting to know that he was not alone.

Silence.

'I'm sorry about your wing. I didn't know what else to do! You pretty much dodged every single punch that I tried to hit you with!'

'Don't sweat it. It was a good move. No one's done that before.'

Rinad smiled to himself.

'But don't get overconfident,' Yuva continued. 'It was just smart. You still can't fight to save your life.'

Rinad nodded as his smile receded.

Silence.

'How long have you been doing this?'

'I've been with Guruji for nearly thirty years.'

'Thirty years! How old are you?'

Yuva chuckled, 'Forty-one.'

'What? You don't look it one bit! I thought you would have been in your late twenties or early thirties, max!' Rinad exclaimed.

'Manwaans age slowly.'

'That's good to know.'

'What are you idiots talking about?' a voice came from behind. Maya approached them from the darkness and stood behind them.

'Doesn't anybody sleep around here?' Rinad jested.

Maya chuckled. 'Move over.'

Rinad and Yuva shifted to either end of the ledge, and Maya squeezed herself between the two of them.

'How about you? How long have you been here with Guruji?' Rinad continued.

'Around twenty years, maybe,' Maya replied

'Damn! What did you guys do all these years?'

'We'd fight petty criminals discretely. Nothing too fancy...we could never reveal ourselves. We'd always have to work at night. That's why we're up so late. But right from the beginning, Guruji told us about the great celestial revolution and how we'd have to be prepared to fight it. So, that's pretty much all we did. Prepare!'

'Hmm...don't you guys ever get out?'

'And go where?'

'Home? To your families, maybe?'

'This is our home. And we don't have any other family. Our parents abandoned us when we were kids—when we had minor realisations and some of our capabilities developed. The world was not too kind, and Guruji... well, let's just say he adopted us. He's been the only parent we've ever known.'

'And the only parent we've ever needed,' Yuva added coldly.

'Oh! I'm sorry to hear that,' Rinad said softly.

'It's been over twenty years. It's chill,' Maya chuckled.

'Right. What about friends?'

'It's not really easy to maintain a social life, doing what we do.'

'Hmm…'

'But we do have a few. We don't see them too often, though. Every time we meet them, we put their lives at risk.'

'I can imagine.'

'It's been ages since I met my buds. I can't afford to lose another friend because of who I am,' Yuva said in a serious tone.

Rinad looked towards Maya, hoping for a detailed expansion of Yuva's morbid statement. But Maya just shook her head, asking him to let it be. It was best to not broach such topics.

'Basically, we keep our distance,' Maya continued, easing out the tension, 'and that's why we've been discrete in the past.'

'Is that also why you wear masks?'

'Yup. Those damn masks!' Yuva grunted under his breath.

Maya chuckled, 'He hates wearing them.'

'It feels like we're going to a birthday party or something, man!' Yuva complained.

'But hold on, doesn't Govinda wear funky costumes in all his movies?' Rinad asked.

'Yes, but he's an actor…playing a character. It's justified. This is just pure silly!'

'Oh, that feels silly?' Maya continued. 'I'll remember to bring that up the next time we encounter a cockroach.'

'What do you mean?' Rinad asked.

'He's scared of cockroaches,' Maya said trying to hold back her laughter.

'What?!'

'He can't stand the sight of them. Every time he sees one, he asks Govi to take care of it for him.'

'Dude…you're like eight feet tall. And you've got arms the size of tree trunks, man!' Rinad laughed in disbelief.

'Look, cockroaches are filthy and disgusting. They've been to the dirtiest of places and can survive a bloody nuclear attack. And when I'm in the bathroom, naked and showering, I don't want to see a cockroach waving its antlers and staring at me. It's just gross!' Yuva whined as his entire body shuddered.

'Are we talking about Yuva and his love for cockroaches?' a voice came from behind. The three of them turned around and saw Ash and Nivi approaching the balcony.

'How are you two up at this hour?' Maya asked.

'You guys are so loud. We came to tell you to keep it down. You'll wake up Guruji,' Nivi said in a hushed, sleepy tone.

'Oops…sorry!' Rinad said. 'You guys sleep early?'

'These children go to bed by 9 p.m. Sometimes 8.30 p.m. too,' Yuva mocked.

'And what would be so wrong about that? We wake up at five in the morning. Unlike any of you guys,' Nivi replied.

'Whoa! You guys wake up at 5 a.m.?' asked a surprised Rinad. Waking up at such odd hours was unheard of to him.

'We've been doing it since we were kids…it's no biggie!' Ash said.

'Is that because you're South Indian?'

'Thanks for stereotyping, man.'

'No…I didn't mean…'

'But yeah,' Ash chuckled.

'That's a great habit, though!'

'Not when it comes to fighting crime at night!'

Rinad chuckled. 'Do you guys have any family or friends?'

'We do…back home in Chennai,' Nivi said. 'But we try and keep our distance. It's really not worth the risk.'

'Man! Staying couped up for all these years…cut off from family and friends…I can't even imagine it!'

'Better get used to it, bro,' Maya said.

Rinad smiled to himself.

A sense of warmth was brewing around him, and he was glad to be here. With the four of them staring into nothingness and being absolutely comfortable with each other in the silence. At this moment, it began to feel like home. While he did find it hard to digest the fact that his social life was officially disrupted, the journey through the bigger picture seemed to be worth the sacrifice. No more Saturday nights with the boys, no more drinking or smoking. He was in great company. People who supported, motivated, and pushed him to achieve the peaks of his capabilities. He couldn't have asked for more.

The five of them remained in tranquillity, gazing at the clear, star-studded sky.

'I had to ask you guys something,' Rinad hushed and broke the silence yet again. 'Guruji didn't give me a proper answer, but maybe you can help me. The night I tried to escape, one of the Asuras called me the leader of the Manwaans. What did he mean by that?' Rinad asked.

'Exactly that,' Yuva grunted.

Rinad frowned.

'Guruji said the same thing. Can you maybe expand on that?'

'According to the prophecy, when the gates of Hell open, the king of the Manwaans will emerge. It'll be his responsibility to lead us and curb the revolution,' Maya said with a straight face.

Rinad grew silent.

'Fancy,' he said with a poker face. 'And why does everyone think I'm that guy?'

'It's more of an educated guess,' Nivi said.

'I have my doubts,' Yuva jested, and all three of them chuckled.

'Me too,' Rinad agreed. 'And where is this prophecy coming from? Is it written somewhere or something?'

'We don't know that…Guruji won't tell us,' Maya replied.

'Hmm…fair enough.'

'Don't let it get to your head, though. You're still terrible.'

'Thanks, man,' Rinad said with a sarcastic grin.

The five Manwaans laughed and continued to stare away into oblivion.

Thirty-five

The next day, Rinad sat under the Banyan tree with folded legs as Guruji strolled back and forth around him. The sky was overcast, but the air was quiet, with absolutely no wind and a pleasant temperature.

While Rinad would have his combat sessions with the other Manwaans, the meditation sessions remained one-on-one. Guruji had to talk him through it, which would have distracted the others. Even though Rinad was getting comfortable with his surroundings, he was far behind when it came to being prepared for battle, and this worried everyone. Guruji could sense that time was running out, and he feared that Rinad would not be able to contribute much on the battlefield. What worried him was the fact that the prophesied leader of the Manwaans would not be able to fight and, thus, not be able to lead.

Rinad sat there with his eyes closed, calmer than usual. The silence around him harboured a favourable environment to meditate in. Additionally, after having stayed away from weed and his medication for several days, his mind was clearer, and he started feeling a sense of peace like never before.

'Good, Rinad. You are doing much better,' Guruji said in his calming voice. 'Now, go deeper. With each breath, feel yourself detaching from your body to become an observer.'

Rinad's breathing deepened.

'Let your mind, body, and soul experience what they need to. Your job is to remain unaffected and simply observe how they respond.'

Rinad's forehead tensed a little.

'Let go, Rinad. You are still holding on. Just let it go.'

Once again, Rinad took a deep breath, and his forehead relaxed as he exhaled.

'Good. Now, bring your attention to your breath. Do not judge but be a silent observer. In…and out…in…and out…in…'

Guruji's voice began to muffle and fade away. The source of the soothing words no longer seemed to be a single point but reverberated around Rinad in his mind. The light started to fade away, and unknowingly, Rinad's head collapsed mildly, almost as if the life force had left his body. He slowly began to feel a slight separation from his physical self, eventually being taken into complete darkness as all the sounds around him drowned out.

Pitch black with pin-drop silence.

He levitated in the calming darkness as he looked around in awe. He had transcended to an unfamiliar place but was at complete peace and had floated away without worry. Relishing every second of it.

Just then, a speck of blue light began to emerge from a distance. The dot seemed to approach him as a humming sound gradually filled the space, and the temperature started to rise.

Guruji had stopped speaking when he saw Rinad's head collapse. He simply stood there and observed.

As the light approached nearer and the sound got louder within his mind, Rinad began to feel the warmth against his skin. He remained calm, but his breathing began to shorten, and his forehead began to moisten. With every second, the temperature rose, and his heart thumped harder. A soft blue glow radiated through his skin, and sweat covered his body with scorching heat. In his mind, the light had almost become blinding, and, in his body, it felt like his skin was being burnt. Unable to bear it, he began to lose focus, and his body started shivering.

The blue light froze, and he began to get sucked away from it. The blinding light and the humming sound faded as he got pulled in the opposite direction. With a crash, he opened his eyes as a shiver ran through his entire body and he collapsed to one side. His clothes were wet, his head throbbed, and his eyes began to water.

Guruji immediately sat next to him and used the sleeves of his robe to wipe Rinad's face.

'There you go…it's alright …calm down…everything will be fine,' Guruji said in his calming tone as he stroked Rinad's head while he shivered feverishly and wept.

Panic had assumed throughout his body—the warmth against his skin, palpitations, the sweat, all of it came screaming back. His heart felt like it was about to explode through his chest as he buried his face into Guruji's lap and wept like a baby.

'Why is this happening!' Rinad cried out. 'I've not smoked or taken any medicines…why the hell is this damn anxiety not leaving me!'

'Just calm down…breathe…do not think about that right now,' Guruji said as he patted Rinad.

By then, the silence in the air had been disrupted by a mild drizzle. The overcast sky got thicker as the day plunged into clouded darkness. The rain began to get heavier, and the wind howled.

Not a good sign for Rinad.

He buried his face deeper to darken out everything.

'Can we go inside, please?' Rinad said in a muffled voice.

'Of course,' Guruji helped Rinad stand. A bolt of lightning struck in the distance, and the world around them flashed with momentary brightness.

'Aargh!!' Rinad yelled and collapsed to the floor. He covered his face and curled up on the ground. By now, both were drenched because of the incessant rain and Rinad, frozen to the grass, was covered in muck.

'Guruji, please take me inside…' Rinad whimpered.

Guruji lifted him and guided him indoors as Rinad refused to take his hands off his eyes.

* * *

Rinad sat wrapped in a blanket on his bed, and Guruji sat beside him. His shivering had reduced, but a fever had caught up, and Rinad had still not recovered from the trauma. No one said anything for several minutes, and the room was filled with just the sound of Rinad's shivering breath.

'Would you like some chai?' Guruji softly broke the silence.

Rinad shook his head fervently.

'Would you like to tell me what happened back there?'

Rinad took a minute and tried to catch his breath, 'I have this condition called selaphobia…' he said with no energy in his voice.

'I know that.'

'How do you…'

Guruji gave him the same expression he had given many times in the past. One that meant, "I know everything about you."

'Right. Of course.'

'I meant, what happened while meditating?' Guruji asked.

'I don't know…it was really strange. I was floating in a dark, silent place…but I was at complete peace. I loved it, but then I saw this blue light coming from afar. But as it got stronger, the anxiety started taking over, and I just snapped out of it. I could feel the same warmth against my skin…'

'You mean how you feel during your panic attacks?'

'Yes…and that's so strange. For the first time, I felt something different while meditating, and then I landed right back into panic. It's almost as if my body remembered how it felt during my attacks, and as soon as it felt a similar sensation, it transported me back to that feeling. It felt like a trigger.'

'Hmm…' Guruji had a soft smile.

'What?'

'It seems like you've had a breakthrough, Rinad,' Guruji said as his smile grew wider.

Rinad frowned.

'You sound like my therapist, you know.'

'Perhaps…' Guruji chuckled, 'but whatever you saw in your mind…it was probably a baby step towards your realisation!'

'You mean I'll be having a panic attack every time I attain it?' Rinad asked with a displeased look.

'Rinad…do you feel hungry when you've not cleared your stomach?'

'What?' Rinad squeaked.

Guruji stared expectantly without flinching.

'You mean…like go to the toilet?'

Guruji nodded.

'Of course not. Everything is still in my stomach. How will I feel hungry?'

'Precisely,' Guruji smiled.

It took a minute, but when it hit Rinad, he slowly nodded in agreement.

'You know, Guruji...sometimes your ways are a bit unorthodox. Disgusting, in this particular case,' Rinad chuckled.

'I am cool like that, you see,' Guruji said with an unusual façade.

Rinad laughed, amused with his teacher. And with a heightened respect for him.

'But I still don't know my celestial parent...or my capability,' Rinad said dejectedly.

'Don't worry...you will figure it out,' Guruji concluded.

Of course, he made a conscious decision not to reveal what he had witnessed under the tree.

The mild glow that radiated from Rinad.

The educated guess that Guruji had made regarding Rinad's capabilities was substantiated with evidence.

After the proceedings of this evening, Guruji felt a newfound confidence coursing through him.

Thirty-six

'Can't any of you get one simple job done? Must I do everything myself?' Usur roared at one of the weekly midnight meetings.

'My king, something extremely strange happened,' one Asura hesitantly said.

'What?' Usur growled.

'We saw our comrades you had sent out to execute the Manwaan leader.'

Usur was baffled. 'Then why aren't they here? If they think they're here to party and have a good time, I swear, I'll rip them…'

'My king…' the Asura interrupted, 'they were not Asuras anymore.'

'What do you mean?'

'They did not recognise us, and we did not see our comrades in them. They were just regular humans.'

'How is that even possible?'

'I swear, my king. And one more thing…'

'Hmm?'

'We went to the his apartment and found their liquid forms splattered against the walls. It's almost as if the hosts were relieved of them. The hosts were set free...and our comrades were...killed.'

Usur fell silent. A chill ran down his spine.

This could mean only one thing, he thought to himself.

Usur!

A voice echoed in his head.

'Usur...I have not heard from you. What are the updates, my trusted commander-in-chief?'

It was Mihaara speaking to Usur. He had devised a way to communicate with the king of the Underworld one on one, so they didn't have to meet in person each time to exchange updates.

Usur shut his eyes to converse with the Fagir.

'Mihaaraji! It is so lovely to hear your voice.'

The Asuras looked at each other in confusion as they saw their king standing there with his eyes shut. Seemed odd, especially considering they were amidst a predicament.

'Apologies for not sending across an update, Mihaaraji. Our progress has been good, but we have encountered an obstacle. Any chance I could see you in person and have this conversation?'

'Hmm...alright. Come on down.'

Usur opened his eyes and looked at the confused faces of his comrades.

'Wait here. I need to meet Mihaara,' he said and bolted towards the portal, leaving the Asuras confused and worried.

A meeting with Mihaara was not a good sign.

Usur reached the portal area. He stood there, shut his eyes, and began to murmur a mantra.

Khalo bhumi bhasonayaan
Jago bhumi bhasonayaan
Idho bhumi bhasonayaan

As he did, the portal opened, and he jumped into it, landing in the passageway that connected the portals to the Gateway of Hell. He ran towards the circular Gateway, which was partially shut. Once opened, the Gateway could be completely closed and locked only by an angel who possessed the knowledge to do so. As he reached the entrance, he found a stoic Mihaara standing on the other side with his hands behind him.

He did not seem impressed.

'What is it, Usur? Why did you need to come back down?'

'Mihaaraji,' Usur replied as he crossed the doorway and bowed his head in reverence, 'I have a feeling that one of your siblings roams the Earth.'

'Impossible!'

Usur stared at Mihaara with disagreement in his eyes. He was too overwhelmed with fear to say it with words lest he upset him.

'Two of the hosts that my comrades possessed were even relieved of their demonic energy. The hosts walk unscathed, and my fellow Asuras are no more. Only one of your siblings could have done that.'

'But who could it be?' Mihaara grew pensive.

'Can't you sense their radiation, Mihaaraji?'

'I'm afraid not. Just like how we've built a celestial forcefield around Hell, they've built one for themselves to hide from us.'

Usur stayed quiet. This was not his area of expertise, so he let his ally angel figure it out and conjure up the next steps.

'But who could it be…Uraavati, maybe?' Mihaara was thinking out loud. 'No, no…the Gods would never send her. Or could they? Maybe it's Gurgaan…or Milaayak… actually, it could be any of them…Usur, there's only one way to find out.'

'Yes, Mihaaraji?'

'You are my eyes and ears on Earth. I need you to contact me when you are in his or her presence. Through your senses, I might be able to pick up the radiation. Nevertheless, this is a big problem. We need to expedite the annexation.'

'I couldn't agree more, Mihaaraji,' Usur replied gleefully.

'Open up several more portals along the western belt.'

'It would be my pleasure. Just the Asuras? Or…'

Mihaara smirked and shook his head. 'It is time for them to see what we are truly capable of.'

Usur grinned back and began to rally his troops as Mihaara opened the Gateway completely.

'The time has come, comrades!' Usur yelled.

'Let's take it down! Iaj Raakn Ho!'

'IAJ RAAKN HO!!' voices growled back from the darkness.

As Usur stepped to one side, shadows of beasts emerged from the depths of the Underworld. Thousands of floating creatures swarming through the corridors of Hell. Their shapeless forms would soon have flesh and bones. Their red eyes in Hell would manifest as black eyes on Earth. As the members of the Underworld Clan crossed the Gateway of Hell into the passageway, Usur, who stood in one corner, began to recite the mantra.

Khalo bhumi bhasonayaan
Jago bhumi bhasonayaan
Idho bhumi bhasonayaan
Mariho bhumi bhasonayaan

With the continuous chanting, portals began to open up above the floating figures one by one, and a bright blue light shone through them. Even though the Underworld had no discernible ceiling, the portals seemed to appear on an invisible surface. Soon, the infinite passageway of Hell was lit up by the luminescence of the hundreds of portals.

Once the portals opened up to an appropriate amount, the creatures tilted their heads up and began to levitate towards them, almost as if being absorbed by the openings. A reverse-gravitational pull lifted them further up, and eventually, the floating, formless beasts got sucked into the portals one by one, transferring them to the other realm.

As Mihaara stood on the side and watched like a proud master, an ocean of shadows of warriors of the Underworld Clan levitated across the Gateway, stood in the passageway, got sucked into the portals, and were sent to fight the battle that they had long awaited.

The revolution had begun.

Thirty-seven

'Good evening, *chacha*! Do you have a few minutes to spare?' the police officer addressed one of the elderly vegetable vendors in the market in Bandra East. Addressing unknown elders as "uncle" was a norm, and young police officers often made a conscious effort to show respect.

'Sure. What's this regarding?'

'Chacha…roughly ten days ago, certain unusual activities were witnessed here. Could you give us more details about the same?'

The elderly vendor tensed up and began to dart his eyeballs in worry. When he got no response, the police officer looked towards his partner with an affirmation that something extremely unusual had occurred. The two of them were part of the special force, which was under Deshpande's command, and Pawar had assigned them the task of gathering information on the first unusual sighting that had been recorded. They would not leave without having made some progress.

'It's alright, chacha...you can tell us exactly what you saw. We know it may sound abnormal, but we're here to get to the bottom of this.'

The vendor swallowed hard, hesitated a couple of times but finally spoke up. 'You will think I am mad...'

'No, chacha. I promise you...we will not.'

The vendor took a minute, gathered his confidence, and continued, 'I don't know how it started...but I remember these two people—one man who was a vendor, like me, and one lady who was buying vegetables from him. They both suddenly had a fit or something. Their bodies started vibrating and...' he paused midway and broke into a sweat.

'Take your time, chacha. We've heard about it. We just need to confirm the same,' the officer consoled him in a calming tone.

'Their eyes turned black. They had long black nails that started emerging from their fingertips and even black veins on their necks!'

'And then?'

'Then...nothing. They turned normal again and walked away. The vendor left his cart as it was and never came back.'

The officers looked at each other with fear and worry.

'Did you notice...'

Before the officer could complete his next question, he was interrupted by echoes of voracious screams. The two of them ran towards the direction of the screams and were horrified at what they saw on reaching the end of the lane.

Swarms of crazed people were running onto the Western Express highway. Cars and trucks banging into each other, people abandoning their vehicles and running, and some people even being trampled by others. On observing closer, the officers noticed men and women jumping on the cars, running after people, and slashing them with their hands.

Men and women with black eyes and long nails.

'Oh my god! This seems like…' the officer was thinking out loud when his attention was drawn by something utterly strange. There was a particular lane in Bandra West from which these men and women with black eyes were running out.

From the same street, beastly creatures began to emerge.

Red-eyed creatures nearly eight feet tall with black fur all over their bodies. Long ears, black claws, paws instead of hands and feet, and sharp canines but with flattened faces. These beasts were as huge and hairy as bears, vicious as wolves, and roared like lions but ran and functioned like humans.

Rakshasas.

On looking closer, the officer even noticed an active transformation. A man running away from the scene got the black-red liquid leeched onto him. As he vibrated, his entire body turned black, and fur began to emerge all over. His face transformed into something like that of a wolf with a flattened nose, with the ears growing long, black fangs emerging, and hands and feet turning into hairy paws. The five-something-foot man was now a creature towering nearly eight feet that growled as it attacked other unpossessed humans.

'What in god's name are those things?' the officer gasped.

Usur had opened up multiple portals this time, and the locations were spread across Bandra, Andheri, Juhu, Goregaon, Malad, and Borivali, covering a major chunk of the western belt of Mumbai. Asuras and Rakshasas in the form of black and red liquid seeped onto the surface of the Earth and began possessing the nearest available host. Gender, age, height, weight—nothing was a barrier. The warriors almost operated on a first-come, first-serve basis.

In front of them was a buffet, and they could choose what they wanted.

Or rather, who they wanted.

Guttural screams echoed through the pockets of Mumbai. The rage of a large group began to take over as dark clouds covered the sky and submerged the city in rain and thunder. Hundreds of people were slowly being possessed, and no one could make any sense of it.

This time, subtlety was out the window.

The Underworld Clan had one objective—possess as many and kill even more. And that's exactly what they did. As they found and possessed their hosts, they immediately assumed their complete demonic forms and began killing any unpossessed humans in sight.

The Rakshasas did not have a middle ground. The minute they possessed their hosts, they would completely transform into beastly creatures. The Asuras had relatively subtle features like black eyes, claws, and veins, but this wasn't the case with the Rakshasas. They were either in their host forms, as humans, or complete raging beasts. The Rakshasas could even alternate between running on their back limbs, like humans, or on all fours, like animals. Of course, they would run at thrice the speed when on all fours. Some Rakshasas even carried the Asuras on their backs to expedite the attack's spread across the city.

It was chaos, and Mumbai was being rampaged and torn down.

The officer whipped out his phone and dialled a number.

'Hello…Pawar sir…i-it's happening, right in front of our eyes. And there's more, sir. The creatures…th-they've gotten bigger…'

Thirty-eight

'Sir!!' the doors banged open.

'Pawar…how many times must I tell you…'

'Sorry sir, but there's no time to knock!'

Deshpande was taken aback by Pawar's tone. Not once had he been spoken to like that, let alone by his faithful subordinate.

'Kay aahe, Pawar?' Deshpande asked concernedly.

'Sir…Mhatre just called. It's not looking good, sir. You need to come and see this…'

Deshpande stood up and paced after Pawar. As they both exited his office, Deshpande noticed the entire station standing and watching the news on the tiny television that was kept at the top left corner. There was pin-drop silence.

'BREAKING NEWS!'

'Mumbai is witnessing a calamity like never before. Black-eyed men and women and wolf-like creatures are tearing the city apart. There are dead bodies all over the Western Express highway, and these creatures are spreading out like wildfire. No one is able to stop them. What are these things? Why are

they…whoa…hey, look out! Behind you!! Oh no…run!! Help!! Help!!!'

The live feed disappeared, leaving a white noise screen with a fuzzy, distorted sound filling the station.

No one flinched. All the heads turned towards Deshpande, who just stood there.

Speechless.

'Pawar…I want every single officer on the field. Make sure everyone is armed.'

'But sir…we are no match. Bullets don't even affect them!'

'I don't care, Pawar!' Deshpande boomed. 'I'll speak to Kamat, sir. He will inform the defence minister, and the armed forces should be there to help us. But we cannot wait for them. I will not let another person die under my watch! NOW, GO!' Deshpande turned around and paced back into his room.

'Yes, sir,' Pawar responded hesitantly. He was torn between his commanding officer's bravery and the futility of the situation. He knew they were no match for the creatures, but even if they could save one life, they would have attempted to fulfil their responsibility as protectors of the city. And that was the least they could do.

'Alright, men! You heard what sir said. Let's go. Vikrant…' he pointed to one of the junior officers, 'make sure you inform all the other stations as well. Check your guns, wear your vests and let's save our city. This is what we wear our uniforms for. Good luck out there. *Bharat Mata ki…*'

'*Jai*!!!' all the officers yelled in unison. The doubt in the room had immediately transcended into a wave of pride as the officers got ready for the battle of their lives.

Meanwhile, Deshpande walked into his office, whipped out his phone, and called ACP Kamat.

'Hello, sir. Are you seeing this?'

'Yes, Deshpande. It's chaos!' ACP Kamat responded.

'Sir, I am speaking to the other stations and gathering all our men. It would be great if you could put in a word too.'

'Of course, Deshpande. I'm on it.'

'One more thing, sir. I fear we will not be able to face these things ourselves. Could you also have a word with Rathod sir and ask him to mobilise the armed forces? We will need their help, sir.'

'Already done, Deshpande. Rathod sir said that he would send them immediately. Of course, they will take some time. Please go there right away and try to control the situation until they arrive.'

'On it, sir,' Deshpande replied with vigour and cut the call. He walked over to his table, opened the drawer, and removed his gun and the holster that was attached to a belt. He loaded the gun, buttoned it inside the holster, and strapped the belt on. He grabbed a few extra rounds of ammunition and shoved them into his pocket. Lastly, he reached for his hat, put it on, and strode outside his office.

As he led the way, all the officers followed, got into their jeeps, and drove along to save their city from being completely destroyed.

Thirty-nine

Nearly twenty-five police jeeps pulled up at the main Bandra junction on the Western Express highway. The jeeps parked themselves in one straight line, acting as a wall that the officers could use as a cover for defence. All the officers sprang out of their vehicles and got behind one side. Just as they awaited their orders, they saw a battalion of black and red eyes in the distance and froze.

No one had witnessed anything like this before. Not only did they stare in shock at the beasts but also at the sheer number of bloody bodies in their way. The battalion trampled over the bodies and charged with rage.

'Steady, men!' Deshpande commanded. 'Positions!'

All the officers took an offensive stance, loaded their weapons, and pointed them towards the creatures. In terms of numbers, it was a complete imbalance. Roughly a hundred officers versus over 300 Asuras and Rakshasas. But this did not deter the protectors of the city.

The men in uniform held their ground as the beasts progressed towards them.

Some hands shivered; others were rock steady. But there was no turning back now. They waited for orders from their commanding officer as the beasts inched closer and were now nearly fifty feet away.

'FIRE!' Deshpande boomed.

A round of shots was unleashed on the Underworld Clan with nearly a hundred per cent accuracy. Many beasts fell as a result of the force of the impact. A cloud of dust covered the area, and with the added intensity of the monsoons, it was nearly impossible to discern the outcome of the firing.

As the dust cleared, the creatures that were not shot just stood there, presumably waiting for their comrades to rise again.

Rightly so, the few who had fallen stood up and stared. Unscathed.

One of them growled, 'IAJ RAAKN HO!'

'IAJ RAAKN HO!' they all screamed and attacked yet again.

This time, hope began to fade away from the squadron of police officers. Their bullets were futile, and they had no other weapons to fight with.

'LOAD!' Deshpande commanded. 'FIRE!!'

Another round of shots was unleashed, but the enemy was too close for the bullets to have any impact.

The beasts jumped over the vehicles, pounced on the police officers, and began to tear them to pieces, some even ripping the heads of officers with their mouths. A few officers put up a fight, but it seemed pointless. Shots were fired up close, but it only gave the men in uniform a couple of minutes to retreat.

It was a blood bath.

Deshpande watched with moistened eyes as his men were being torn apart like soft toys. Some fled, but as they did, many of them began turning into beasts themselves. The black and red liquid spread rampantly and latched onto the nearest available hosts.

Either people were dying or being converted.

A Rakshasa came and landed a blow on Deshpande's face, injuring him severely. He began to bleed but did not lose hope. He removed his stick and gun, one in each hand, and began taking on the beast. After a few whacks with his stick, the creature stumbled a little, and Deshpande fired multiple shots at his face, hoping to aim for his brain.

But in vain.

The beast took a couple of seconds to recover as Deshpande fired on. Finally, the gun clicked—his bullets were over. He reached for his pocket to load his weapon, but the beast landed another blow on him, launching the gun in one direction while Deshpande flew in the other, falling close to the foot of a police van. He used the tyre to pull himself up, but it was too late. The beast was towering over him, ready to deliver the fatal blow. Deshpande held his hands in front of his face, shut his eyes, and began to pray as the beast growled and raised its hand to execute its opponent.

Slash!!!

Liquid spurted all over Deshpande's face. He opened his eyes in shock to see the beast frozen for a second, followed by its head slowly sliding off and falling to the floor. The body collapsed and vibrated—almost like it still had some life left. Deshpande stared at the ghastly, severed head, wondering what had happened.

'You need to chop their heads off,' a voice came from the side.

Deshpande turned his head to see a man with wavy hair that dropped to his chin in black robes with black marks on his face and hands. He held a long silver sword with a mildly curved tip and a thick black and golden brass hilt. His sword was smothered with gooey black liquid from the beast, and the man wiped the blade on his trousers. Deshpande recognised the man from the videos Pawar had shown him.

'Asuras and Rakshasas cannot be shot. Their heads have to be sliced off,' the man yelled amidst the chaos and extended his hand. Deshpande held onto it and stood up, unsure what to make of "Asuras" and "Rakshasas".

'Thank you,' Deshpande said with a soft smile.

'Don't thank me yet. Inspector Deshpande, right?'

'Yes...' Deshpande said in a confused tone. Clearly, this man had been tracking his whereabouts.

'I'm Jaffer,' the man introduced himself while taking out another sword from his back, similar to the one he held, flipped it, and offered the hilt to Deshpande, 'Here...

you'll also need to inform your reinforcements to bring in swords.'

'Thank you,' Deshpande said as he grabbed the hilt, 'I'll do that. But I don't think this will be enough. We're terribly outmatched,' he said despondently as he observed the massacre unfolding around them.

'I've got some help as well,' Jaffer said with a smirk.

'What?'

Jaffer gestured towards a by lane connected to the Western Express highway.

As Deshpande looked over, he saw a massive battalion of nearly 300 men dressed like his black-robed saviour running towards the battlefield. All were armed, charging with their swords held high.

The Musafir clan had arrived.

Forty

The door banged open, and Yuva entered carrying a bruised and bloodied Jaffer.

'Guruji! I have him!' Yuva yelled, 'Ash…can you come here? Quickly!'

Yuva entered the living room and placed Jaffer on the sofa. Ash, Nivi, Maya, and Guruji walked in briskly. Govi, too flew in and perched himself on Yuva's shoulder.

'Hey Bhagwaan!' Guruji gasped as he saw his blood-soaked friend.

Jaffer, the leader of the Musafir clan, had been a dear companion to Guruji and the Manwaans. He, along with the members of his tribe, had been Guruji's eyes and ears. This arrangement had worked out exceedingly well as the Manwaans had to keep their identity a secret, and any crime-fighting escapades that they would partake in had to be done discreetly.

Jaffer, once a police constable himself, had accidentally witnessed the Manwaans in action many moons ago. When he brought this up with his seniors, they thought him to be mad and dismissed him on the grounds of being mentally challenged and incapable of handling the responsibilities that were expected of a man in uniform. While his immediate response was to silently berate the system for not having faith in him and his word, he was eventually approached by an aged man dressed in a yellow robe. Guruji, a saintly figure who walked into Jaffer's life, picked him up from the abyss he was lost in and began guiding him.

Of course, Guruji made the terms of the arrangement clear from the start.

He knew that Jaffer had seen what he had seen, but at the same time, he realised that it would be many more years before the world would be ready to candidly witness the proceedings of a celestial revolution. Since he and the Manwaans would keep a distance from the public eye, he knew that he would need help when it came to staying in touch with what went on around Earth and staying away from the eyes of the angels, both Fagir and Arinch. He and the Manwaans would, in many ways, report to Milaayak and the other Arinch, and manoeuvring without them noticing, would become nearly impossible. He needed informants who could remain deeply connected with the human proceedings but, simultaneously, not be detected by the celestial beings.

And so began the formation of the Musafir clan—highly skilled warriors who were allies to the Manwaans. Guruji put Jaffer onto one of his trusted associates, who trained him and the newly appointed Musafirs religiously and became the teacher that they needed. From there on, every newly inducted

Musafir was first and foremost made aware of the celestial revolution and all the primary characters of this universal plot. The Musafirs were picked carefully, screened meticulously, and tested rigorously before they could be let in on the bigger picture.

Additionally, Guruji's associate was the one who devised the technique of permanently marking the Musafirs all over their bodies—almost as a protective shield. The markings, which were the equivalent of symbols of several cosmic formulae, would make it extremely difficult for angels to locate them as they acted as a form of shield around the Musafirs. Of course, this played as a mild disadvantage when it came to blending in with regular humans. Mild being the operative word, as most people would assume that these full-body-tattooed-beings were simply huge body art fans and would not spare them with more than a three-second glance.

From then on, a very fruitful collaboration began between the Manwaans and the Musafirs.

'Sorry, Guruji…' Jaffer panted, 'I tried to save him, but was no match for the Asuras.'

Ash sat beside him and placed his palms on all of Jaffer's wounds one by one. Jaffer moaned as the yellow-green light emitted from Ash's palms began to heal the wounds.

'Thank you,' he said as Ash finished.

'No worries. Did you manage to see him? Was he fine?'

'I don't know. I couldn't see inside the vehicle. All I know is that it's a white van,' Jaffer said as he tried to sit up.

'You need to rest,' Guruji said in his calming tone.

'Did you see the number plate?' Yuva asked.

'No…sorry. But there were three of them, and they were heading towards the Sassoon Docks.' Jaffer grew pensive. 'I lost two of my trusted men…'

'I'm sorry to hear that, Jaffer,' Guruji consoled him. 'Please stay for a while. Recover properly before you leave.'

'I can't, Guruji. I need to alert my fellow Musafirs.'

'I understand. At least have some food?'

Jaffer remained quiet and thought for a few seconds. Eventually, he realised that he would need the energy to carry on. 'Sure…' he said as he shut his eyes while trying to catch his breath.

'Good. Maya, Yuva…you need to rescue him. We cannot afford to lose him. And bring him here…he needs to start his training. I fear he will not have enough time to attain any level of realisation.'

'Yes, Guruji,' Maya said firmly.

'Try and slice their heads off. Nothing else seemed to work,' Jaffer suggested.

Guruji darted a speculative glance towards Jaffer.

'I'm sorry, Guruji. We have no other choice,' Jaffer continued unapologetically.

Guruji sighed, shook his head, and forced the words out of his mouth, 'If that be the case, do what needs to be done.'

Maya nodded. She and Yuva proceeded to suit up and went on their way to rescue the prophesied Manwaan leader.

'How many men and women do you have, Jaffer?' Guruji continued.

'Around 300.'

'Hmm…'

'And each one is at your service, Guruji. We will not rest till the battle is won. Either we die, or they do,' Jaffer said with newfound energy.

'I admire your passion and bravery, Jaffer. You have been a true ally. Make sure you are ready. The outburst may begin anytime.'

'We've stood by you all these years, Guruji. Waiting. Training. This is what we were made for. Asura or Rakshasa…nothing can get in our way. We will be ready.'

Guruji smiled.

'I believe you, my friend. I always have.'

Forty-one

'*BHAGWAAN KE NAAM PE*!' Jaffer shouted as he raised his sword.

'*BHAGWAAN KE NAAM PE*!!!' the Musafirs yelled in unison as they charged towards the Asuras and the Rakshasas.

The sudden attack took aback the Underworld Clan. The arrival of the Musafirs instilled a great sense of confidence in the remaining police officers, who also began to fight back.

The Musafirs knew their way around a war. While they had learnt how to operate guns, swords acted as extensions to their bodies, and they wielded them with great proficiency. Heads were being sliced all over, and pools of black liquid began to cover the roads.

Deshpande and Pawar fought side by side. Pawar, too had been handed a sword by one of the Musafirs. Even though he had not trained with one extensively, he rose to the occasion and fought valiantly. Their bodies were wounded, but their spirits had been lifted with the arrival of their newfound allies.

It finally seemed like a fair fight.

Just then, the sound of helicopters was heard from a distance, mixed in with the buzzing noise of truck engines. Deshpande recognised the sound—the armed forces had arrived.

Five helicopters covered a large section of Bandra and began to fire away. Even though the bullets would not kill the Asuras or the Rakshasas, they would slow them down and give the police officers and the Musafirs an opportunity to slice their heads off.

Meanwhile, twenty green army trucks pulled up along the highway, from which nearly a hundred and fifty army men stormed out. All holding swords. The wave of soldiers overpowered the Underworld Clan with ease.

Deshpande smiled with a mild sense of relief.

Besides the Musafirs, no one knew what these creatures were. All they knew was that they were wreaking havoc and tearing the city apart. And that was enough. The remaining police officers, the Musafirs, and a section of the Indian Army fought side by side against the black and red-eyed beasts. There were heavy losses, but victory was inevitable.

The creatures began to realise that they were being overpowered. The nature of their attack had transitioned from an offensive one to more of a defensive one. On seeing that the humans outnumbered them, they had no choice but to retreat towards the alleys of Bandra. All the

Asuras and Rakshasas stopped midway through the battle and fled in the opposite direction.

A sigh of relief and cries of victory were let out by everyone present on the battlefield. Everyone raised their swords and danced in joy. Army men hugged the Musafirs without even knowing who they were. Deshpande placed his arm around Pawar.

'I can't believe it, Pawar. We did it! We actually did it!' he said with glee.

'It had to happen, sir! Good will always triumph over evil!' Pawar responded. Deshpande stared at him in awe. These were possibly the wisest words his subordinate had uttered.

Triumph was in the air as the winners celebrated their victory.

Deshpande looked over Pawar's shoulder and noticed a poker-faced Jaffer standing and staring in the direction the beasts had retreated in. He tried to follow Jaffer's vision and noticed that the Asuras and the Rakshasas had only fled to a certain extent and had stopped after that. They were not out of sight.

And then, something eerie happened.

The Rakshasas lifted their heads and began to howl. A raspy, guttural howl. Each Rakshasa took the cue from the other and joined in, and within seconds, the howls echoed through the streets.

The celebrations ended abruptly, and everyone looked around, wondering what these sounds were.

Jaffer knitted his brows and clenched his jaw. Deshpande realised that something was off, and Jaffer was possibly the only one who had an answer.

'Hey...Jaffer!' Deshpande yelled as he ran over. 'What's going on? What are they doing?'

'Calling for backup,' he said without batting an eyelid.

Deshpande froze.

The howling carried on for a few more minutes and finally stopped. The echoes on the streets faded away as a deathly silence took over, barring the sound of heavy rain in the background. Everyone looked around, and no one moved a muscle.

The sun had descended and plunged the city into darkness, and everyone waited silently, looking at the mayhem around them.

Suddenly, the Earth began to rumble. It felt nothing short of an earthquake. Everyone looked over to the creatures who had retreated towards Bandra, but they all stood still.

Grinning.

Jaffer ran over to get a view of the Western Express highway. So far, the battle had been contained in the Bandra cross-section of the highway, as that was where all the Asuras and Rakshasas were.

Or so they thought.

From the distance and the darkness, hundreds of red eyes began to emerge. The rumbling grew louder, and the number of eyes began to steadily increase as the cloud of dust surrounding them got thicker.

Eventually, hundreds of red eyes were joined by hundreds of black eyes.

Jaffer gasped at what he saw.

A wild stampede of Rakshasas carrying Asuras on their backs was charging towards them, the total number of which seemed twice as many as the police officers, army men, and Musafirs combined.

Leading the army, atop a Rakshasa and with a cocky smirk, was Usur, king of the Underworld.

Usur had opened up portals across several locations on the western belt, with a larger focus on Bandra. He planned to draw most of the attention there, urging all his opponents to rush to its defence. The battle would ensue, many would die, several would be injured, and they would be completely underprepared and overwhelmed when the entire force from across Mumbai attacked together.

His plan worked to the T and elicited the exact response he hoped for.

When the army grew closer, the creatures who had retreated towards the roads of the hyper-locality of Bandra started charging once again.

Nearly a thousand from the main highway and around a hundred from the perpendicular road joined the cross-section. The humans were surrounded. This was a meticulously well-planned attack with no room to escape.

'May the Gods be with us,' Jaffer shut his eyes and whispered to himself. He then raised his sword and addressed all those present there with ferocity in his voice, 'IF WE DIE...WE DIE WITH HONOUR! WE DIE FIGHTING THE ENEMY!! WE DIE PROTECTING OUR MOTHERLAND!!!'

All the officers, army men and Musafirs yelled in agreement.

'*BHAGWAAN KE NAAM PE*!' Jaffer boomed.

'*BHAGWAAN KE NAAM PE!!!*' A resounding response from everyone present there.

The Underworld Clan charged with full force, and the humans took a defensive stance. As they inched closer, dust filled the air, and the two armies collided.

The bloody battle of the great revolution had begun.

Forty-two

'Okay...hold on tight. Whatever happens, don't let go!' Yuva said as he flapped his wings slightly and maintained his horizontal position six feet off the ground.

'I hate this!' Ash groaned as he latched on tightly to Yuva's left foot. Rinad held onto the right foot, Maya to the left shoulder, and Nivi to the right. The boys were dangling from Yuva's feet while the girls had his broad back to rest on.

'Alright...now, going up...' Yuva announced, flapping his wings harder. Guruji watched his students working together as a team for the first time as the wind from Yuva's wings brushed against his face and disrupted his neatly combed facial hair.

'Are you sure we're not too heavy?' asked a concerned Rinad, who was doing this for the first time.

'Na...this is a piece of cake,' Yuva ground his teeth arrogantly and flapped his wings even harder. The team of five were over ten feet above the ground.

'Okay...we're going to try moving now,' Yuva said, slowly progressing in one direction. Once the other four seemed comfortable, he increased his pace and flew around in circles. Guruji watched and smiled from one corner of the room as the five of them smoothly glided through the training arena.

'Can we not do circles, please?' Rinad yelled.

'Don't tell me you're going to throw up,' Maya smirked and yelled back.

'Kaww…Kaww…' Govi said as he followed his master around the room.

'He's asking why the boys are on the legs and the girls on my back.'

'Good question,' Rinad frowned.

'Courtesy…apparently!' said Ash.

'And Ash lost a bet to me. He will be dangling on the leg forever,' Maya said gleefully.

Just then, a loud sound of wings flapping was heard. The sound overpowered the flapping from Yuva's wings, and the room lit up with a bright golden-white light.

'What the…' Yuva lost focus and nearly crashed into a wall. Others lost balance and fell from a height of almost ten feet. Maya, Ash, and Nivi landed smoothly on their feet, owing to their training, while Rinad, who tried to manoeuvre himself mid-air, failed nevertheless and landed on his rear.

'Ouch!' he moaned as he rubbed the area of impact.

The light faded away, and the five of them looked towards Guruji, only to notice Milaayak standing next to him with concern in his eyes.

'I'm sorry to barge in like this, brother,' he said in a gentle but serious tone.

'You're always welcome, Milaayak. Tell me…what brings you here?' Guruji responded.

'I'm afraid we're out of time. It has begun.'

Guruji fell silent.

No one flinched.

Everyone knew what that meant.

Guruji took a deep breath in and let it out to calm down. This was one of the few times Rinad had seen him slightly tensed. 'Well…I guess it's time then,' he replied, looking at Rinad worriedly.

Rinad had been training his level best, and while his meditation and general combat had improved, he was still far from having his realisation or being battle-ready, for that matter. Guruji had given his complete, undivided attention, and even the other four Manwaans trained regularly with him, but it was not enough. He did not know his capabilities and would be chewed up in a battle against the Asuras and Rakshasas.

'Get ready,' Guruji told everyone sternly.

Without a word being said, everyone began to walk towards the room which had their attires.

'Not you, Rinad,' Guruji continued. 'You will need to stay back.'

'But Guruji…how can I not go and fight?'

'You are not ready.'

'So do I just sit around and do nothing?'

'Unfortunately, yes,' Guruji responded and turned away towards Milaayak.

'Milaayak…I hope you will fight with us?'

'Of course. I will have to.'

Guruji lowered his head despondently. Milaayak's comment had given him a sense that he had failed to live up to his responsibility as a Manwaan teacher—finding all the Manwaans, training them to attain their realisations and being prepared for war. He knew what was coming. He knew the prophecy. And yet, he felt like he had not done his bit. Now, humanity would suffer, and Guruji could not help but bear all the guilt.

Milaayak sensed this.

'I did not mean it that way, brother. Forgive me,' he tried consoling Guruji.

'No, Milaayak. I have failed. I had one responsibility, and I could not fulfil it successfully…'

'That is what you think,' the Arinch replied. 'For all you know, this was how it was meant to unfold. My friend, I need you to believe that this was all meant to be. Even if you tried, you could not have done it differently.'

Guruji nodded. 'Thank you, old friend. I would have been lost without you.'

'I'm going nowhere,' Milayaak responded, exchanging a soft smile.

'Are you ready?' Yuva boomed as the four of them gathered in front of Milaayak.

'My boy…I've been ready for two millennia,' Milaayak said with a strange seriousness. Under different circumstances, one would have misconstrued this as a joke, but this was far from one.

'Right…of course,' Yuva smiled respectfully.

The four of them had their attires on, costumes with colours of their choice; black and purple for Maya, orange and white for Yuva, and a black and white combination for both Ash and Nivi—along with simple masks to cover their faces and protect their identity.

Each even had their weapons on them. Maya had her double-bladed spear, and Ash and Nivi had a boomerang blade and a nun chuck each, along with their newly invented Audicapitator. Yuva never used a weapon. He felt it only slowed him down.

'Alright…hop on,' Yuva continued.

'Oh! Hold on!' Ash interrupted and ran into the lab. Everyone watched him go curiously.

'What's that?' Maya asked, pointing to the new device in Nivi's hand.

'We call it the Audicapitator. It will basically generate an ultrasound frequency capable enough to temporarily handicap whoever it's pointed towards,' Nivi replied.

Maya nodded, approving the value add that such a device would have during battle.

'Here guys…take this,' Ash panted as he handed out tiny earbuds with small grey metal bodies attached.

'What's this?' Yuva looked at the tiny piece, careful not to crush it between his giant fingers.

'It's a micro transistor walkie-talkie for us to communicate,' Ash said. 'You need to just touch the surface to speak into it.'

Rinad stood outside, rubbed the mole on his jawline and observed the entire conversation as everyone pushed the device into their ears.

'We made six of them. Two are kept on top of the table as soon as you enter the lab,' Ash told Rinad softly. Of course, Rinad just dropped his head. He wasn't going into battle, so the earpiece would be useless to him.

'Are you all ready?' Guruji croaked.

'Seems like it, Guruji,' Maya replied.

They had all gathered around in a circle. Maya, Yuva, Ash, Nivi, Rinad, Milaayak, and Guruji. As always, Govi flew in and perched himself on Yuva's shoulder.

'You need to stay here, buddy…' Yuva said as he stroked his sidekick. 'It could get too dangerous out there.'

'Kaww…Kaww…'

'I'll be fine. You need to take care of Guruji and Rinad. Will you do that for me?'

'Kaww…Kaww…'

'Shabaash!'

Everyone focused on Guruji, who just stood there looking each one straight in the eyes.

'Before you go, I just want to say…' Guruji stopped midway and choked as his eyes welled up.

'We know, Guruji…' Maya said with a soft smile.

Guruji took in a deep breath and composed himself. 'Keep each other safe. And remember, underneath the demonic energy, they are still innocent human beings. You must consciously try to save as many of them as possible.'

Yuva opened his mouth to protest.

'I know they all cannot be saved…' Guruji calmly silenced him, 'but there is hope,' Guruji looked towards Milaayak, cueing him to speak.

'I will be able to relieve them of their demonic energy. I will try and save as many as possible. But some will have to die,' Milaayak said pragmatically.

Guruji nodded and smiled in agreement. 'Even if we can save one soul, it would be a victory. And remember… you are neither God nor human. You are the best of both. You are Manwaans!'

A silence swept into the room as everyone stared at each other. Absorbing in the calm before the chaos.

'Good luck out there,' Guruji added.

'I'll see you on the field,' Milaayak informed the Manwaans and tilted his head. His magnificent wings spread out, and he started levitating. There was a burst of golden-white light, and in a flash, he was gone.

The four Manwaans walked up to Guruji, took his blessings one by one by touching his feet, and ran upstairs.

Govi perched himself onto Guruji's shoulder and, along with Rinad, watched as the four realised Manwaans left to partake in the battle they had long prepared for..

Forty-three

On the battlefield, casualties had drastically increased on both sides, but the Underworld Clan had more than enough beings to spare. Rivers of blood flowed, bodies of humans lay dead and severed heads of the creatures, along with their bodies, were all over the Western Express highway. The Asuras and Rakshasas left no stone unturned and killed every human in sight. Police officers, army men, and Musafirs had suffered far greater losses than their opponents, but no one retreated. Everyone stood their ground and fought till their last breath.

Jaffer, Deshpande, and Pawar fought side by side under the main bridge. They had positioned themselves against a wall so as to keep the fight in front of them. A smart move, considering the sheer number of beasts and the fact that they could attack from anywhere. This way, at least one side was blocked off.

The only saving grace in this entire situation was the helicopters. They held their positions and fired away, slowing down the Underworld Clan to a great extent and giving the humans a chance to fight back.

However this, too, was short-lived.

The battle had spread out and began to consume the adjoining hyper-localities that were primarily residential areas and housed several short, dilapidated buildings, with the helicopters hovering around and firing at their targets from a distance. On noticing that they were being a hindrance, a few Rakshasas stealthily began to make their way up the buildings to take their opponents down.

They ran all the way up to the roof and broke the doors open, and in just a few minutes, the terraces of two of the buildings that were closest to the helicopters were swarming with Rakshasas.

Towards one side, an occupant of one helicopter noticed the roof being flooded by the beasts and realised what their next move would be. They roared and charged, ready to jump across into the flying vehicle and destroy it.

'Pull away!! They're going to take us down,' yelled one of the officers to the pilot.

But it was too late.

By the time the pilot steered, attempting to fly the helicopter away, several Rakshasas had leapt onto it. Some slipped and fell while others dangled for a couple of seconds before climbing in and ripping the heads of the occupants of the helicopter.

All were killed.

The helicopter, now without a pilot, began to descend directionless. The force increased as it inched its way towards the ground and finally crashed into the highway, breaking the road to bits and crushing many defending humans beneath it.

All of this happened within minutes. Too quick for anyone to process.

Another helicopter witnessed this and saw the Rakshasas charging towards them from the roof of the building close to them. Once again, they tried to pull back, but it seemed too late, yet again.

The helicopter began to move away, and two Rakshasas leapt from the terrace. Their aim was spot on, and their jump was about to conclude right into the helicopter. Just as they were about to enter and take down the helicopter, a huge, winged creature swept them away.

Yuva had made it just in time.

'Rakshasas…fantastic,' he commented with sarcasm.

He caught both the Rakshasas with claws on their feet and flew high up. One of them bit him, but it didn't affect him much. He grabbed it by his hand claws and lifted it in front of his face.

Slash!!!

He severed its head and threw it away, along with the headless body. The other Rakshasa witnessed this and began to whimper.

'Now your turn, buddy…' Yuva snarled, and this time, using just his feet's claws ripped the Rakshasa's head off.

The occupants of the helicopter that he had just saved saw all of this with their jaws dropped. Never before had they witnessed such a marvellous being—eight feet tall with claws and wings.

Of course, they were glad that he was on their side.

Yuva then flew onto the terrace and began working his magic there.

Meanwhile, Maya, Ash, and Nivi arrived at the scene on the ground and began fighting side by side with the Musafirs, officers, and army men.

'It's about time!' Jaffer yelled as he pierced an Asura.

'We got here as soon as we could!' Maya shouted back. She whipped out the spear from her back and pressed the black buttons on either end of the hilt, and a long silver blade emerged from each end. As she turned, she noticed a group of roughly fifteen Asuras and Rakshasas running towards her and Jaffer, who were almost back-to-back.

'Run!' Jaffer yelled.

'No!! Wait for my signal!'

'What signal?'

'Just wait!'

As the mini battalion inched closer, Maya pointed her left arm at them, and all fifteen froze and held onto their stomachs. Black liquid came from their mouths, and most of them dropped to their knees and began to throw up.

'Now!' yelled Maya.

Jaffer and Maya lunged towards the handicapped crowd and sliced away. In a couple of seconds, all the heads were severed.

'Finally, I get to see you in action!' jested Jaffer.

'I know, right?' Maya chuckled. 'Watch out behind you!'

A Rakshasa was about to land a blow on Jaffer when it was intercepted by a muscular arm. Milaayak held the beast tightly, twisted its arm, and placed his angelic palm on its head. A golden-white radiation emerged from his palm and was shot through the Rakshasa. As it passed through its body, it began to vibrate. The skin turned brown, and the fur on the body began to recede as the wolfish face morphed back into its original form. Finally, the black and red liquid spurted out of the body, and a young girl in her late teens stood in place of the Rakshasa.

'What's going on?' the girl yelled frantically as she looked around and witnessed the battle around her. 'Oh my god! What's that?' She pointed behind Milaayak. Another Rakshasa came and landed a blow on Milayaak. The Arinch did not flinch but calmly turned around. The beast whined and was about to retreat when Milaayak grabbed hold of its neck with one hand and relieved it of the demonic energy with the other. Once again, black and red liquid spurted to reveal a man in his late forties.

'Who are you? What am I doing here?' he panicked.

'I'll explain later,' Milaayak responded, lifting the young girl and the man off the floor, extending his wings, and flying them safely.

'That must be Milaayak?' Jaffer asked, intrigued.

'How did you guess?' Maya grinned sarcastically and ran off to fight her next target.

Jaffer turned around and noticed a shell-shocked Deshpande and Pawar covered in the black and red liquid. From their expressions, it was clear they had witnessed the unbelievable act of the demonic energy being relieved.

'It's a long story…I'll tell you later,' Jaffer said and ran off.

Pawar spat out the liquid from his mouth, shivered with disgust, and turned to his commanding officer, 'Sir…what in god's name is going on?'

'I have no idea, Pawar. Just be thankful that they are on our side. *Chala*!' Deshpande commanded, and the two stood up, ran back in, and continued slicing heads.

* * *

While Jaffer and Maya handled the east side of the highway, Ash and Nivi fought on the west side. The twins operated with a bladed nun chuck and a boomerang blade each, and it was time to put their newly invented Audicapitator to use.

At first, the Rakshasas and Asuras were all over them. Ash kicked the stomach of an Asura and then used the blade of the nun chuck to slice its head off. Another Rakshasa came snarling at Nivi. She dodged a bite from it and hopped onto its back. It shook its head vigorously, making Nivi lose her grip. Before she landed on the ground, it kicked her, throwing her away.

'Nivi!!' Ash yelled, defending himself from another Asura.

'I'm fine...' Nivi moaned and got back up on her feet. Only to find the Rakshasa coming towards her. She immediately pointed the triangular body of the Audicapitator at it, locked her target using the yellow monocle, and pressed the button on the handle. The raging beast stopped midway and held its ears with its hands, disturbed by the ultrasound waves being released towards it. It momentarily lowered its head as a reaction to the pain. Taking this opportunity, Nivi launched the boomerang blade at it. The blade cut through the air as it travelled in a circular motion, sliced the beast's head off, and returned to Nivi, covered in black liquid.

She then looked over to Ash, who was struggling with two Asuras and one Rakshasa. She toggled the settings on the device that was attached to the yellow monocle and targeted the three creatures. Once they were locked in, she raised her hand and pushed the button on the handle again. The three creatures were immediately handicapped and began stepping away from Ash, owing to the unbearable pain in their ears. She hurled her boomerang blade again, slicing the three heads off. As the three headless bodies fell, Nivi ran over to Ash and helped him stand up.

'Dai...what's the point of all these fancy inventions if you cannot use them when required?' Nivi said with raised eyebrows.

'They were too close to me. And I was worried about you,' Ash replied and continued, 'I thought the Rakshasas had you.'

'Oh please…I can take care of myself!'

'But the devices are pretty neat, eh?'

Nivi nodded with a soft smile.

'I can't believe we're actually fighting Rakshasas, man!' Ash continued as he dusted himself off. 'We've only studied about them in theory.'

Nivi chuckled, 'That's true! Oh no…'

She turned around and noticed a group of twenty Asuras and Rakshasas in front of them.

Ash pressed into the earpiece and spoke, 'Guys…this is getting out of hand. There are way too many of them. Any ideas on mass eradication?'

Yuva, who was busy dodging and attacking Rakshasas on the roof, pressed into his earpiece, 'Nothing is working on these bloody creatures. Just keep slicing heads. I'm almost done up here. Who needs help?'

'Under the bridge!' Maya yelled while pressing onto her earpiece. 'There are a couple of police officers and army men who could use the help.'

'Alright! Be there in five!' Yuva responded and continued slicing.

* * *

'How many men did you come with?' Maya yelled as she sliced off a head and went to the next. She and Jaffer continued fighting off the beast on the east side of the highway.

'Men and women,' Jaffer yelled back as a Rakshasa came to bite his head off.

'What?'

'Men and women! We have men and women as part of the Musafir clan. Nearly 300,' he clenched his teeth, dodged the Rakshasa, and passed his sword through his mouth. When he removed it, the creature bled but continued to attack. Jaffer then dodged it again and sliced its head off.

'Well…I think we'll need more help,' Maya yelled. 'Who is commanding these creatures anyway? They seem to be doing their own thing.'

Jaffer froze for a second.

He sliced off one more head and looked in all directions. He then ran over to the west side and looked again in all directions.

Usur was nowhere to be found.

Even though Jaffer had never interacted with Usur, he had heard about him. And after he saw him leading the Underworld Clan, he put two and two together.

'What happened?' Maya yelled.

Jaffer ran back with fear in his eyes, 'This is just a distraction…'

Maya gasped, 'From what?'

Forty-four

'Guruji…what's the point of all this?'

Rinad broke the twenty-minute silence that had seeped into Manbhoomi since his four comrades had left for battle.

Guruji stood at the balcony threshold and stared into oblivion while Rinad sat on the sofa, and Govi, who didn't utter a sound, cosied himself next to him.

'The point of what?' Guruji responded without moving a muscle. Clearly, a lot was on his mind, and he did not want to clutter it further with trivial discussions.

'Even if we win the battle, we would have killed so many of our kind. Countless dead…countless families ruined… what's the point of fighting? And even if we do win, at what cost does it come?'

'It is your duty, Rinad. Our duty,' Guruji said sternly and turned around. 'Everyone has a responsibility to fulfil. You were bestowed with responsibility of being a Manwaan for a particular reason. Your job is to live up to that. Act on it. Do not question it. Questioning it would be questioning the Gods and the destiny that has been written out for you. That never leads to any answers. And do not worry about the outcome. Just keep doing what you were made to do, and you will see the light at the end of the darkest tunnels. However long it might take.'

'But how do you know you're destined to do this?'

'You would feel it. You would feel complete, and the sense of longing for identity would cease to exist,' Guruji said softly.

'Hmm…'

'Did you feel at ease with the life you were living before this?'

'Not really…'

'Precisely. And how do you feel now?'

'Much calmer.'

'And that is because you are fulfilling your destiny. Your life's purpose. You are living the life that you are meant to live.'

Rinad grew silent.

'You do not seem convinced. What is the matter, Rinad?'

'Something does not feel right, Guruji. While I agree that I feel like I've found my identity and can make the world a safer place by being a Manwaan, something about killing the Asuras and Rakshasas is not sitting well with me,' Rinad responded pensively.

Guruji smiled. 'Then search for the answers you seek, and you shall find them.'

As they looked at each other in silence, a sudden seriousness dawned upon Guruji's face.

'What is it, Guruji?' Rinad asked.

Guruji grabbed his walking stick resting against the sofa and paced towards the doorway leading to the living room. He looked towards the entrance of the house. Something did not feel right.

Bam!!!

The door blasted open, and a platoon of ten Asuras and Rakshasas stormed in.

'Run, Rinad!' Guruji yelled, flipped his stick, and held it like a sword.

Rinad stood up and darted towards the open balcony, only to be intercepted by a second platoon of ten. Govi flew off to one of the higher shelves and hid himself there.

They were surrounded.

A Rakshasa slapped Rinad, who went flying and landed on the couch. For a brief second, Rinad looked over to Guruji, who was wielding his walking stick like an expert swordsman. Nearly ten Asuras and Rakshasas tried getting to him, but the Manwaan teacher defended himself.

An Asura unleashed a punch, and Guruji ducked and responded with a low roundhouse kick while tackling two more. When three of them were on the floor, he dodged a kick from another Rakshasa and whacked the stick on his head, following it with a summersault in the air. The Rakshasa fell, and Guruji landed on him, pinning him down. He then jumped again and bounced off two more Rakshasas while kicking them to the floor.

Rinad watched his tiny, aged teacher beating the living daylights out of an entire platoon with awe. Meanwhile, another Asura landed a slice on his face, and Rinad started to bleed. He tried to fight back, but the Asura pinned him down.

'Hold him,' he growled, and two Rakshasas caught hold of his hands, and another caught his neck, choking him mildly.

'You move…you die!' the Rakshasa holding his neck snarled.

Guruji, who seemed to be faring well till now, finally got tired and took a hit from one of the Asuras. Five Asuras picked him up and pinned him against the wall. Both Guruji and Rinad were restrained and could not move a muscle.

From the open door, another group of four walked in, led by Usur.

He walked in, stood right in front of Guruji, and smirked.

'Guruji! *Pranaam*!' he jested and folded his hands to greet the Manwaan teacher with respect. Of course, it was all theatrics. 'I've heard so much about you!'

'I'm afraid I can't say the same,' Guruji replied while being choked.

'Of course, where are my manners? Let me introduce myself. My name is Usur.'

Guruji gasped.

'Ah! So, you have heard of me! I'm honoured! Maybe you didn't recognise me in this host I'm currently in. I had to make do with what I could find, unfortunately. After everything is over, I should find a new piece of meat to latch on to,' he chuckled, cueing his audience of subordinates to snigger along.

Guruji, who had a line of blood dripping from his mouth, didn't utter a word.

Usur turned towards Rinad. 'Oh, the great leader of the Manwaans,' he bowed his head mockingly. He excitedly bounced towards him and jumped onto the sofa, placing himself beside him.

'You have made my life hell, young man. And that's a big achievement, considering I am from Hell!' he chuckled. 'But not to worry, it'll all be over soon. If only you had given in right at the beginning, none of your beloved Manwaans or Guruji would be in danger.' Usur stood up with vigour and looked towards Guruji. 'But your city is ablaze. Your humans are now, well, ours, if not dead, and the Manwaans can do nothing about it. That sounds like a happy ending to me. What do you think, Guruji?'

'You will never win,' Guruji muttered under his breath.

'How strange! Because it looks like we've already won,' Usur inched towards Guruji with his hands behind his back.

'The Gods are with us. They will never let you win…' Guruji replied as he gasped for breath.

'The Gods are too busy for you, Guruji. They're too busy to fight their own battles. Why do you think they created Manwaans? So that they could have someone do the dirty work for them. I know...I know...they can't step on Earth like the angels...blah blah blah...but they could have figured out a way to do so by now, right? It's been over two millennia since the great celestial fallout. Are you telling me that the Gods are stupid enough not to figure out a way to come to humanity's rescue themselves? They're smarter than you think, Guruji. This is all just showbiz for them. Now they're going to watch the angels fight each other. Only the Fagir have the support of the entire Underworld Clan. And with barely any Manwaans remaining, who do the Arinch have?' Usur grinned. 'And besides, what you are witnessing today is merely just a glimpse of what the Underworld is capable of,' he continued, 'If I start talking about some of the other creatures we have down there, you will start shitting your pants,' he turned and told Rinad, who was drenched in sweat.

He turned back and stood a few inches away from Guruji. 'But I'm glad we won't have to go that far. Considering the job is nearly done.'

He paused and smirked. 'Time to put an end to this.'

Usur began to assume his complete demonic form as his eyes, nails, and veins turned black. He raised his hand and, using his extended claws, landed a fatal blow across Guruji's neck.

Guruji's severed head slid off, rolled onto the floor, and the lifeless body collapsed.

The great Manwaan teacher was no more.

Forty-five

'No!!!' Rinad screamed. 'I'm going to kill you for that!!!'

'Tch tch…so much rage! It's cute, actually,' Usur responded arrogantly.

'What kind of an animal are you?' Rinad began to weep.

'I just returned the favour, boy. You Manwaans are the ones who started slicing heads off. I'm just doing my job,' Usur grunted and walked up to Rinad. He bent down and got close enough to feel Rinad's warm, palpitating breath on him, 'And let it be clear that if you get in my way, this will be the result,' he concluded, turned around, and began to walk away. 'Finish him. Properly, this time,' he boomed and walked out, followed by the mini platoon of four that came with him, leaving Rinad alone with nearly twenty Asuras and Rakshasas.

The Rakshasa holding his neck released him, and Rinad immediately went in for a punch, but the creature dodged it with ease and slashed him with the back of his hand.

'Kaww…Kaww…' Govi flew in to do his bit in helping

out the prophesied Manwaan leader. He pecked the eye of one of the Asuras.

'Ouch!!' the Asura yelled. 'You stupid bird!'

'Kaww…Kaww…' Govi returned for a second peck aimed at another Rakshasa but failed to notice another Asura hand that came his way and whacked him to the corner of the room, slamming him against the wall.

'Kaww…' his voice grew feeble as he fell to the floor. A pool of blood began to form around him.

'That should take care of it,' the Asura growled.

Another Asura boxed Rinad, and he fell to the floor.

'Let's have some fun, shall we?' she smirked.

All twenty Asuras and Rakshasas started taking turns kicking Rinad, who lay on the floor. His face was scratched up, and he moaned and cried harder with each kick that landed on him.

A Rakshasa then lifted him and pinned him against the wall.

One by one, they took turns and laid punches on him all over. Rinad started coughing blood, and the world started fading around him. Finally, to finish him off, an Asura lifted him all the way up and slammed him to the ground.

The Underworld warriors laughed, leaned in, and looked over Rinad as he lay on his back with his eyes shut, drenched in blood and sweat.

'It's almost done,' an Asura snarled.

'Who'd like to do the honours?'

Forty-six

'This is just a waste of time, Guruji. I'm not getting anywhere. Let me just train in combat with Yuva. At least I'll get better at fighting. This meditation business is not meant for me. I'm not the Manwaan leader…perhaps I'm no Manwaan at all,' Rinad complained as he paced back and forth under the tree in Manbhoomi garden.

Guruji sat in stillness in a cross-legged position on the circular stone ledge around the tree, with one palm resting on the other between his legs. He didn't flinch and simply watched his student complain.

'It is stated in the prophecy,' Guruji replied calmly.

'Oh god! Stop it with the prophecy! You know what…I'd like some proof of this so-called prophecy. Where is it written? Who has written it? Show me the book, or scroll or leaf that it's been written in…'

'Only the angels will have the answer to that.'

'That's very convenient, Guruji.'

'It's true. They give us the information. We simply pass it on.'

'So, some angel said I'm supposed to be the Manwaan leader?'

Guruji nodded.

'How can that be expected of me? I can't fight for nuts. How am I supposed to be the strongest Manwaan?

'Correction…you are not meant to be the strongest. You are meant to lead them,' Guruji said with a smile.

Rinad grew pensive.

'Well, maybe I'm not meant to have any heightened capabilities. I mean, I'm pretty good at strategising and stuff. Maybe that's my capability,' Rinad said while doing the air quotes with his fingers.

Guruji simply shrugged his shoulders. 'Maybe!'

'What?! You mean I could work my ass off, attain my realisation and still not be able to do anything effective?!'

'I do not have those answers, Rinad. But I do know that you will have at least one heightened capability, if not more. The angels would not tell us about you if you were not a Manwaan. They do not have so much time to spare.'

'Then why didn't you start training me earlier?'

'It was not meant to be…'

Rinad frowned.

'What do you mean?' he whined.

'Had I done so, I would have intervened with destiny's plan, you see,' Guruji replied.

'Whatever…' Rinad dropped his shoulder and sat on the ledge next to his teacher.

Guruji placed his hand behind Rinad's back and smiled.

'You must not stop believing, Rinad,' he said.

'I believe it,' Rinad replied in a grumpy tone.

'No. You do not.'

'Well, I want to…'

'That is a good start, but you still do not believe your path has been chalked out for you. You refuse to believe in your destiny.'

'What do you want me to do, Guruji? I'm trying. I'm really trying to believe!'

'I do not need you to try. Do not try to believe. Just believe. Do not push towards it. Let the forces pull you instead.'

Rinad grew silent.

'Rinad, you may think you are believing, but if you do not believe it from the deepest chambers of your gut, it will not manifest itself. If you truly wish for it to manifest, you must believe it with every cell in your body. Not try. But do.'

'Believe that the universe has a plan…'

'Believe that you have a role to play in this life of yours…'

'Believe what destiny has in store for you…'

'Believe…'

'Believe…'

'Believe…'

Forty-seven

'I'll do it,' said a Rakshasa excitedly. 'I've been looking forward to it…'

All the Rakshasas were huddled in a circle as they leaned in and towered over Rinad's motionless body. The Rakshasa raised its hand to severe its target's head, and Rinad's eyes opened to reveal two fluorescent blue sockets.

Bright light radiated from his eyes.

'*Believe…*' Guruji's words echoed in his head.

'What the…' the Rakshasa lowered his hand.

'Kill him…fast!' another growled.

Three more from the surrounding platoon raised their hands for an attack.

'Aargh!!' Rinad began to scream, tears rolling down his cheeks. His back arched, his palms forcefully opened up while his body tightened.

As he continued to scream vehemently, his entire body began to glow from the blue radiation. The radiation got stronger by the second, and by the time the Rakshasas landed their hands on him, the radiation shot out in all directions from his entire body and flooded the room, decimating all the creatures in the vicinity into pieces.

The heat from the radiation had reduced the creatures to ashes and wrecked the house's structure. The walls and ceiling had cracked along with the furniture, with an impression on the ground where he lay, similar to a meteor strike.

At the centre of the impression—a glowing Rinad.

The radiation began to return and eventually got sucked back into Rinad. Just as the last bit subsided, he sat up with a start and heavy breathing while covered in sweat. As he panted, he lifted his palms and looked into them.

Nothing.

However, he could still feel the tingling warmth against the surface of his skin. The same feeling he would get every time he got a panic attack. The same feeling he got when he was floating in the darkness in his mind during one of his meditation sessions with his teacher, while being faced with a blue light.

Warmth from within him.

He sat there with his back hunched and no clothes on him. The radiation had shredded all that he was wearing to pieces.

Once he gathered himself, it struck him. *Guruji!*

Still weak from the pounding he had received, Rinad mustered up whatever energy he had left and crawled towards Guruji's lifeless body. As he inched towards it, he looked at the head that had rolled away from the body, drenched in a pool of blood that had oozed and formed around it.

Rinad pulled the head in and placed it next to the body. He stared at it and burst into tears, burying his head into his teacher's body and howling. Both rage and sadness had taken over, and Rinad lost himself.

As he wept incessantly, he once again felt the warmth against the inside of his skin. This time, he brought his attention to it. He lifted his head and noticed that the blue radiation had reappeared, and his body was glowing again. He shivered with rage, and the intensity of the radiation got stronger.

He could not get Guruji's voice out of his head.

His words.

His teachings.

'*Believe…*' kept ringing within him.

As the voice grew louder, sweat began to drip from his forehead, and his breathing escalated rapidly. Finally, he yelled out loud, filled with anger and pain, and almost as a reactionary measure, raised his hands.

A thick wave of the same blue radiation shot out from each palm, destroying the wall in front of him. The force of the beam caused a recoil, and Rinad got pushed back and fell to the ground, following which the radiation subsided.

He could still feel the warmth from Guruji's body. He placed his hand on top of the lifeless leg and wept silently.

From another corner of the living room, away from the area of impact, an injured Govi witnessed all the events that had unfolded.

Forty-eight

The four Manwaans from the battlefield flew back to Manbhoomi. Jaffer had figured out Usur's strategy and asked them to go and check on Guruji and Rinad while he, along with the Musafirs, Milaayak, officers, and the army men, fought the Underworld Clan.

The Manwaans and Milaayak had definitely strengthened the humans' position in battle, but they were still ill-matched in terms of numbers. Countless Asuras and Rakshasas were swarming all over, and now that the Manwaans had left, the situation began to worsen.

As the Manwaans approached Manbhoomi, they could all sense that something had gone horribly wrong. The front door was busted open, and the balcony window shattered. Of course, these seemed trivial when they noticed that one section of the house was almost burnt to a crisp. As Yuva landed and Maya, Ash, and Nivi jumped off him, they darted inside, only to find the entire house dilapidated. The Asuras and Rakshasas had torn the place down and wreaked havoc. The dining table had been shattered to pieces, the walls broken, and lights, fans, and air conditioners were pulled out from their places and dismantled. It felt like a hurricane had swept through the place.

They were horrified at what they saw as they ran into the living room. Guruji's head and body. As two separate pieces. With Rinad lying next to it. Without any clothes, weeping, and covered in Guruji's blood.

All four were speechless.

Maya and Ash collapsed to the floor, Nivi fell back and slid down against the wall behind her, and Yuva stood there motionless as his eyes flooded with tears.

All four wept for their teacher.

The only person in the world who had understood them.

Who fought against all odds, took them under his wing, and trained them to survive in a world that would not accept them.

Who loved them unconditionally and taught them how to love.

That person was no more.

And without him, once again, the world began to feel like a cold and unfamiliar place.

For several minutes, all of them just wept.

'Kaww…' a feeble sound came from the corner.

'Govi!' Yuva said in a choked voice and followed the sound. Against the wall, he found his beloved sidekick gravely injured and unable to move. He picked his little friend up and held him close to his chest.

'Don't worry, buddy. You'll be fine,' Yuva whispered as he stroked Govi.

'Kaww…Kaww…' Govi said in a feeble voice.

Yuva grew suspicious. 'You killed twenty Asuras and Rakshasas all by yourself?' he turned his head towards Rinad and asked in disbelief.

All heads turned towards Rinad.

Rinad, who was lying down the entire time, finally used his hands to sit himself up and nodded solemnly.

'How? What happened?' Maya continued.

'And where are your clothes?' Ash added.

Rinad did not reply.

'Kaww…Kaww…' Govi said.

A tear rolled down Yuva's cheek and met with a soft smile that his lips had assumed. He wiped the tears off and sniffed.

'He had his realisation…'

Maya, Ash, and Nivi looked towards Yuva and then at Rinad. A sudden wave of hope had taken over the room. In the silence, Ash ran into Rinad's room, brought back a fresh pair of clothes, and laid them next to Rinad on the floor. Rinad silently stood up and got into them.

Following his cue, the other four rose and stood in their tattered clothes and masks. Ash placed his palm on Rinad's injured areas while Nivi did the same for Govi. As soon as Govi was healed, he perched himself back on his usual spot—Yuva's shoulder.

Rinad too felt a new strength surging through his veins. But it wasn't because of being healed.

He had, indeed, attained a level of realisation.

All five gathered around Guruji's lifeless body and stood with their heads bowed.

'What now?' Nivi broke the silence.

'Now we fight,' replied Rinad after taking a breath to process his thoughts. 'They've crossed the line, and we won't let them get away with this. But we need to remember everything that Guruji told us. Even though these Asuras and Rakshasas have taken over our city, they still possess innocent humans. And we can't let them die. We have an Arinch fighting by our side, and we need to use his ability to relieve as many bodies of demonic energy as possible. It's what Guruji would have wanted.'

'But there are way too many of them,' Maya replied. 'We'll be forced to kill more than we can save, and we'll have to make peace with that. Unfortunately, there is nothing else that we can do about it.'

'We need to think harder. There must be a way. We need to believe there is a way, and I promise we will find one. But we need to keep each other safe. And if that means killing them, then so be it. But be on the lookout for ways to save them. Once Yuva flies us in, let's spread ourselves out. Our priority would be to rescue the people in danger. We'll then need to coordinate with Milaayak and figure out a strategy to speed up the relieving of the possessed bodies,' Rinad paused and took a deep breath in. 'This is our world. And no one's going to take it from us. Be it Asuras, Rakshasas, or Fagir. And if required, we'll die protecting it,' Rinad concluded with grit.

His four peers raised their heads and looked at him with strength and hope in their eyes. A smile grew on their faces. They were proud to see their comrade believing and fulfilling the destiny carved out for him.

'Ash…' Rinad continued, 'I'm going to need that earpiece.'

Ash smiled and nodded.

'But what's your capability?' Yuva asked.

'Kaww…Kaww…' Govi responded and gestured towards the burnt section of the house and the hole in the wall.

'No way!' Yuva gasped with a smirk.

Forty-nine

Back on the battlefield, the human death toll had increased swiftly since the Manwaans' departure. Lifeless bodies of police officers, army men, and Musafirs lay all over. No civilians were to be seen, as most had either been possessed by members of the Underworld Clan or managed to flee from the scene. Most buildings around the now-battlefield were also infested with Asuras and Rakshasas rather than their original occupants.

The helicopter crash had broken down the flyover, and the broken bits had fallen and crushed the abandoned vehicles under it. Bandra smelt like a concoction of a graveyard and Hell—blood infused with rot—and the roads had now assumed a black and red colour from the mixed blood of humans and beasts. Visibility had also greatly reduced owing to the thick overcast, and incessant rainfall accompanied by thunder and lightning, a normal occurrence during the peak of the monsoons.

Deshpande and Pawar led their remaining fifty-odd battalion of police officers and army men on the eastern side. At the same time, Milaayak fought side by side with Jaffer and the hundred-odd Musafirs on the western side of the highway.

By now, all the officers and army men had swords. Throughout the battle, they learned that the most effective way to operate was to hold a pistol in one hand and a sword in the other. The guns would slow down the creatures, and the sword would finish them. And this strategy proved to be relatively more effective than any other. The men teamed up and fought in pockets of four and five, making sure all sides around them were being manned.

'Aargh!!' Pawar yelled as one Rakshasa pinned him down. Deshpande and his other two small group members were busy tackling their beasts and Pawar continued to scream as the Rakshasa kept biting, hoping to get a go at its victim's head. Fortunately, Pawar had inserted the sword horizontally into its jaw, almost acting like a restraint. Nevertheless, the beast kept biting and inching closer, with its saliva drenching Pawar.

'You disgusting beast! Get off me! Your mouth smells!!' Pawar yelled with shivers of disgust. He then held the hilt of his sword with his right hand and used his left leg to push against the edge of the sword. Once it seemed like he had a somewhat locked position, he removed his pistol from the holster and pointed it right into the back of the creature's throat. The mouth opened and closed persistently. Pawar waited for the opportune moment.

When the creature decided to take a break from the biting and let out a wide-mouthed roar, Pawar fired his rounds deep into the Rakshasa's throat. With the multiple shots, the beast got pushed back by a couple of steps, and in the few seconds it took to recover. Pawar swung his sword and sliced its head off.

'You're getting good at that, Pawar!' Deshpande yelled as he stabbed an Asura.

'I'm enjoying it, sir. This is a good vent for my stress. I should do this whenever I fight with my wife,' Pawar jested.

Deshpande laughed and pulled the sword out of the Asura. The Asura looked at the wound the sword had engraved on its body and looked back up. Unaffected. It came at its target when it suddenly met with gunshots from the side, straight to the head. Its head was pushed to one side with the force of the bullets, and before it could recover, Deshpande severed it off. He looked over towards the direction of the bullets and saw Pawar standing there, holding up a gun with a grin on his face.

Deshpande grinned back. 'So, shall I go home? You seem to be in control of everything.'

'I'm just getting into the groove, sir!'

They both chuckled amidst the sounds of gunshots, clinks of swords, and heads and bodies being ripped apart.

'Look out! Behind you!' Deshpande yelled, instantly pulling out his pistol and shooting at an Asura running towards Pawar. Meanwhile, the latter removed his pistol and shot at another Rakshasa that was charging towards Deshpande.

'I think I spoke too soon, sir...' Pawar yelled as he suddenly found himself shooting three creatures, alternating between each one. Deshpande, too, was now confronting four creatures.

The two officers began stepping back towards each other until they were completely back-to-back, ambushed by a platoon of seven beasts, with more approaching. The beasts growled and snapped at Deshpande and Pawar, who were caught in the centre.

The officers were surrounded.

* * *

On the western side, Milaayak was handling the situation much better. An Asura or Rakshasa was no match for the celestial power that coursed through an Arinch's vein. Or whatever he was made of. The only problem was that he attracted more creatures, putting Jaffer and some of the Musafirs around him in imminent danger. The Musafirs, however, were extremely skilled swordsmen. They danced with their swords and were a fair match to the Underworld warriors.

Even though the Musafirs had guns and were trained to use them, they never really chose to do so. They could use the swords to defend themselves and even slow down the creatures before landing their fatal blows. Their swords clinked with the claws of the beasts rapidly, and the high-pitched sounds echoed through the streets leading in from the western side.

Milaayak would handle almost ten creatures at the same time with ease. At one point, when three of the creatures charged at him together, he kicked one in the gut, punched the other in the face, and pinned the third one down to the ground. By the time the other two recovered from his blows, Milaayak pinned each one on top of those already down. He held all three Rakshasas down with one hand as they roared and tried to break free. A mini platoon of four more came towards him, but with four easy punches with his free hand, he sent them flying too. He then placed his palm on each of the three Asuras he held down and passed the celestial radiation through them, relieving them of their demonic energy. Before the three now-humans could realise and react to the ridiculous journey that their bodies had been through, Milaayak flew them to safety and returned in seconds.

With all this, Milaayak attracted much attention on the battlefield, and news eventually reached the king of the Underworld.

Usur, now back on the battlefield, was partaking in the joy of plundering the city. When an Asura informed him about a so-called "invincible being", Usur suspected that it might be the Arinch that had gotten in their way earlier.

He walked onto the highway from one of the tiny lanes to get a closer look. He ensured he was not visible to the angel, as that would put his existence at risk. He hid behind an overturned truck and looked between the wheels. When he witnessed his comrades being relieved from their hosts, his suspicion was affirmed, and he immediately ducked down, shut his eyes, and called out to his ally Fagir.

'What is it, Usur?' Mihaara communicated from Hell. *'How is the revolution progressing?'*

'We're making good progress so far, Mihaaraji. I got in touch with you as I can see the Arinch fighting with the Manwaans,' Usur replied in his mind.

'Well done. Show him to me…'

Usur slowly stood up without opening his eyes. The radiation was enough for an angel to be identified by his or her siblings.

'Milaayak! That swine!!' Mihaara boomed.

Usur ducked back down and shut his eyes. *'I need to go back in, Mihaaraji. I hope you can take some action against this…'*

'Try and stay away from him, Usur. Let me see what can be done.'

Usur opened his eyes and went back into the lane, making sure he didn't get noticed by the Arinch.

* * *

Meanwhile, Milaayak continued overpowering several Asuras and Rakshasas when he suddenly heard a scream.

'Help!! Somebody!!'

A large platoon was ambushing Pawar and Deshpande from the eastern side, and the odds were looking slim for them, with no one near enough to come to their protection. The other officers fighting with them had been ripped apart, and they were now surrounded.

The Asuras and Rakshasas had pinned down Pawar and Deshpande and were gnawing ferociously at them, but before they could taste their blood, Milaayak flew in and cleared the zone.

Deshpande, Pawar, and Milaayak stood back-to-back with nearly fifty Underworld warriors charging at them from all directions. While this was a piece of cake for Milaayak, Pawar and Deshpande slowly struggled. The smart creatures realised that the two officers were the weaker links and began to focus on them, and eventually, Milaayak had the added responsibility of ensuring their safety.

When the beasts realised that this new plan was working, they called in for reinforcements, targeting the two officers. With the creatures completely onto them, Milaayak had no choice but to make the two officers curl up to the ground while he covered them with his body and used his expanded wings to surround them like a shield. With no way to attack, the creatures started jumping and piling over the angel.

'Aargh!!' Deshpande yelled as he was crushed under the heap of Asuras and Rakshasas piled on the Arinch's glorious wings. They kept biting Milaayak, and although it did not affect him, he could not retaliate with any form of offence. Nearly a hundred Underworld warriors were onto them, and more kept jumping in.

The three of them were trapped with no way to escape.

Fifty

As the battle ensued, hope seemed to fade away for the humans. With just a handful of officers, army men, and Musafirs remaining, the possibility of victory leaned largely towards the Underworld Clan.

Pawar, Deshpande, and Milaayak were trapped under a ginormous heap of Asuras and Rakshasas with no way to escape. The two officers squealed as they were being crushed by the building pressure.

Zap!!!

A strong beam hit the heap and cleared the pile like the first shot of a game of Carrom. Before the creatures could react, more beams came at them and kept knocking them out.

The Manwaans had finally returned.

This time, all five realised.

Yuva approached the heap and Rinad let go of his leg, landed down, and started beaming the creatures one by one, slicing their heads off.

Yuva came closer to the heap, and Rinad released his grip on his leg. After a mild stumble on landing, he quickly gathered himself and proceeded to beam down the creatures one by one, slicing off their heads. Maya and Nivi held each other's hands and hopped off Yuva's back, landing adjacent to Rinad. Finally, Yuva nudged on the foot that Ash held onto, and the two of them landed in the remaining empty spaces.

The Manwaans had strategically surrounded the heap.

While they had positioned themselves perfectly, the challenge was clearing the heap on the inside while fighting off the creatures that attacked from the outside.

Maya and Nivi took turns and switched sides to battle the creatures. Maya wielded her double-bladed spear, but she began to struggle, considering she had targets on both sides. A Rakshasa landed a blow on her face, scarring her as she fell to the ground. But before the Rakshasa could proceed with its attack, Nivi sliced its head off with her bladed nunchuck, and Maya quickly hopped back on her feet. She then held her spear out in front of her, twisted the middle of the hilt, and pulled it apart. The spear split into two—one for each hand. She pushed the black buttons on the bottom of each hilt, and additional blades popped out from the other ends.

Maya now stood there with two double-bladed mini spears.

'I was waiting for you to use that,' Nivi jested.

'I keep it only for emergencies,' Maya retorted, slicing the creatures on either side.

'Well, if this is not an emergency, I don't know what is!'

* * *

On the other side of the heap, Yuva was having the time of his life. He was finally being presented with a challenge befitting his size and potential. As he floated mid-air, his feet would rip apart the creatures attacking from the outside while he cleared the heap by demolishing those on the inside. Ash worked side by side with Yuva and used the ultrasound device to handicap creatures, following it up with a swing of his boomerang blade.

Rinad too assumed a side stance and beamed creatures on the outside and the inside. When it shot out of his hands, the blue radiation could burn through anything that came in its path—like the walls of Manbhoomi or the flesh of an Asura or Rakshasa. The initial burst that Rinad had during his realisation was not something that could be called upon repeatedly. While that would reduce everything around in his vicinity to dust when emitted from his hands, the shiny blue beams would have the diameter of his palms, and the damage would be contained to the direction they were being pointed at, having a scorching effect, nevertheless.

Of course, he had no clue what it was made up of and was not completely aware of how to use his newfound capability effectively.

As he pointed his arms and beamed, the force from the radiation would cause a recoil, making him lose his balance, causing him to lose his flow and waste his energy on recovering from the fall. Now and then, the creatures would land a blow on him, but all Rinad had to dodge the blows, beam back, and recover. He certainly was no match for hand-to-hand combat and depended entirely on his capability.

While focusing on the heap, Rinad managed to sneak glances occasionally to defend himself from the outside, and during an Asura's attack, he let out a beam and zapped the waist, slicing it in half.

* * *

On the other side, Maya and Nivi were managing well at first. Still, they eventually began attracting many more creatures towards them and realised that they needed a more effective plan. They glanced at each other and, without saying a word, mutually agreed on the strategy that they should adopt.

Maya stood sideways and held out her hands on either side. The creatures on the heap started holding their stomachs and throwing up the black liquid, along with many who came from the outside. As the number of creatures increased, Maya started panting and dripping with sweat. She clenched her jaws as she held control of nearly twenty creatures on the outside and over ten on the inside.

Taking this as a cue, Nivi sent her boomerang blade towards the creatures under Maya's control on the outside and whipped out her bladed nun chucks. She proceeded to behead the creatures on the inside, and after hopping from one beast to the other and executing them, she returned to the place where she started and raised her hand. The boomerang blade returned into her grasp perfectly, and the platoon of twenty on the outside fell to the floor in perfect sync, with their heads sliding off and rolling to the floor.

Maya released her hands, looked at Nivi, and smiled as she panted. The unspoken strategy that they had agreed upon had worked perfectly.

Slowly, the heap kept reducing as the heads of the creatures were being severed, and when the burden was lightened, Milaayak used all his might and broke free from the heap, sending all the creatures flying away. Deshpande and Pawar fell to one side panting and recovering from the claustrophobia.

'Quick…everyone around the officers,' Rinad yelled, and the five Manwaans, along with Milaayak, formed a circular wall around the two officers and continued fighting off the creatures.

At that point, Rinad noticed something. The top half of the Asura that he had beamed across the waist earlier was still moving with a full life. It was using its hands to crawl away from the scene. It's almost as if it did not need its lower half. And that's when it struck Rinad.

'Guys…we need to handicap them!' he shouted.

'What do you mean?' Yuva yelled back.

'Chop their legs off. Even one would do. That way, they'll still be alive but won't be a threat.'

'But they'll still be Asuras or Rakshasas,' Ash replied.

'Yes, but Milaayak will be able to relieve them after that. Right now, we just need them to stop attacking,' Rinad persisted.

'I'm not too sure about this,' Maya said hesitantly.

'Trust me…it's the only way to save as many of them as possible. Guruji would have wanted this…'

The last line did it for everyone. They had to do it for Guruji.

'For Guruji!!' Nivi yelled and sliced the legs off an approaching Rakshasa. As predicted, the handicapped creature whimpered and used its hands to crawl away and escape.

'Oh my god! It worked!' Nivi affirmed excitedly.

'Alright, let's do this!' Yuva added.

'Milaayak, you try to relieve as many of them as possible,' Rinad continued.

'Got it,' the angel replied with a smile. He was glad to see the leader rising in the newly realised Manwaan.

From there on, the scene took a drastic turn. The Manwaans now felt they were fighting for Guruji's cause and attacked with newfound vigour.

Everyone went for the legs. At least one, if not both.

Rinad beamed, Ash and Nivi used their boomerang blades and bladed nun chucks, Maya used both her double-bladed mini spears, and Yuva used the claws on his hands and feet. Soon, hundreds of Underworld warriors were handicapped and crawled around like headless chickens. Or rather, legless warriors.

At the same time, Milaayak focused on relieving the creatures of demonic energy and flying them to safety. The plan seemed to be working perfectly well.

The only problem was that the handicapped humans, former members of the Underworld Clan, risked bleeding to death. Taking a cue from this, Ash and Nivi would heal as many humans as possible amidst the battle.

The Manwaans would handicap, Milaayak would relieve, and Ash and Nivi would heal as many as possible.

The team worked like a highly efficient, well-oiled machine.

Fifty-one

Usur isolated himself from the Manwaans and Milaayak. He may have been a great leader when it came to strategising for the revolution, but he refused to get his hands dirty. In his head, that's the way it needed to be. He had to see things from afar and plan and order accordingly. Or at least, that's how he justified his cowardice to himself.

When informed about the turn of events, Usur ran towards the primary zone to get a look at the situation first-hand. He saw hundreds of his handicapped comrades crawling to safety. In disbelief, he gawked at the sync with which the opposing team worked and noticed that his army numbers were drastically reducing.

From a distance, Rinad, busy beaming the creatures, noticed Usur standing from afar and gauging the situation intently. Usur looked towards Rinad, and their eyes met. A pang of fear seeped through Usur when he saw the blue radiation emerge from Rinad's palms.

'THAT'S HIM!' Rinad yelled, pointing out to Usur. 'THAT GUY KILLED GURUJI!'

All the eyes focused on the direction Rinad pointed out, so they could get one good look at him. At the creature who had killed their beloved teacher.

Usur did the smartest thing he could have done in that situation.

He bolted in the opposite direction.

'He's getting away!' Yuva yelled.

'Milaayak! Milaayak!!' Rinad yelled out but could not find the Arinch. Milaayak was at the other end, relieving and rescuing, and the chaos was too much for him to take notice of Usur.

'RETREAT!!!' Usur yelled. 'You…come here!' he commanded one of the Rakshasas as he ran. The beast went on all fours, Usur hopped onto it, and it bolted in the direction it was ordered to. The king of the Underworld could not have outrun a flying creature like Yuva himself, but on the back of a Rakshasa on all fours, the chances seemed higher.

As they ran in the opposite direction, the warriors of the Underworld Clan took the cue and started following them.

In a matter of seconds, the tables turned, and the remaining 300 creatures began to retreat.

Usur closed his eyes and lipped a mantra.

Khalo bhumi bhasonayaan
Jago bhumi bhasonayaan
Idho bhumi bhasonayaan

All the portals across Mumbai began to open, and the beasts began jumping back in—their only chance at safety.

'What's going on?' Ash cried out.

'He's opened the portals,' Maya yelled. 'They're all returning to Hell. Once they enter, we won't be able to do anything. We can't go after them!'

'Don't let them escape. Try and hold off as many as you can!' Rinad shouted.

'What about Usur?' Nivi added.

'Leave that to me…' Rinad growled, 'Yuva…let's go.'

Yuva grinned, and after a quick run up, Rinad hopped onto his back. Yuva leapt, flapped his wings, and they began to chase down the king of the Underworld. Meanwhile, Milaayak joined Ash, Nivi, and Maya and helped them prevent the creatures from escaping back to their abode.

Usur turned his head back to notice the two Manwaans gaining up on him.

'Stop them, you fools!!' he commanded, and the creatures started jumping onto Yuva to slow them down. Rinad held on with one hand and beamed the creatures out of their way with the other while Yuva flew higher to escape from the creatures on the ground.

Just then, a Rakshasa pounced on them from an adjoining building and threw Rinad off Yuva's back. Rinad managed to latch on to Yuva's neck with one hand while dangling. The Rakshasa had also slipped and dangled from

Yuva's neck on the other side. However, he pierced his sharp claws into Yuva's neck to ensure he didn't fall off.

'Aargh!!' Yuva yelled in pain and started to bleed from his neck.

Both Rinad and the Rakshasa were dangling from Yuva's neck on either side and kept clonking into each other.

At one point, the Rakshasa tried to scratch Rinad with the claws on his feet Rinad, who was about to fall, held on with his other hand and pulled himself up slightly to overlook the Rakshasa, but could not use his hands to emit his radiation. Seeing this, the Rakshasa pulled itself up and launched towards Rinad. His ferocious snapping jaw slowly approached Rinad's face.

The helpless Rinad started getting infuriated.

Just as the Rakshasa's jaws opened to chew its opponent's head off, Rinad's eyes began to glow. The radiation got stronger, and a pair of blue beams shot out of his eye sockets straight into the creature's throat, tearing it apart as it fell.

'Whoa! You can do that with your eyes too?!' Yuva exclaimed.

'I guess so!' Rinad panted and sat back up as the chase towards Usur continued.

They flew quickly and followed Usur into an alley in Bandra East, the closest portal to Usur's last location.

It was a fair chase. The Rakshasa's speed on all fours was a good match for Yuva's flight.

Usur turned into another alley where there were multiple abandoned vegetable carts. He was getting close to his exit point.

'Faster!' Rinad yelled.

'I'm trying!' Yuva flapped harder while dodging the carts.

Usur made the last turn, and the open portal was at the end of that lane. He had timed it perfectly. The portal had just begun to close, giving him enough time to jump in and away from the Manwaans.

'Faster, you imbecile,' he growled at the Rakshasa that carried him.

Yuva turned into the alley.

'That's his portal!' Rinad shouted as he saw the glowing circular portal at the other end from a distance.

As Usur approached the opening, he carefully stood halfway up on the Rakshasa and held its neck to keep his balance. Ready to make his exit, looking behind repeatedly to check on the Manwaans chasing him.

'We're not going to make it,' Yuva cried.

Seeing this, Rinad placed his feet on Yuva's shoulders and held onto his neck for balance.

When Usur was just a couple of feet away, he jumped, aiming perfectly for the portal, feet first. His legs entered the portal. He was about to escape; the portal was growing smaller and was about to close. Taking the cue, Rinad pushed off Yuva, darted into the air, and shot a single beam from his hand, zapping his target's neck.

The portal had closed, but Usur's head did not make it.

Rinad had severed the head just before it could leave the surface of the Earth. The body fell in, but the head rolled onto the surface of the Earth as Rinad crashed and fell from his heroic jump.

The king of the Underworld was slayed.

Fifty-two

'Jaffer, do not let them escape!' Milaayak yelled out.

Jaffer raised his sword and yelled, 'KILL EVERY LAST ONE OF THEM. NO ONE ESCAPES! *BHAGWAAN KE NAAM PE*!'

The Musafirs raised their swords, '*BHAGWAAN KE NAAM PE*!!'

They all yelled their war cry in unison and gave every last bit of energy to ensure that the warriors of the Underworld Clan did not return to their abode.

Maya, Ash, and Nivi stood guard at the portals and took care of the Asuras and Rakshasas that came their way while Jaffer and Milaayak chased as many as possible.

Meanwhile, Deshpande, Pawar, the remaining twenty-odd police officers, and army men collapsed on the floor in disbelief.

They had won the battle.

Tears of joy began to roll down their cheeks. They felt they had achieved the impossible.

Deshpande and Pawar had no energy left to chase any more Asuras and Rakshasas. They sat in the middle of the battlefield with moist eyes, watching Maya, Ash, Nivi, Milaayak, Jaffer and the remaining Musafirs do what they were born to do.

'I think I've seen everything, sir,' Pawar said, panting.

'I hope so…' Deshpande replied as he wiped off a tear and collected himself.

'What do you mean, sir?'

'Pawar…the world will now be a different place. These people…with these powers…these superhumans, or whatever they are, are our strongest allies. We need answers, Pawar. We still don't know anything. And we don't know what else is out there,' Deshpande said as he watched some of the Asuras and Rakshasas jump into the portals that led to Hell.

This caught Pawar's eyes too. 'Where do you think they are going, sir?'

'Where do you think?' Deshpande replied without batting an eyelid.

Pawar chuckled and replied in jest, 'I hope they all go to Hell.'

Deshpande turned his head coldly towards Pawar.

His eyes said it all.

Pawar abruptly stopped chuckling, 'You m-mean…they all c-came from H-Hell?' Pawar gulped and stammered.

'Anything is possible…' Deshpande turned back and observed the scene.

'We can speak to that man with the black markings on his face…'

'Jaffer…' Deshpande nodded.

All the portals eventually closed, and the access to Hell was sealed off. Many of the warriors of the Underworld Clan had escaped. Some went back into Hell, and some ran off into the city. If they did not assume their demonic forms and stayed as humans, they could easily blend in and live life amongst the common person.

While many had been killed or relieved, many still roamed the Earth, and many more had escaped into the Underworld.

The humans might have won this battle, but the war had just begun.

Fifty-three

Meanwhile, Rinad recovered from his fall in the alley and slowly stood up, holding his back. His body had been through a workout that he was not prepared for, and he was now starting to feel it.

'That was a pretty cool move, buddy,' Yuva grinned and extended his hand. Rinad took his help, stood up, and dusted himself off. 'Do you believe it now?' Yuva continued.

'I'm starting to…' Rinad moaned from the body ache. He turned to look at Usur's head, which was not two feet away from him. 'I wish I could have saved him, though…'

'You had no choice. He would've escaped. You did what you had to,' Yuva said with a matter-of-fact tone.

'I guess so…'

'Come on, let's go see what the others are up to,' Yuva gestured towards his back. Rinad smiled, hopped on, and they flew back to check on their comrades.

* * *

The city of Mumbai had turned into a massive bloody battlefield. Bandra looked like Bandra no more, with bodies lying all around, black and red rivers flowing, and dilapidated buildings. Even though the city was saved, the cost that it came with was huge, and it would be a long time before they could recover from it.

When the situation had calmed down, Deshpande immediately called in the paramedics. While waiting for them, he got a last glimpse of the heightened capabilities that surrounded him.

Milaayak was relieving some of the legless creatures. He scanned the entire premises as the Manwaans and the Musafirs had handicapped them all over. He would go to each one and place his hand on the head. The bottom of his palm would begin to glow, and golden-white radiation would be passed through the creature, resulting in the black-red liquid—the demonic energy—spluttering all over. The now-humans would be flustered and have no recollection of how they got to this point.

Following this, Ash and Nivi would heal as many as possible. They would place their palms on the handicapped areas, yellow-green radiation would emerge, and the wound would heal.

Deshpande and Pawar witnessed all of this first-hand.

Only Milaayak's and Jaffer's faces could be discerned clearly. The Manwaans still wore their tattered masks, so only part of their faces could be seen.

* * *

From the alley in Bandra East, Rinad and Yuva flew into the main area of the battlefield. On seeing them, Maya, Ash, and Nivi ran towards them, and there was a moment where they held each other's hands and smiled contently as their eyes welled up.

Guruji might have left them, but his spirit was still there with them.

At that moment, sirens were heard from a distance, and multiple ambulances began to arrive at the scene.

'We need to leave before more people see us,' Nivi said in a choked voice.

'What about the handicapped people?' Yuva asked.

'We've healed most of them. The paramedics should be able to handle the rest,' Ash replied.

'Let's go,' Maya added.

All took their positions on Yuva. Just before he took off, Rinad looked behind and noticed Deshpande, and their eyes met. Rinad did not have a mask on, and it was the only Manwaan face Deshpande could see clearly.

They stared at each other, with blank expressions, as Yuva took off and they flew towards the horizon.

Deshpande watched them fly away as the paramedics rushed in and attended to the injured.

With a soft smile, he rested his head on the wall behind him.

Fifty-four

The funeral pyre burnt strongly as a pundit chanted the necessary mantras. The five Manwaans, along with Govi, Milaayak, and Jaffer, had gathered around to say their final goodbyes to their beloved Guruji. All dressed in white. Except Milaayak, of course, who was dressed in his regular angelic cloak. And Govi, who was never really dressed.

Milaayak and Jaffer stared into the fire with stern expressions. Govi, as always, had silently perched himself on the shoulder of Yuva, who stood there with folded hands, a cold expression on his face and tears welling up in his eyes. Rinad, too, welled up but was more pensive, while Maya, Ash, and Nivi could not hold back their streams of tears.

As a tribute to Guruji, the Manwaans wanted to hold the funeral at Manbhoomi. Even though their house had been destroyed, they felt it had to be done here and had arranged for it to take place in one corner of the outside garden.

This felt nothing short of losing a parent, particularly for Maya and Yuva. They both had been abandoned as children, and Guruji was the one who had taken them under his care and raised them. The three of them had been together for nearly twenty years, and the fact that Guruji would not be around anymore was not sinking in. Their relationship was doubly special, as the two Manwaans had been cast out from the world. When they felt like they were a burden and undeserving of affection, Guruji stepped into the shoes of a parent and showered them with the unconditional love they needed and deserved.

Even for Ash, Nivi, and Rinad, Guruji was the one who helped them find and come to terms with their identities. They were lost souls, meandering the world with no purpose, and Guruji instilled that sense of "belief" within them.

He had taught this odd bunch of misfits to accept who they were and wear their idiosyncrasies as a badge of honour.

For nearly two hours, they all stood there without saying a word and watched till the fire was no more. Ultimately, the pundit collected the ashes into a small clay pot, covered it with a yellow cloth, and handed it to Maya, who was nearest to him. Maya held it in her shivering hands and sobbed profusely.

Nivi and Ash comforted her; the others watched with broken hearts and shared pain. As Rinad continued to look at Maya, his attention was drawn to something else.

In the distance, an old frail lady stood at the other end of the garden under the Banyan tree. She, too, was dressed for the occasion, wore a white gown, and had straight white hair tied into a clean, tight knot. When she noticed Rinad looking at her, a soft smile grew on her face.

'Guys…who's that?' Rinad asked softly.

Everyone turned and looked at the lady cluelessly.

'She's waiting for you,' Milaayak said in an undertone. 'I need to take care of some things. The revolution has begun, and things will not be the same anymore. Take care. I'll see you soon.'

Yuva stared at the lady as he replied to Milaayak, 'Do you plan on giving us updates or…'

Whoosh!!!

Yuva turned around, and he was gone. 'Can't he at least say goodbye?' he grunted.

From a distance, the old lady's smile grew bigger, and she bowed her head as if greeting someone. From his peripheral vision, Rinad noticed Jaffer bowing his head and bringing his palms together in a namaste.

'You know her?' Rinad asked.

'I do,' Jaffer replied sternly.

'Who is she?'

'I think it's best if she explains it herself. I need to go and rally the Musafirs. We need to prepare for the next battle,' he said, turning around and jogging away.

When Yuva turned back to look at Jaffer, he was gone.

'Don't these guys ever say goodbye?' he said as he shook his head.

The five Manwaans walked towards the lady who stood there with her hands behind her back and without moving a muscle. Her face seemed mildly familiar, but no one could recall any memories of her. They all got closer to the tree and stood there.

'I'm sorry for your loss,' she said in a soft, cracked voice.

'Thank you,' Nivi said gently. 'Did you know our Guruji?'

She nodded. 'I'm his sister,' she said as her eyes welled up.

'Oh!' Ash replied in surprise. 'We're sorry, but he never really spoke about you...'

'He was not supposed to. But Shashikant asked me to contact you if he were ever to move on...'

The Manwaans gasped and fell silent.

'Guruji had an actual name?' Yuva whispered to Maya, who shrugged in response.

'You didn't think his name was just Guruji, did you?' the lady chuckled mildly.

Yuva smiled sheepishly.

'Why don't you all come with me...I can tell you more about him. You can too. Besides, we have a lot of work to do. The revolution has begun, and we need to train harder,' she said with determination.

The Manwaans silently agreed.

'You can come live and train with us,' she continued.

'Us?' Maya asked.

'My students. Your Manwaan brothers and sisters.'

'Oh…I thought they had all been killed?' Nivi said.

'Not all. And Manwaans are being created as we speak. We need to train together and prepare ourselves for what's coming.'

All of them nodded in unison.

They turned and looked at the half-destroyed Manbhoomi. A place some of them had grown up and had their realisations in—a place filled with memories. Possibly, the only place most of them could truly call home.

'Don't worry…' the lady continued, 'we can return and fix it. It's not going anywhere. Come,' she smiled, turned around, and led the way.

The Manwaans slowly followed her.

'Sorry, but…do you have a name?' Yuva asked hesitantly.

The lady turned around and smiled, 'I'm Shaanti.'

Fifty-five

'Mumbai has witnessed the most catastrophic fortnight to have taken place in its history. From the reports, over five hundred have been confirmed dead, over 700 injured, and over 300 are missing. The Battle of Bandra, as it is now being called, not only witnessed creatures that many claim to be from the Underworld or Hell but also witnessed humans with special abilities or superhumans. All these are speculations, and many are still opposing the notion that creatures from Hell were the ones who tore down the city of Mumbai. According to many people from the event, the superhumans were the ones who saved all the officers and the armed forces, and…'

'Sir…' Pawar banged open Deshpande's door and barged in.

'Pawar! How many times have I told you to knock!!' Deshpande boomed as he closed the news video that was playing on his phone and put it aside.

'Terribly sorry, sir…' Pawar said sheepishly, 'but this came in for you. There is no address…two of those men with black markings came and gave it to me and asked me to give it to you,' he added and handed Deshpande a sealed envelope.

As Deshpande flipped the envelope, he noticed an 'M', designed with a tribal aesthetic, used as the seal. He looked at it for a second, and just as he was about to rip it open, his phone rang—an unknown number.

'Pawar…' Deshpande gestured towards the door. Pawar shut the door and stood in front of his desk.

'I mean, you need to leave, Pawar!' Deshpande grunted.

'Oh…sorry, sir,' Pawar chuckled and walked out.

Deshpande rolled his eyes, shook his head, and answered the call.

'Hello?'

'Inspector Deshpande…it's Jaffer here. Hope you've recovered?'

'Oh…Jaffer! Yes, much better. Thank you. How are you?'

'I'm ecstatic,' Jaffer said in a cold tone.

'You don't sound it,'

'I was being sarcastic.'

'Oh,' Deshpande said awkwardly, not knowing how to respond.

'I called to say that this is my number. My people and I…we're called the Musafirs, and all you need to know, is that we're fighting to protect our motherland. We are on your side, Inspector.'

'That's good to know. But what are we fighting against?'

'The letter will answer that. The Manwaans had asked me to get it sent to you.'

'The who?'

'Again, the letter will explain it all.'

'Hmm...'

'Call me if you see anything unusual. I'm sure by now you know what to look out for,' Jaffer said with a slight chuckle.

'Yes, I'm relatively well-versed.'

'Very well then. Take care, Inspector. See you on the battlefield.'

'Wait...what battle...'

Jaffer hung up.

Deshpande stared at his phone, not knowing how to react.

After a few minutes, he wiped the sweat off his forehead and dialled another number.

'Hello, Kamat sir. How are you? That's great. I'm getting better, sir. Thank you for asking. Sir, I have a favour to ask. I need to recruit a special task force of a hundred officers. We don't know what's out there and are extremely underprepared. A hundred won't be enough, but it's a start. They will be under my command, and I would like them to go through special martial arts and arms training. They will also need specially designed swords and will train with them extensively,' Deshpande insisted. 'Apparently, the battle is not over, sir. And we need to be prepared for whatever shows up tomorrow...Thank you, sir.

I look forward to it,' Deshpande concluded, putting the phone down.

He then opened the letter and began to read it.

Hello, Inspector!

I'm sure you have a hundred unanswered questions in your head. We'll try and clear as many of them as possible. In case you have more questions, you have Jaffer's number.

Inspector, we've been plunged into a new era. An era that you will need to embrace as the new normal. An era where nothing may make sense, yet anything may be possible.

We are not alone, Inspector. There are inexplicable forces that are greater than us, and unfortunately, the human race is intertwined with them. I'll keep this concise, but just know that everything you're about to read is absolutely true.

From what we know, the universe can broadly be divided into three realms (although there are many more)—the human realm, the celestial abode (or Heaven), and the Underworld (or Hell). The human realm, as you may have guessed, is Earth. There is a celestial abode where the Gods (yes, they do exist) and the Arinch (Worthy Angels) live, and the Underworld is where all the dark forces of the universe thrive. The Asuras and Rakshasas are some of those dark forces that you have already witnessed.

Roughly two millennia ago, a major fallout took place, and seven out of the fourteen angels of Heaven were cast out and sent to Hell. The Fagir (Fallen Angels), as they came to be known, formed an alliance with the Underworld Clan and orchestrated a revolution against Earth and Heaven.

Against the Gods.

A revolution that has already begun.

The start of which you have already witnessed, Inspector.

The Gods can never set foot in the human realm as it would lead to our complete extinction. When news of the revolution reached Heaven, the Gods feared that the seven remaining Arinch, would be no match for the newly formed coalition between the Fagir and the Underworld Clan. And to build their alliance on Earth, they created us.

Manwaans.

To say the least, we're a hybrid between man and God and have been bestowed with the responsibility of safe keeping our motherland.

The media may call us superhumans and whatnot, but we don't care for names. In our world, we're called Manwaans; maybe you could try using that too!

We cannot speak for others, but the five of us who fought at the so-called 'Battle of Bandra' would like to pledge to serve humanity. Unfortunately, we do have loved ones that we need to keep safe and, thus, cannot reveal our true names.

The gates of Hell have been opened, Inspector, and we are now neck deep in the Kalyug or the dark ages. While there have been many definitions of this term, all you need to know is that it is simply the period where the Underworld takes over.

What we witnessed a few days ago was a glimpse of what may follow. And while this may scare you, we want you to know we are with you—all the way!

We have been created to protect the human race, and that is exactly what we shall do till our last breaths.

We will die before we let anything happen to any of you.

This is our motherland.

And we will not let anyone take it away from us.

Yours truly,
The Manwaans

Fifty-six

'I'm telling you, Ajit…we are lucky that our houses are intact. Most of the buildings near the Western Express have been reduced to pieces! Did you ever imagine that we would see such a day!' Rinad's dad exclaimed to his usual suspects, who had gathered weeks after the Battle of Bandra for an evening dinner. Present there were Ajit and Ramita, the older couple, Karan and Aruna, the younger couple and their kids, Rinad's parents, and Rinad himself.

'I agree,' Aruna said, sipping her gin and tonic. 'We are truly blessed. What would we have done if something had happened to us?'

'But honestly, the situation was handled very poorly,' said the pessimistic Karan. 'I mean…look at the number of deaths and casualties! And hundreds of them are handicapped! Their lives will not be the same anymore!'

Rinad sat there twiddling his thumbs and shaking his feet. Having fought the battle himself, he found it quite futile and annoying to listen to this privileged bunch complaining about the method by which Mumbai was saved. Apparently, the fact that it was saved was not good enough for these elitists.

'I'm just extremely grateful that we are all okay,' Rinad's mom said. 'In fact, when Rinad did not answer his phone that day, I got extremely scared!'

'What were you doing then?' Ramita asked Rinad.

'I was…umm…sleeping,' Rinad lied.

'I still don't understand how you were able to sleep. I was losing my mind for those couple of days,' Rinad's dad said.

Rinad just shrugged his shoulders and sipped on his orange juice, waiting for this horrendously boring evening to come to an end—a complete waste of a Saturday evening.

'But those creatures…these superhumans…none of it feels real,' Ajit said.

'And yet it is! We would have all been dead if it weren't for those…umm…what are they called…Marwa or something…' Ramita asked.

'Manwaans!' Rinad's mom corrected her promptly. 'Thank god for them!'

Rinad chuckled at the reality of that statement. Truly "God" had to be thanked for the creation of Manwaans.

Just then, the lights began to flicker. Just a short-lived one, though. With a couple of flickers, it was back on.

'They must be doing some maintenance work,' Rinad's dad commented, sipping his whisky.

And that's when it struck Rinad.

He was unaffected by the flicker!

Normally, his selaphobia would have caused panic, and he would have been having a meltdown by now. But nothing. Rinad heaved a sigh of relief and pretended to be interested in the meaningless conversations unfolding in front of him.

It itched him even more, as he still had so much work to do. He had had one level of realisation, but it wasn't his peak. He still hadn't identified his celestial parent, and to achieve all this, he had to go deeper into his meditation and training. He was meant to be the leader of the Manwaans, and he had to prepare himself to be worthy of that title. But even though he was half celestial, he was still half-human, and finding a balance to live both lives was the true challenge. To hang on to the sanity that the "normal human" world presented, he made it a point to live up to his Saturday routine, today being the first day he would resume it after the long hiatus.

Besides that, weekends were meaningless as they were nothing different from weekdays. He had been fired from his job, but he couldn't care less. He loved his parents and his friends and chose to spend as much time with them as possible.

'Well…now that things have settled down, have you decided the next steps, Rinad?' Ajit asked.

Rinad shook his head and stroked the mole on his jaw, 'I actually want to take a year off…just to figure things out.'

'A year off? Be careful. It would be extremely hard to get back in.'

And that set it off yet again.

The world began to blur, and Rinad's chest became heavy as his palms moistened and his heartbeat rose. A sense of confusion dawned upon Rinad as he hung his head and tried to process the anxiety creeping in.

Why is this still happening to me!! I thought I would be over this by now!! He screamed within his mind.

He shut his eyes and consciously brought his attention back to his breath.

In, 2, 3, 4…hold, 2, 3, 4…out, 2, 3, 4…hold, 2, 3, 4…

He carried on, and as suspected, his shoulders relaxed, his jaw unclenched, and his breathing slowly returned to normalcy.

I'm getting pretty good at this breathing thing. He thought and amused himself.

The anxiety had still not permanently departed, and triggers would still set it off. Rinad quickly realised that it would never leave him for good, and he would just have to learn to deal with it, which he was gradually getting better at.

'I'll figure it out... you don't need to stress,' he replied with a smile to Ajit, who bobbed his head and returned to his drink.

Rinad's phone rang at that moment, and he pulled it out of his pocket.

Jogi calling…

The expected phone call had arrived!

'What's up, bro?' Rinad answered excitedly.

'Yo, bro! Are we on for tonight?' Jogi replied from the other end.

'Of course, man! It's been a while!'

'Yeh, man!! I haven't seen you since I picked you up from Dahisar! Let's meet at yours? Smoke one-two doobs and then head to Sagar?'

'I actually don't drink or smoke anymore, man. How about I meet you guys directly at Sagar? You can drink on my behalf,' Rinad jested.

'Whoa! That rehab centre really seems to be having its effect on you, man!'

Rinad chuckled, 'I guess you could say that!'

Fifty-seven

As the portals closed, many Asuras and Rakshasas jumped back into the passageway connecting to the Gateway of Hell and recovered from their humiliating defeat. Not only did they have to return to Hell, but their leader, their king, was no more. However, one thing was different this time. The surviving Asuras and Rakshasas now had hosts and could migrate between Hell and Earth. The next time the portals opened, they would not enter as black-red liquid but would already have a form to move about. Not just that, many of their comrades did not make it back in time and were already roaming the Earth.

They had company in case they decided to go back.

The nearly five hundred Asuras and Rakshasas gathered around the headless body of their king and mourned his loss. They picked it up and proceeded towards the circular gate. They marched with their heads held high, celebrating their leader. They all assembled inside as they crossed through the door, and Mihaara appeared.

On seeing the body, a mild sadness took over his eyes. But only momentarily.

'Mihaaraji, here is the headless host of Usur,' a female voice spoke up from the crowd. The gathering parted, and she walked to the front. 'I'm afraid he is no more.'

An eerie silence took over the chambers of the Underworld.

'And you are?' Mihaara said calmly.

'I am Areez. I served as Usur's first-in-command.'

Mihaara slowly nodded, stared coldly at the body, and said nothing.

'What is your order, Mihaaraji?' Areez continued.

A sudden hiss echoed through the chambers. Multiple hisses followed, and the parted crowd moved even further to give way to a large cloud of dark green shadows that levitated between them. The shadows slithered to the front, and the woman stepped aside.

Mihaara smirked.

The shadows proceeded to grow in size. They began to take shape as they expanded, and defined bodies could be discerned. Scaly hands, feet, and abdomen, but the faces were different.

A reptilian head that resembled a dragon but with a flat nose. Long whiskers above the upper lip drooped nearly to the chin, along with hair-like growth from the chin and ears. Lean, muscular bodies, long sharp tails emerging from just above their rear with a black, thin, cloud-textured covering wrapped around the crotch that dropped till the midpoint of the thigh, almost like a short towel.

As the shapes formed completely, the creatures opened their eyes.

Venomous, dark green sockets.

The group leader stepped up and touched Mihaara's feet and placed the same fingers on each eye and then on the middle of her chest.

'Mihaaraji...after all these millennia, it is almost insulting that you did not once ask us to help you in the revolution that we have long waited for,' the leader hissed with her fangs flailing out of her mouth as she spoke.

'I waited for the opportune moment, Nagdor.'

'And?'

'And this is it,' Mihaara sneered.

Nagdor smiled. 'The Najasura tribe is at your service, Mihaaraji.'

'And the Najakshasas?'

'They await our orders,' Nagdor calmly replied, extending her right hand to one side as if gesturing towards something.

From far behind the crowd, thunderous steps boomed as the walls of the Underworld shook.

Mihaara lifted his head. He could see multiple pairs of green eyes in the distance, nearly a hundred feet high.

The beasts roared in the dark, and the Asuras and Rakshasas shivered with fear on hearing the sound they dreaded, despite it being the sound from an ally.

Mihaara grinned. 'Perfect.'

Fifty-eight

'You disappoint me, Mihaara,' a voice boomed.

'I assumed Usur was capable. I should not have,' Mihaara replied with a tinge of sadness in his eyes.

Indeed, Usur had not lived up to his expectations. Mihaara had groomed Usur for thousands of years, and all that effort seemed to be in vain. The first phase of the annexation was a relative failure. Heaven was made completely aware of the revolution, and the Arinch roamed the Earth on high alert. It would only be more challenging from here on.

The seven thrones were arranged semi-circularly, and the Fagir Council meeting was in session—three chairs on either side, with one in the centre towards the back of the room. Dark smoke floated throughout, and none of the faces could be discerned. Just the tips of the hands and feet.

'But the Najasuras and Najakshasas have lined up. Earth will crumble against them,' Mihaara continued.

'Will they be able to fight our siblings?'

Mihaara hung his head shamefully. He was still not certain if those creatures could take down the Arinch.

'We will face them ourselves. The Najasuras and Najakshasas can easily take care of the Manwaans.'

'You said that the last time. Look where we are now. The whole damn universe has been made aware of our plan. All because of your negligence!' the voice growled.

'I apologise. But we will now strike with the totality of our strength. We will unleash the Underworld's fury upon them. They will not stand a chance!' Mihaara said.

An eerie silence followed.

'I love arrogance, but I hate futile promises. I do not trust your capabilities anymore, Mihaara. It seems to me that you could do with some help,' the voice commanded.

From the shadows, a beautiful, dark-skinned woman stepped into the light and stood beside Mihaara. Golden-brown hair and violet eyes. She spread her glorious violet wings and smirked.

Mihaara smiled back at his elder sister politely and respectfully.

'Emakeni will fight with you, Mihaara,' the voice boomed.

Mihaara took a second, looked towards the direction of the voice, and bowed his head.

'As you command, Saatan.'

A few weeks later...

Shaanti stood silently in the open grounds of Manbhavan. Her mind was elsewhere.

Whoosh!!!

She heard the sound of a swift flap of wings behind her.

'I do not feel right about this,' Shaanti said sternly without breaking her stillness. She was expecting company, and the company had arrived.

'I can understand, but it is for the best,' Milaayak replied in a consoling tone. 'It is a service towards the cause…'

'Damn your cause!' Shaanti boomed.

'Calm down, Shaanti.'

'Do not tell me to calm down. You cannot play with someone's mind like that. What is to happen to that poor child?!' Shaanti was almost in tears.

'I'm sorry you feel that way,' Milaayak replied coldly.

'No, you are not,' Shaanti snapped.

Milaayak looked away. He was, in fact, unapologetic. He couldn't care less. All he could see was the finish line, which was tainted with Heaven's name on it for him.

'I understand this is difficult for you, Shaanti. But I am afraid I am not here to console you. We have bigger issues,' the leader of the Arinch spoke in a matter-of-fact tone.

'The resistance has grown strong, and the situation has gotten out of hand,' Milaayak continued. 'They are recruiting as we speak. We must act now, lest it be too late.'

Shaanti stared without flinching. Almost as if she had no stamina left for any form of rebuttal. She crossed Milaayak and walked over to the other end of the room. By the doorway, attached to the wall, was a small glass box, and enclosed in it was a wooden circular button. She opened the glass box and pressed the button, which led to an arpeggiating wooden chime that rang and echoed throughout Manbhavan's campus.

The dining and meeting lounge was within the central structure of the campus, and surrounding it were smaller accommodations with huge expanses of empty ground in between. All the structures were hut-shaped but made of concrete and painted in a beige-cream colour, giving a sort of Greek feel to the entire campus of Manbhavan.

As the melodic alarm rang, all the Manwaans started marching towards the central structure, almost as if on cue.

Rinad and Yuva walked in with their new comrades. Maya, Ash, and Nivi had gone on a mini vacation, but they would receive time-to-time updates from their buddies on campus.

Shaanti darted her eyeballs to make sure the attendance was complete.

Thirty-six. All are here, she thought to herself.

She nodded to a young girl at the back of the room. The girl turned her head and waved her hand mid-air, following which the door began to close without any physical contact.

The room grew silent.

Shaanti placed her hands behind her back and looked towards Milaayak, who stood behind her left shoulder. Milaayak nodded, and Shaanti cleared her throat.

'Students…I apologise for calling you in suddenly, but I am afraid I have some bad news to share with you.'

The room grew tense and immediately transitioned to pin-drop silence.

'Some of you may be aware, but let me present a quick recap for the uninformed. Over the past few months, many Manwaans have united to consolidate their feelings of rebellion against their pre-ordained destiny. They call themselves the Resistance and disagree with the Gods and the Angels. More and more Manwaans are joining their cause, and we fear they could threaten our role in the great revolution,' Shaanti concluded and looked towards Milaayak.

Milaayak stepped forward. 'They have even managed to capture Ralimaan. They went to the extent of staging a battle amongst themselves, and when he arrived to settle the dispute, they overpowered him and held him hostage. They are now on a quest to retrieve the scattered pieces of the sword of Arampira.'

A sudden collective gasp echoed through the room as the audience stood shell-shocked. The information was limited, but enough to put two and two together.

Ralimaan was one of the Arinch, and the sword of Arampira was the only weapon that could kill an angel.

Some Manwaans had heard about the Resistance, a rebellious group that began forming after the Battle of Bandra. Still, the fact they would go to the extent of attempting to exterminate an angel was something they could not digest. Additionally, their ability to hold an angel hostage proved their strength.

Milaayak stepped back. His job was to convey the information, not motivate the troops or arouse an emotional response. That was expected of the Manwaan teacher.

'We need to march towards Delhi,' Shaanti continued. 'The Resistance has headquartered themselves there, and we must face them before it is too late. I will leave you with that. I will keep you informed on our exact date of departure,' Shaanti paused and let out a heavy breath. 'Be prepared. Thank you.' she concluded, dismissing the gathered bunch.

The Manwaans looked at each other, nodded determinedly, and exited the room. Shaanti watched Rinad leave, once again, with concern in her eyes.

Once the room was empty, she returned to her original pensive position and continued staring.

'He's smarter than you think. Rinad will find out,' Shaanti said calmly. 'And when he does, it will get ugly. You have used him as bait.'

'It may seem immoral now, but it will pay off. And he did not die, did he? I ensured his safety,' Milaayak cut in.

'And what about my other students? They, too, are being misled. They need to be made aware that the leader of the Manwaans is with the Resistance. If not, they will end up killing him. Rinad may end up killing the leader! And who will be blamed then? The poor kid thinks he is the leader...'

'I agree with you completely. They will need to know that their leader fights with the Resistance. And when the time is right, they will know who it is. Rinad, too, will know the truth. Until then, things stay as they are,' Milaayak commanded.

Shaanti shook her head in disagreement. 'Will you at least tell me who this "Manwaan leader" really is? Is he even aware of it?'

Milaayak smiled. 'She, Shaanti. *She*.'

End

Character List

1. ACP Kamat - Senior officer of the Police force
2. Ajit - Rinad's parents' friend
3. Amit - Karan and Aruna's son
4. Areez - Asura, Usur's first-in-command
5. Aruna - Rinad's parents' friend
6. Ashwin Iyer - Manwaan
7. Asuras - Creatures from the Underworld
8. Emakeni - Fagir
9. Govi - Yuva's pet crow
10. Gurgaan - Arinch
11. Guruji - Manwaan teacher
12. Inspector Manohar Deshpande - Senior officer of the Police force who reports to ACP Kamat
13. Jaffer - Leader of the Musafir Clan
14. Jogi - Rinad's friend
15. Karan - Rinad's parent's friend

16. Maya Irani - Manwaan
17. Mihaara - A Fagir, Saatan's first-in-command
18. Milaayak - Leader of the Arinch
19. Mr. Mukherjee - Rinad's boss
20. Mr. Shah - Rinad's father
21. Mrs. Shah - Rinad's mother
22. Nagdor - Leader of the Najasura tribe
23. Najakshasas - Creatures from the Underworld
24. Najasuras - Creatures from the Underworld
25. Neena - Karan and Aruna's daughter
26. Nivedita Iyer - Manwaan
27. Param - Rinad's friend
28. Rakshasas - Creatures from the Underworld
29. Ramita - Rinad's parents' friend
30. Rinad Shah - A hyper-anxious, pot-smoking, twenty-six-year-old male
31. Saatan - Leader of the Fagir
32. Shaanti - Manwaan teacher
33. Sub-Inspector Virat Pawar - Senior officer of the Police force, Deshpande's first-in-command
34. Uraavati - an angel
35. Usur - King of the Underworld
36. Vinay - Rinad's friend
37. Yuva Kanojia - Manwaan

Acknowledgements

"People will forget what you said. People will forget what you did. But people will never forget how you made them feel."

Maya Angelou

I truly hope that this book has been able to provide a memorable experience and, hopefully, taken you a step towards your realisation. Of course, crafting it would have been impossible without the support of many, who are, in my opinion, the legit Manwaans of my life.

My mum, Valli, dad, Gopal, and brother, Anurag, for being my pillars through it all.

My aunt, Kala, and my sister, Keerthana, for always being my cheerleaders.

A host of people, in addition to the above, took the time to share their valuable feedback (on various things)—Vedika, Divya, Akshith, Sameer, Manvi, Vinita, Rohan, Aditi, Palak, Riya & Gautam.

Shreya Punj, thank you for believing in the book and helping me manoeuvre the world of publishing more effectively.

A special shout out to a special person—Sukrutee Bhosale, for always sharing my enthusiasm (even for the silliest or smallest of things), being my forever sounding board, and just being the best colleague one could wish for.

Another special person—Nidhi Kaushik. I really would've been a blindfolded puppy meandering through the dark if it wasn't for her. Right from providing her thoughts for the first few rounds of edits to see the book all the way through, she's someone who I certainly could not have done this without. For any author looking for some guidance—look no further and get in touch with her!

And, of course, the folks at NuVoice Press – Kevin Missal, Vini, Navya, Abhijeet, the design team, and so many more, for making this book what it is today.

There have also been several people who've helped spread the word, and to those, I say I'm very lucky to have you in my life. No need for names; you know who you are!

And finally, you! To all the readers of this book—a big thank you from the bottom of my heart for taking the time out and diving into this experience. I hope you enjoyed reading it as much as I enjoyed writing it. The journey of the book would certainly not be complete without you.

I'm very eager to know your thoughts, so please do leave a review on Amazon.in or reach out to me directly on Instagram (@abhishekrishnan).

I look forward to building this universe and telling more stories. Hopefully, I'll get a bit better each time!